In Loving Memory of
Sarah Rainwater
"I sat alone grasping at shards of darkness; now I have the
illumination of your memory to brighten my life."

Our time was far too short.

Special Thanks to:

Mom and Dad, Jack Whisner, Jeff Burgeson, Carrie Ingraham,
Celeste Ferguson, Josh Barnwell, Riley Brown, Russell Parman,
Jason Keen, Franklin Ward, Hannah Morgan, Tammy Fathera, my
aunt Lainie and Uncle Jerry, my sister Bethany, and as always my
very favoritist cousin in the whole wide world.

Very Special Thanks to:
Dave and Antoinette for always being there. I couldn't make it
without the two of you.

Kaylee

Kaylee

ISBN: 978-0-578-00914-8

"It is not length of life, but depth of life."
Ralph Waldo Emerson

Prologue:

"**I** can't get it to stay on the hook." Kaylee fumbled with the worm.

"You have to put the hook through it." Her grandfather told her.

"Eww, that's gross." She exclaimed, piercing the side of the slippery worm with the silver hook, causing a brown substance to ooze out slightly. Her grandfather watched her and smiled. He'd hoped that she would enjoy fishing. It was a safe pastime for her. He didn't think that she would though, not unless she was successful at it, which he doubted she would be. Children, especially rambunctious ten year olds who were just discovering the complexities of the world usually didn't enjoy such things as boring as fishing, not unless they proved extremely lucky in the endeavor.

"Good, now we have to throw the line, remember what I taught you?"

"Yep Grampa." She threw her arm behind her and tossed the hook out onto the water. It didn't go far but it was far enough for the little girl to feel satisfied with her first attempt.

"Not bad," Grampa shrugged, "maybe we'll make a

fisherman out of you yet?" He said with delight.

"Uh-oh!" Kaylee looked down at her burn scarred hand. The tip of her finger, the one she'd used to place the worm on the hook was now decorated with a single drop of her blood. Grampa looked over at it and felt a small amount of relief. He was thankful that she noticed it so quickly, she usually didn't. "I see red, gotta stop." She spoke the line she'd memorized. "Red means stop."

"Aww, it's just a little pin prick. It will be alright." He took her finger and wiped away the blood. "See it's already stopped bleeding." Kaylee smiled at his words and nodded before turning her attention back to her fishing line. Her bobber was sitting peacefully on the morning water, she could just make out the red line that dissected it's radius, the white top clearly visible.

"You think the fish will like that worm?" Kaylee asked her Grampa.

"Maybe, if they're hungry." Grampa told her.

"If I was a fish, I wouldn't like worms, they're icky." Kaylee proclaimed.

"Then what would you eat?" Grampa asked.

"I don't know, normal food, like cookies, I think I'd like cookies no matter what animal I was."

"But you couldn't eat them, fish don't have teeth."

"I'd eat them anyway, they'd be soggy cause they'd be in the water." Kaylee answered.

"Can't beat that logic." Grampa chuckled. "Why don't you

reel it in, see if the fish like it more if it's moving?" He suggested. Without a word she began reeling the line in as fast as her little arms could operate the rod. "Slowly, slowly, you want the fish to be able to catch it."

"Okay." She said, slowing the spinning of her hand. Soon the bobber was at the top of the rod and Kaylee threw the line out again, without any prompting from her grandfather. This time it went further than the first. "Look at that." Kaylee said, proud of her accomplishment. Grampa put his arm around her and pulled her over the arm of her beach chair and hugged her.

"You're a natural." He told her, which made her smile. The two sat silently, gazing at the beautiful morning sun coming over the horizon and shedding its beams of light onto the crystal blue water.

"Do fish only eat in the morning?" Kaylee asked after several minutes of silence.

"I suppose they eat anytime." Grampa answered.

"Then why do we have to come out here so early to catch them?" She asked.

"Well, I think because they don't expect us to be looking for them this early, they think it's safe." He answered. Without warning, a loud shot ring out behind them. A flurry of shotgun pellets slammed into Grampa and threw him forward into the water while Kaylee was showered in the back left shoulder and was pushed out of her chair, spinning her to the ground.

Hearing the pump of the shotgun, Grampa picked his head

out of the water. His back and arm were in burning pain. He tried but couldn't quite conjure the strength to stand. He felt a hand on the back of his shirt pick him up and drag him back onto dry land. A boot rolled him over. He looked up to see Rick Olsen, the man he sometimes worked for standing over him holding the shotgun in his left hand and wiping his right on the side of his jeans.

"Where is it?" Olsen demanded.

"Where is what?" Grampa feigned ignorance.

"You know what you took from us Randy, tell me where it is." Olsen reiterated before turning his head to see Kaylee getting to her feet and training her eyes on him. Grampa's concern switched from himself to his granddaughter and he conceded.

"Alright, alright, I'll tell you, but don't hurt her." He said quickly to be sure that Olsen didn't target his granddaughter. Olsen responded by putting his foot on Grampa's chest and pushing down, causing all of the air in the old man's lungs to expel.

"You don't seem to understand who you stole from." Olsen told him before taking a .357 Magnum revolver from his belt and shooting the little girl in the chest, just to the right of her heart.

"No!" Grampa wrenched in pain. The force of the blast flung the little girl into the water. Olsen replaced the pistol and pointed the shotgun at Grampa.

"Tell me!" Olsen calmly ordered. Grampa looked up at his assailant, hate filling his eyes. The saltwater and blood mixed in his wounds causing immense pain in his back. His heart raced and his mind thought only of Kaylee. He decided that this was his time to die.

"No." Grampa said in a calm, clear tone. Olsen nodded, put the barrel of the shotgun against his nose and fired. Grampa's head erupted in a deafening explosion of blood, brains and dirt. Olsen stepped off the murdered man and flung the shotgun over his shoulder.

"What did you do?" He heard Kaylee yell at him. She was making her way out of the water. His head and body turned simultaneously to the sound of the voice. At first he thought it was someone he hadn't yet seen but it was the little girl. She was walking normally out of the water as though nothing had happened to her. Blood was pouring from her chest wound but she didn't seem to notice. "What did you do?" She repeated.

Olsen stood shocked, watching the girl make her way over a few rocks. He told himself that his eyes must be lying to him. That he must be imagining this. Kaylee stopped her approach when she was out of the water and stood straight. Olsen, in an attempt to regain his composure, pumped the shotgun.

"You killed my Grampa! You killed my Grampa!" The little girl screamed and pointed at him accusingly. Olsen's shock overwhelmed him again, he stood motionless watching that which he thought impossible. "You're a bad man!" She screamed repeatedly at him. "You're a very bad man!"

Olsen couldn't take it anymore, he began slowly backing

away from the little girl. With each step he took, she took a step closer, screaming all the way. Olsen's shock rolled over into fear and the only thing his legs would do was scurry him away from the child that should be dead but wasn't.

1

"The Raid"

At exactly seven o'clock in the morning the alarm clocks in rooms 214 and 215 went off. The occupant of room 214 immediately got up while the occupant of room 215 hit the snooze button. The occupant of room 214 wiped the sleep from his eyes, started brewing his complimentary coffee and turned on the shower faucet. The occupant of room 215 went back to sleep. Room 214's occupant was almost finished with his shower by the time the snooze feature on 215's clock/radio reactivated the alarm. This time the occupant got up, wandered half asleep to the shower, got in, turned it on, squealed when he found the water was cold, lathered up, rinsed and stepped back out.

Room 214's occupant brushed his teeth and shaved before he donned a sleek pair of black slacks, a light blue button up dress shirt, brown belt and brown hiking boots. 215's occupant gargled with mouthwash, threw on some jeans and a t-shirt that read: "I like big fish, big trucks and big girls (not necessarily in that order)." Both slipped Smith and Wesson .45 Caliber Police Tactical pistols and badges onto their belts.

At exactly 7:21 a.m. both motel room doors opened. David Jackson and Jesse Owens stepped out onto the second floor balcony. Jackson took in a deep gulp of the fresh morning air while Owens reacted negatively to the light of the severely overcast morning before putting on a pair of sunglasses and taking a long swallow from an extra large bottle of Pepto Bismal.

The two men standing on the balcony couldn't be more different. Jackson stood at six foot two inches, his skin was a dark black, his frame stout and muscular. He was approaching forty years and his face was beginning to show the crisp edges that age brings. Owens was considerably younger, still in his twenties, his face continued to maintain the youth of a newborn, occasionally showing red in his cheeks whenever he was embarrassed. His slender frame only reached five foot nine, his pale skin even more so this chilly morning because of the hangover he was attempting to shake off.

Once the Washington State morning environment was examined, both cops went back into their rooms, obtained their suitcases and carried them downstairs to Jackson's car. Owens was sent with the room keys to check out of the motel while Jackson warmed up his metallic black 1967 Ford Mustang Shelby GT-500.

Their first stop was next door to the motel; one dozen doughnuts were acquired and the two were fast on their way out of town. They were happy to leave North Bend Washington for a number of reasons, the first being that they simply didn't like the small town atmosphere that permeated the little city of about five thousand people. People there were actually kind and considerate, something that Jackson wasn't used to and Owens had forgotten. The second reason was that they could finally accomplish what they had come to the country town nearly 40 miles east of Seattle for. They headed down a narrow two lane highway that led east from the town and into even more sparsely populated country than they had just left.

About twenty miles out of North Bend was a farm. While most farms raised chickens or apples, this farm had no livestock whatsoever and its only plant life, besides the customary Washington blackberries, was of the Cannabis variety, though that was only grown for recreational purposes. The real use of the farm, where it made its profit, was in chemicals: Methamphetamine, a synthetic derivative of Amphetamine.

At first look, the farm was quite normal, it contained a house, barn, a greenhouse for the few Cannabis plants grown there and a few other miscellaneous buildings. It was inside the barn that the

Meth Lab was set up. Methamphetamines can be made with fairly easy to obtain chemicals, which makes the drug a favorite among small time outfits.

Most of the chemicals used in synthesizing Meth are highly volatile and the synthesis itself produces highly toxic waste. This operation was no exception. Because the chemists producing the drug had only a little experience, they had inadvertently been producing large quantities of Phosphine gas, which was highly explosive.

Those running the farm had gotten off to an early start this particular morning because they were due to send off a shipment that afternoon and hadn't yet made all the drugs expected. The usual breakfast was therefore skipped and the two part-time chemists went straight to work producing Crystal Meth or "Devil's Dandruff" as it would be called when passed off on the streets of Seattle.

Jackson and Owens arrived at the staging area just before eight in the morning. Since they were scheduled to begin their briefing at eight and be operational by nine, everyone had already arrived. The Seattle Narcotics Squad would be running the primary operation with backup coming from the King County Sheriff's department. Emergency services and Hazardous Material disposal came from King County also. King County encompassed all of

Seattle and even North Bend, since the farm was outside of any city limits, King County had jurisdiction. Seattle Police had been the department that had generated the information for the warrant and a deal had been worked out to let the more experienced Seattle Narcotics Squad conduct the operation with King County Sheriffs in reserve.

King County sent a total of six cars and twelve deputies to assist with the raid. Lieutenant Jackson, who was in operational command decided to place four of the cars on nearby roads to institute a roadblock in case anyone might flee the scene. He held the two other cars, each with two Sheriff's deputies, in reserve in the event that assistance might be needed at the farm.

Jackson couldn't bring the entire narcotics unit with him so he chose to bring his best and brightest team, Narcotics Squad One. N.S.1. consisted of five of Jackson's best narcotics detectives.

Ben Casteel was a veteran officer who had been on the force almost twenty years. Casteel stood straight, but not tall, he was slightly shorter than Owens but made up for a lack of height with girth, a revered combination of fat and muscle that allowed him to intimidate suspects while simultaneously putting victims at ease that their Officer could handle himself. He wore glasses, even on raids. He refused contact lenses because they irritated his eyes. He broke many pairs and kept at least half a dozen spares in his car at all times.

Casteel was the official commander of the N.S.1. team.

While Jackson ran the entire squad, each team had a Sergeant in charge of them. Casteel made Sergeant after only five years on the force and was very proud of that but had since not been promoted, something that hardly bothered him. He preferred being in charge of only a small group, the extraneous amount of paperwork required of the higher grades didn't appeal to Casteel, who would always consider himself an old fashioned beat cop.

Kimberly Mason had only been on the job six years but what she lacked in experience she made up for with tenacity. Her deep voice, short hair and butch appearance often made her the butt of jokes, though never to her face. It had been said that she was the toughest woman in the police department and probably the meanest.

Mason detested most of the other female officers on the force. They were weak in her view, propagating the double standard that she was known to rant and rave against. She believed that to be an officer, anyone, regardless of gender, should be required to perform the same physically demanding tasks. That was something the other female officers weren't made to do since the department's physical fitness test had a different standard for females than for males. While a cadet, Mason had easily taken the test under the male standards and beaten it.

Marcus Holloman had been an engineering student at the University of Washington before he heard the call of public service or that was what he frequently told people. Besides Jackson he was the only African American in the Narcotics Unit but where he'd thought he would find racism he'd actually discovered was where he fit in the most.

Holloman was as tall as Jackson but much more toned. His only hobby was body building. He organized every part of his life around the sport. Anytime the team needed to reach him in his off-duty hours, all they had to do was check the gym, where they often found Kimberly Mason spotting him.

Ari Rothstein was short and fat, his long black hair parted in the center and thin goatee made him unlikely to be mistaken for anyone else. He'd been a cop a little over ten years. Born into a wealthy Jewish family he'd decided to become a cop after being bullied in college and because his degree in computer programming wouldn't buy him a cup of coffee in Seattle after the Seattle computer programming market flooded when the dot.com's fell.

Joel Johnson was the straightest shooter in the squad. The stereotypical cop: caucasion, six foot, two hundred pounds, brown hair, brown eyes, 20/20 vision. Joel Johnson had never disobeyed a single rule in his life. He could be found in church every Sunday and Wednesday. He'd never been married, never had a girlfriend, rarely got a date, and when he did, disaster happened. The rest of the squad joked that every time Johnson went out with a woman, they sold all of their stock in whatever restaurant he was taking her to. Johnson took the teasing in stride, he realized that his honesty and lack of vices was what often hindered his love life, but he didn't want to change any of those things about himself.

When they saw Jackson's Mustang pull into the assembly area, the Sheriff's deputies and Seattle officers slowly migrated toward it. Jackson and Owens got out, Owens more slowly than Jackson who opened the trunk and handed Owens a bulletproof vest with the word "POLICE" written in white across the front and back.

"How you feeling this morning Jesse?" Casteel asked the approaching Owens.

"Yeah, how's your singing voice?" Kimberly Mason joined in.

"Singing voice?" Jackson asked, fastening the straps to his vest.

"Last night at that bar Hank Williams here decided he was going to do the drunk version of Achy Breaky Heart." Holloman informed. Jackson laughed and turned to Owens who was popping a couple of Aspirin.

"It was a bet. They had karaoke and Johnson bet me I wouldn't do it." Owens told him.

"And what did Joel have to sing?" Jackson asked.

"Ice Ice Baby." Owens replied.

"Did he?"

"I don't recall, I kinda passed out." After Owens' answer everyone turned to look at Johnson who was standing in the back of the group and smiling.

"Nope, he weaseled out." Ari Rothstein informed.

"Hey, it wasn't my fault he got trashed and wasn't conscious to collect." Johnson said defensively.

"You owe me one rap song." Owens returned flatly.

The King county Sheriff's deputies had now gathered around Jackson's Mustang and everyone was ready for their final brief. Sergeant Bill Bramble, the highest ranking King County Deputy turned to his men and spoke.

"Ok, lets get started, we went through assignments yesterday, lets do this exactly the way we planned it." He said with Jackson beside him. "For you two that weren't here yesterday, this is Lieutenant Jackson, he's the Seattle O.I.C." Jackson smiled and nodded. Bramble turned toward him, lowered his voice, and whispered into his ear. "Speak slowly, they're just country bred white boys." Jackson looked at him confusingly but Bramble walked away and blended into the clump of deputies before Jackson could ask about the comment.

"Alright, just like we walked through yesterday. My team's going to take point. Johnson, Mason, Holloman and Casteel will approach on foot from the north. Rothstein, Owens and I will be in the Explorer and we'll enter from the northwest." Jackson said and pointed to the black Ford Explorer that N.S.1. brought with them. "I want your two cars to come in from the west down the driveway." Jackson told Bramble, who nodded. "I'll be on the radio and will tell you when I want you to come in. The other four cars will be covering the adjacent roads to make sure nobody gets out. Hopefully we'll have a clean safe sweep here, I don't want anybody getting hurt. We know that the barn is where they're making the meth, its filled with gases, so stay away from it. Under no circumstances is anyone to enter the barn, that's what our resident HazMat team is here for." Everyone nodded. With a signal from Jackson, Owens took a picture out of a folder he was holding and showed it to the deputies, it was of a red headed man in his early twenties.

"Our primary objective is the narcotics, but the man we want is this man here." Owens said, showing everyone the picture. "His name is Eddie Collins, his older brother used to be a major player in Seattle and now junior here thinks he's going to pick up where his bro left off. We know he's going to be here today to take possession of a large amount of Meth. It is imperative that he doesn't escape. Consider Collins armed and dangerous. He's a bad boy in every sense of the word. He likes to brag to his friends that he'll never be taken alive and his favorite hobby is shooting at cops. Use extreme caution with him." Everyone nodded again.

"Alright, let's get into position, we'll go on my mark." Jackson told them.

While the team members moved into their respective positions, the northwestern sky slowly opened up to produce the large thick raindrops it was famous for. Mason, Holloman, Casteel, and Johnson were dropped off along an adjacent road that ran along the north of the farm and began making their way through the thick undergrowth. Ari Rothstein held the search warrant and drove the

Explorer. Jackson and Owens sat in the vehicle until they got to the trail that led to the farm from the northwest, once there, they prepared to move in by getting out, standing on the step bars and holding onto the roof side rails for easier deployment. Two of the marked cruisers stopped just out of sight of the main driveway and readied to move. The other four cruisers took up their assigned positions, one set of two on the adjacent road to the north and the other set on Interstate 90, which was very close to the farm. Once everyone was in position, Jackson gave the order to move in.

The team that was on foot moved up to the farm, slowly and quietly, through the underbrush, their weapons out and at the ready position. The Ford Explorer moved equally slowly and quietly along the northwest dirt path. The Sheriff's deputies waited for Jackson's signal to move.

The foot team was the first to have eyes on the farm. Everything looked normal from their position so they continued to move in. Each member knew that soon they would be free of the undergrowth that was their cover and they'd have to dash to the structures.

Just before Holloman approached the end of the undergrowth he noticed something slight catch his leg. He was suddenly lifted into the air by his left ankle and suspended several feet off the ground, upside down from a tree.

The trap activated a battery powered, waterproof radio that was attached to a very large loudspeaker which began playing

"Every Breath You Take" by Sting and The Police. Not only did the rest of the team hear the music but so did everyone on the farm. Massive activity ensued around the barn and farmhouse.

"Everybody move!" Casteel yelled at the other team members. They all started running. Mason was the first out of the undergrowth and immediately upon clearing the trees found that she too had stepped into a trap. It was a six foot pit dug into the ground that was covered by a large piece of green carpet camouflaged with grass and foliage. Because of the rain and water that was previously in the pit, Mason was immediately bathed in mud and bugs.

Casteel and Johnson dashed from the tree line toward the chaos that was ongoing around the barn. They inadvertently tripped a wire that activated an elaborate pulley system which eventually led to the opening of a cage that held a very large, very hungry, very angry rottweiler. A dog that instantly honed its attention on the pair of approaching cops.

Casteel and Johnson stopped in their tracks when they saw the ferocious animal sprinting towards them and headed back to the tree line. They scrambled around for a second before one of them hastily suggested climbing a large tree that split into two about three feet up. They climbed and the rottweiler attacked the tree below them, barking and clawing for his supper.

The Explorer quickly arrived and all three cops wondered where the rest of their team was. Jackson saw Eddie Collins run from the house toward the barn while several of the other men moved toward the three cars parked beside the house.

"Jesse, get them! Ari, get the others!" Jackson yelled and jumped to the ground from the still moving SUV. Owens jumped also, drawing his weapon and starting for the cars.

"Backup units move in!" Jackson yelled into his radio. He pursued Eddie around the barn. Rothstein slid the Explorer to a stop and darted to the tree line to find the rest of the team.

Owens arrived at the group of cars just as two of the suspects sped off down the driveway. Another two suspects saw him and darted in the opposite direction with Owens in pursuit.

The two marked cruisers raced down the long gravel driveway until they reached the spikes that Eddie had activated when he heard the warning music playing. The spikes punctured all four tires of the first vehicle carrying Sergeant Bramble and it slammed into a nearby tree. Though the second vehicle saw what had happened to the first, the combination of speed, reaction time, rain and uncertainty as to what had caused the wreck caused it also to be struck by the spikes, sending it into the back of the first car.

Eddie saw that his operation was in danger and knowing that everything inside the barn would be used as evidence against him, decided to activate his contingency plan. He looked over his shoulder and saw Jackson approaching him. Quickly he darted to the side of the barn, fished a tiny electrical switch out of the ground and flipped it. The fuse was connected to a single stick of dynamite, which in turn was tied to a beam above the chemical soup. Jackson saw Eddie stand back up and ordered him to halt. Eddie ignored the command and ran away from the timebomb he'd just activated.

"Quit running damnit, I got a hangover!" Owens chased two men around the house for the second lap.

Marcus Holloman had now cut himself out of the tree that had been holding him prisoner and was helping Kimberly Mason out of the slippery muddy pit that she'd fallen into.

Casteel and Johnson stared down the tree at the giant rottweiler that was barking and clawing at them. The dog's attention was phased for just a moment when it realized that someone was approaching it. The animal turned around with the intention of attacking the new person encroaching its territory but was struck with three .45 Caliber bullets. Within a few seconds Ari Rothstein was standing over the dying animal and looking up at the tree.

"What's the matter with you two?" Rothstein asked with contempt. "Didn't they give you guys guns?"

"That's low man." Casteel jumped out of the tree and landed on his feet. "You can't shoot a dog."

"That was in point of fact going to be my next move." Johnson climbed down. "Beat me to it is all." All three men headed for the farm.

Eddie Collins was heading for a tree line that was past the farmhouse but Jackson was too fast for him. When Jackson caught up, he grabbed Eddie by the shirt and flung him into the mud.

The fuse that Eddie had activated finally reached the

dynamite, detonating it and with it the noxious chemicals inside the barn.

Jackson pointed his weapon at Eddie but his arrest was halted by the barn exploding into a huge fireball that knocked him to the ground.

"What do you think is going on?" One of the Sheriff's deputies on the I-90 perimeter asked his partner.

The partner watched the massive fireball followed by a plumb of black smoke erupt from over the trees. "I'd say it aint good."

Everyone at the farm was showered with wood and debris, some moving faster than bullets, amazingly however, no one was hit head on and the explosion only caused cuts and bruises. The team that was heading toward the action from the tree line was knocked off their feet but quickly picked themselves up.

The two chemists who had made their escape in one of the cars flew down the driveway but were unaware that Eddie had activated the spikes that had disabled the two marked cruisers and soon found themselves driving on four flat tires. Unable to maintain control of the vehicle, the driver attempted to overcorrect and sent the car into a small ditch. When the vehicle came to a stop, the two chemists unbuckled their safety belts and jumped out of the vehicle. Their plan to leave on foot. They instead found two sets of Sheriff's deputies, weapons drawn, who were not in a pleasant mood.

Jackson shook off the deafening bang that was ringing in his ears and scanned the area for Eddie. He found that his prey had recovered much faster than he had and was now heading for one of the parked cars in the driveway. Eddie chose the only car he had keys for, a blue Ford Aerostar minivan, which he'd brought to transport the drugs in. Jackson jumped to his feet, preparing to chase. Eddie threw the van in drive and spun off toward a small dirt path.

Jackson headed for the police Explorer and saw Owens starting his third lap of chasing the other two men around the farmhouse.

"Jesse, the truck, get the truck!" Jackson yelled to his partner who saw Eddie speeding off and understood. Owens was closer to the Explorer than Jackson and jumped in the driver's seat. When Owens brought the Explorer past him Jackson jumped onto the driver's side step bars and grabbed the roof side rails. They followed Eddie into the shrubbery where Eddie's Aerostar was cutting its own trail.

The two suspects running around the farmhouse soon realized that their pursuer was no longer after them and stopped, each taking in deep breaths. They turned around and headed for the last vehicle in the driveway, until they saw the rest of the narcotics team rushing them.

Jackson was whacked with branches, shrubs, rain, and mud as Owens followed Eddie through the woods. He held on tightly to the slippery roof side rails and concentrated on keeping his feet on the step bars every time Owens hit a bump, which was frequent. After narrowly avoiding several trees, the vehicles found themselves in a large open field that led to I-90. Eddie's Aerostar was moving through the tall grasses with Jackson and Owens not far behind.

"What the hell?" One of the deputies on vigil on the interstate watched the two vehicles bounce through the field.

"C'mon!" The other deputy exclaimed before he hit the gas and turned on his flashing lights. The second car followed suit.

"Where the hell are those chaser cars?!" Jackson yelled at Owens after he saw Eddie plow through a fence and make a frantic turn onto the Interstate. Owens concentrated on going through the same part of fence Eddie had already knocked down for him, then made his own turn onto the interstate, barely missing the deputy's cars and forcing them both into the median before they returned to the road.

"Found'em." He told Jackson.

The narcotics team had finally cornered the two slippery suspects in a pincer movement around the house. The suspects looked in front of them to see Mason and Holloman, then behind them to find Casteel and Johnson. They immediately went to their side in the direction of what was left of the burning barn. The four detectives all grabbed at the suspects, slamming one to the ground. The other made it halfway to the barn before Rothstein tackled his legs and sent him sprawling into the mud. Before he knew it his hands were cuffed behind his back and Rothstein was turning him over.

"By the way," Rothstein got to one knee, took out a folded piece of paper and dropped it on his suspect's chest, "Seattle Narcotics, executing a search warrant."

Eddie's Aerostar sped along I-90 with Jackson and Owens right behind it. Jackson was glad to be free of the forest but now had to contend with the sting of the rain at such high speeds along with the backwash Eddie's tires were spewing him with.

The group of vehicles were approaching two very large obstructions, the first was a tractor trailer in the right lane that was being passed by a station wagon in the left. What concerned Jackson even more than that was the highway construction that he knew was ahead.

The station wagon was almost past the truck but Eddie didn't care. He passed the wagon on its left, going onto the shoulder of the interstate, then cutting across in front of the station wagon before he was actually clear of it. Owens saw what Eddie was attempting and

decided to follow, he started to pass the station wagon just as Eddie
cut into its path. Eddie was too close and the wagon veered right to
avoid hitting him. The wagon's front bumper caught between the
tractor's two back tires The entire front end of the wagon was
sucked into the wheels of the truck which began crunching.

The tractor trailer slammed the forward section of the station
wagon into the road and the wagon's rear section lifted off the
ground and spun directly into the path of the Explorer. Owens
whipped to the left and the rear bumper of the wagon impacted with
the top left hand side of the Explorer's windshield, cracking it and
cutting through part of the passenger side door. The Explorer
fishtailed for a moment before Owens regained control and kept
going. Jackson's feet slipped from the step bars. He barely hung on
with his hands.

The tractor trailer hit the brakes and one of the chase cars
stopped to render assistance.

Jackson slipped twice before replanting his feet on the step
bars, then reinforced his grasp on the roof side rails. Owens sped up
behind Eddie's Aerostar.

"And you talk about *my* driving!" Jackson screamed at his
partner through the open window. Jackson could now see the signs
warning of the construction zone and knew they had to act quickly.
"Get us up beside him on the right." He ordered Owens. The
Explorer sped up until its bumper almost collided with Eddie's but
didn't, then Owens, a Nascar fan, slipped the vehicle to the

Aerostar's right and began to pass.

When the cars started passing the familiar red cones that signified a construction zone they were almost side by side but with Eddie's Aerostar still only slightly in the lead. The Explorer was now in Eddie's blind spot and noticing that he couldn't see it, he turned his head to see it coming up on his side. Eddie figured that he could take Jackson out by ramming his car into theirs.

Eddie turned his steering wheel and the gap between the vehicles quickly closed. Seeing what Eddie was doing, Jackson released one hand from the rail and opened the sliding door on the Aerostar's side. Before the two vehicles slammed together, Jackson jumped into the Aerostar.

Grabbing the passenger seat headrest for support, Jackson sideswiped Eddie with a punch which caused Eddie to slam into the Explorer again. Owens temporarily lost control on the wet pavement and let off the gas, taking out several of the warning cones.

Jackson grabbed at Eddie but lost his balance when Eddie veered from the last collision. Jackson fell out the open door, and was only saved by grabbing a seat belt. Owens regained control of the Explorer and took up a position behind the Aerostar, careful not to hit Jackson if he fell.

Jackson held onto the belt with both hands. He tried to get his feet back inside the speeding vehicle. Once that was done, Jackson catapulted himself onto Eddie, slamming his head into the steering wheel and forcing Eddie to lose control of the vehicle.

The Aerostar's rear wheels lost traction. Owens, much too close, veered right, losing control of the Explorer and becoming airborne when he hit a small clump of dirt. The Explorer was lifted a few feet off the ground, slammed into an electronic construction warning sign and came to rest in a large mound of gravel that was eventually going to be used to make pavement.

Jackson reached down, turned the key to the vehicle, shutting it off, and tried to use Eddie's head to steer until the vehicle slowed. Eddie didn't like that plan and decided that he was going to devise a second. He reached up with both hands and twisted the steering wheel, sending the vehicle spinning off a sharp embankment that led up to an overpass that went over a local road. The Aerostar flipped down the embankment spewing mud, glass and metal everywhere it went. It finally settled at the bottom, next to the road, on its roof.

Eddie opened his eyes to see that he was upside down, his shoulder blades propping him up from the ceiling of the vehicle. He could hear the sounds of the wreckage coming to rest and the mud dripping from the tires. He put his hand on the driver's side door window, which was already full of cracks, the extreme light pressure from his hand caused the window to shatter, spitting glass all over him. He slowly crawled out of the vehicle and after a moment's respite propped himself up on the Aerostar to get to his feet. He turned his head to the rear of the Aerostar and saw nothing but Jackson's fist, which dropped him again.

"Guess what Eddie?" Jackson rolled his suspect onto his chest and took out his handcuffs. "You win the race. Know what that means?" Jackson cuffed Eddie. "First place is a trip to jail." He informed with a smile.

Just off the interstate, Owens pushed and pulled to get the now deflated airbag out of his face. He saw that the entire front section of the Explorer was covered with gravel. "We're gonna be in soo much trouble." He rested his head against the steering wheel.

2

"Homefront"

The cleanup effort took about seven hours. The family of four in the station wagon was for the most part alright, though the matriarch was taken to the hospital with neck pains. The driver of the tractor-trailer was unharmed but understandably not very polite about the situation. All five suspects, the two chemists, plus two more suspects at the farm and of course Eddie Collins all sustained minor injuries from the explosion. Eddie was treated at a local hospital under guard and then taken back to the King County jail in North Bend to await transportation to Seattle.

None of the police officers or Sheriff's deputies sustained injuries that caused them to go to the hospital except Jackson who suffered a particularly bloody gash on his head from the car accident.

He was treated and released from the hospital. By the time he arrived back at the scene, everyone was wrapping up the investigation into what had happened.

Six more traps were found around the farm, Eddie's ingenious way of warning him if anybody was snooping around. The barn had been completely destroyed, all that was left was one free standing wall and trace evidence, which was picked up, processed and placed in the back of one of the King County patrol cars that was to be loaned to the Seattle unit.

The search conducted on the farmhouse revealed nothing but a closet full of stored chemicals. They too were processed because they were mostly the household cleaners and over-the-counter medications used in making Methamphetamine. A search of Eddie's Ford Aerostar minivan revealed the most confusing item of the day to the detectives. Inside the glove compartment was a neatly folded sheet of paper wrapped in a thick plastic cover. On the paper was the exact chemical makeup of the drug Cozaar along with very detailed directions in making the prescription medicine.

The Narcotics team's Ford Explorer had to be towed from the gravel mound and was sent back to Seattle, its collision with the construction sign most likely totaling the vehicle. After the scene was cleared, Jackson's team left the Fire Department and Haz-Mat teams to finish the cleanup and went back to the King County Sheriffs office in North Bend to complete their paperwork, a job that lasted several hours. Once that was done, Eddie and his men went before a Magistrate Judge in North Bend, where they were remanded into the custody of the Seattle Police Department and transported to that city.

Upon arrival in Seattle, Casteel, Johnson, and Holloman checked the prisoners into the King County Correctional Facility and made sure they were processed. Mason and Rothstein returned to police headquarters that was located in the North Precinct and the adjacent building, which had been rented out to the Police Department while Police Plaza was being rebuilt. They turned the Ford Explorer in to the motor pool, which was not pleased to receive it, then turned in their paperwork.

Jackson didn't get home until after 9 p.m., upon walking in the door, he found his wife Marcy sitting on the couch in her house clothes watching television with their youngest son, Trevor, who was four. Before Jackson could put his bags down, Trevor had hopped off the sofa and along with Crispy, the family Collie–named that because of his dark brown coat–ran to Jackson. Jackson dropped his suitcase and picked the little boy up.

"How's my boy?" Jackson asked his son, who replied by wrapping his arms around him tightly and telling his father how much he missed him . "I missed you too." Jackson replied.

"Did you get the bad guys?" The boy asked.

"We did." Jackson responded proudly.

"What happened to your head?" The boy pointed to the bandage taped to the side of his father's head, which caused Marcy to look over at her husband.

"Well, the bad guys didn't like me very much." Jackson responded.

"Did you beat'em up?"

"Better, I arrested them." Jackson told him, not wanting to reveal too much. He put the boy back on his feet. "It's just a scratch." He said, crossing the room and planting a kiss on his wife's lips. "Where is everybody?"

"The drama queen is upstairs on the phone as usual and Tyson is in the den on the computer." Marcy answered, staring at his bandage. "Battle scar huh?"

"Yeah, there were a couple of problems. Nothing big." He reassured her.

"Well you better talk to Tyson, he's been going on about this camp thing ever since you left." Jackson nodded and stepped into the den. Trevor jumped back onto the sofa with his mother.

"Hey Dad." The 8 year old on the computer said without turning his head.

"You don't greet your dad at the door anymore when he gets home from a trip?" Jackson hugged his son from behind.

"I wanted to show you something." The boy replied. Jackson focused his attention on the screen. "It's the summer camp's website, they just got it up, we're gonna go swimming, and play football, isn't it awesome? Maybe I can play football for the school, just like you did?"

"Well I think you have a few years before you get into college, you gotta get through regular school first." Jackson responded, pleased by what he saw on the website.

"I can't wait." Tyson responded enthusiastically.

"It won't be long." Jackson rubbed the top of the boy's head. "Why don't you shut her down and head to bed okay?"

"But Tonya gets to stay up late?" Tyson argued.

"Take your brother with you too." Jackson left the room and went up the stairs. He found Tonya in her bedroom with the cordless telephone gossiping about boys and giggling furiously. Jackson stood at her door, watching his 12 year old daughter and smiling at her comments.

"He's so goofy and I think he likes you..." She was saying into the phone, oblivious to her father's presence. It wasn't long before she felt her father's eyes on her and turned to see him. "Dad!" She said covering the receiver. "I don't listen to you when you're on the phone."

"I just wanted to let you know that your old man was home but I see you're busy." He smiled.

"I'll be off at eleven like I'm supposed to." She said assured. Jackson turned to walk back down the stairs. "How'd your thing go?" She asked him.

"Good." Jackson replied. He was getting used to his daughter ignoring him. When she was younger, her father meant the world to her, but as she got older she had been discovering the larger world around her, which barely included him. He knew that he needed to expect that but he missed her attention.

He took the trash out before he took his suitcase up to his room and unpacked it. He showered because it had been a long day and he'd spent most of it soaking wet. He changed his bandage, the stitches he'd gotten at the hospital hurt but he popped a pain pill. By the time he was finished the kids had gone to bed.

When Jackson emerged from the bathroom, he found his wife just getting into bed. "A few problems?" She asked. He crawled under the sheets next to her.

"Just a couple." He took her in his arms. It was an unspoken rule that they not discuss such things in front of the children and the rule had also seemed to roll over between the two of them. Marcy didn't mind, she knew who her husband was and what he did for a living. She actually liked it. It turned her on that her husband was occasionally in dangerous situations. Early in their marriage she'd worried about him but that had seemed to pass after a time and she accepted his need to do what he did.

Jackson didn't mind her attitude at all, he enjoyed that he could come home to a loving family after a long day's work. It was as though his job was a normal one. He only wished that he could work banker's hours to spend more time with them.

"Looks like more than a couple." Marcy, a Registered Nurse, opened the fresh bandage and gazed at the stitches. "About half a dozen I'd say." She replaced the bandage and kissed her husband. "No concussion?"

"Just a cut."

"Because that sounded like a nasty wreck?"

"How did you know it was a wreck?" He nibbled on her neck.

"Jesse called me when you were at the hospital." She informed.

"Really?" He moved his hand inside her nightshirt. "I'm going to have to have a talk with him."

"Nope. He's under orders to call if anything happens to you." She caressed his back. "He knows what'll happen if he doesn't."

"At least I'll know I'm being watched from now on."

"Yeah, you'll have to curtail your late night rendezvous." She said in jest.

"I'm not curtailing this one." He returned.

The sun rose on the Seattle skyline. Its light shined through the window and onto the bed, waking Jill. She opened her eyes but didn't move, the slightest movement would wake her partner. Instead she kept her head on his bare chest and enjoyed the moment. She had predetermined that this would be the last such moment with him and she wanted to maintain it. She closed her eyes again and listened to his heart beat. His hands were wrapped around her slender body, one at her hip, the other on her back. He was so peaceful when he was asleep; she didn't want it to end. Soon it was time and she slowly lifted her head.

Owens opened his eyes to look at her, when she saw that he was awake, she sat up. The sunlight from the window shadowed her perky breasts as the sheets slid down to her waist. She was beautiful, her brown hair resting on her shoulders, the sun illuminating her small nipples. It lasted only a moment before she moved and the scenery changed but Owens would remember it for quite some time.

"Good morning." He said in the standard southern accent she liked so much.

"Morning." She whispered. She gently rubbed his chest until she got to a sore spot.

"That hurts." Owens playfully shrieked.

"What happened yesterday?" She asked, she knew he hadn't wanted to talk about it the night before.

"I got blown up again." He replied nonchalantly.

"Does that happen a lot?"

"Happened twice last year." He told her.

"Ouch." She laughed.

"In the same day too." He told her, which elicited a strange look. "Then I got shot. I had a bad day."

"Bad day?" She repeated. Her feet hit the cold floor of his

apartment and she began gathering her clothes.

"You gonna stay for breakfast? I don't have to be at work for a while." He asked. "I make a hell of an omelet."

"No, I got a job of my own you know." Jill replied. "Jesse? Where are we going?" She had decided that she was going to do this, just not how to start it and this seemed the most pertinent question.

"I don't know, I guess we can go to dinner tonight if you want." Owens answered, not really getting the question.

"No, I mean us, where is this going?" She asked. Owens laid his head back on the pillow, realizing what she was talking about.

"I don't know, what's wrong with the way things are?" He said, wiping the sleep from his face.

"It's not going anywhere, that's what's wrong with it Jesse. I can't keep doing this." Owens didn't reply and the room fell quiet while she buttoned her blouse. Jill didn't like what Owens' silence was implying so she sat back down on the bed and rubbed his ear. "Do you care about me?"

"Of course."

"Do you love me?"

Owens shied away at the question and took a moment to respond. "Look, there are a lot of things..."

"That's what I thought." She said, her tone different.

"I care about you, I do, but love is something different, I just don't think..."

"That's ok." She said, getting her purse. "But I can't keep doing this Jesse, all I find is men who only want sex and I need more than that."

"I don't just want sex." Owens defended himself.

"But that's all we do Jesse." She brushed her hair with her fingers in the mirror. "I think I love you but if you can't offer more than a weekly fling? Well, I just can't do that."

"Ok, we'll do more than that. We'll go out. Let me take you to dinner tonight? It's just that my job...I don't want you to get caught up in it. Almost everybody I know is divorced and I don't want that." Owens said, trying to salvage things.

"That's just an excuse. It's what you said last time and the time before that. You try way to hard to be a movie cop, that's not how real people do things Jesse, you've gotta take a chance every once in a while."

"I don't try to be a movie cop, if I did I'd be an alcoholic. Come out to dinner with me?"

"Jesse, I need more than you're offering. I'm sorry." Jill said, determined to stick to her guns and not be lured back like the last time.

"It's not like that." Owens said. After putting her purse over her shoulder, she sat down on the bed again.

"I know." She reached down to his mouth with hers but just before their lips touched, she changed direction and kissed his forehead. "I don't consider sex a sport." She got up and walked out of the room.

"Ok, what about a hobby?" Owens asked. He heard his front door open. "Leisure?" The door closed. "A sweet diversion?" Nothing. He laid his head back down onto the pillow and sighed, partly in relief. "Maybe?" Silence. "Think about it?"

"I'm waiting." Assistant Chief of Police Bethany Knox tapped her pen on her desk. Knox was in her late fifties, she had salt and pepper hair and crow's feet, which she used makeup to try to disguise. A career police administrator, Knox had grown discontent with the business of late. Her reputation had been tarnished in the last year because she had become the scapegoat for certain operational inadequacies resulting from the police handling of a terrorist incident in Seattle. She believed that she had done nothing wrong during the attacks and was unjustly made the patsy for superiors who had failed to act correctly.

That was why she looked forward to retirement, which wouldn't come for several more years but it wouldn't be soon enough for her. Retirement would mean that she had finally escaped the pressure put on her by maintaining the position that she'd carried for several years, that of Assistant Chief of Police in command of the Criminal Investigations Bureau. A position she realized that she would never move beyond.

"Well?" She asked the two officers sitting in front of her desk again.

"Things didn't go exactly as planned." Jackson replied, not knowing what else to say.

"I hope not, I'd hate to think that one of my most experienced unit commanders planned a complete and utter pooch screw."

"Bethany, there was absolutely no way we could know that they were going to go all Deliverance on us with the man-traps." Jackson replied.

"I understand that, I really do." Knox returned. "But you did more than that. Let me read you a little." Knox turned her eyes toward the file in her hands. "You caused a massive explosion, which involved noxious gases. You caused a two car accident involving a tractor-trailer and a family of four. You completely destroyed one very expensive road warning sign."

"That was me, sorry." Owens raised his hand. Knox peered at him angrily before continuing.

"You totaled one of our SUV's, sent two King County Sheriff's vehicles to the repair shop with four flat tires each, plus other damage the cost of which is undetermined as of yet but I'm sure we'll get a bill. One suspect went to the hospital, along with you. Oh, and let's not forget you lost most of your evidence and killed a dog."

"You of all people know that these things rarely go exactly to plan." Jackson defended.

"Yeah, we tried to save the dog." Owens helped. "Johnson did mouth to mouth on it and everything." Knox didn't reply, she stared at Owens a moment before standing up, walking over to his chair and bending over next to his ear.

"You're. Not. Funny." She whispered with a tone that almost killed Owens in his chair before standing upright again and sitting on the corner of her desk. "Speaking of the dog, there's something strange in your report." She picked up the folder. "The Chief was asking me about this. Casteel and Johnson shot the dog and rightfully so but they were still the last to arrive at the house. Why is that?"

"Mouth to..." Knox shot her stare at Owens. "Nevermind."

"I really don't know, I was chasing Collins." Jackson answered. "I'll ask and find out."

"You'd better, because I think you really needed their help up there sooner than when they got there. I have to explain this mess to the Chief and I'd better not find out that something stupid happened..." Knox quickly searched her mind for the most ridiculous thing she could imagine. "Like that dog chased them up a tree or something. Believe me, heads will roll."

"I'm sure it wasn't anything like that." Jackson told her.

"There's also the matter of you jumping on a suspect's vehicle during a high speed pursuit?"

"Eddie was endangering people's lives by the way he was driving, we had to get him off the road." Jackson had already thought up the excuse.

"I don't have to tell you how dangerous that was. It is not the policy of this department or any other that I know of, that we put our officers in situations like that. What if you'd missed, or God forbid, been killed? As stress free as it would make my life, I'd still hate to have to attend your funeral."

"I didn't think about it, I'm sorry." Jackson lied.

"It's not enough that we've got the highest per capita homicide rate in the state, but our guys are now going out of the city, running around like Starsky and Hutch, blowing things up and jumping on cars!" She continued.. "I have three separate complaints from the Washington Department of Transportation alone for the construction site business. I have another two from environmental agencies and four from the King County Sheriff's office, including one about ethnically insensitive remarks made the day before the raid, during the planning phase and dry run."

"Look, Jesse, he sometimes says some things that get misconstrued, he's from Tennessee..." Jackson said in defense of his partner.

"The complaint was about you." Knox returned. Owens sighed in relief.

"Oh." Jackson said.

"Let me see here." She picked up the folder and opened it.

"Apparently you called the deputies 'country bred white boys?"
Knox stopped and grinned. "How clever."

"Oh, ok," Jackson snapped his fingers, "that's what that was
about."

"Of all the policies you completely ignored, that one will be
the one to get you fired Dave." Knox told him. "Now I get to break
the really bad news to you two."

"Jesus Christ, there's more?" Owens said aloud without
thinking.

"Much more." Knox replied. "I got a call from ADA Burke
this morning. Collins' lawyer is filing a motion and she thinks the
judge is going to grant it, that all charges be dismissed with
prejudice."

"What? Why?" Jackson's jaw dropped.

"Apparently the informant you used to get your warrant, the
one that was hunting and accidentally stumbled onto the operation.
He was over his limit."

"Oh that's bullshit!" Jackson replied.

"That's right he was poaching and since he didn't have a
legal reason to be there, the warrant is null and void. That makes
everything you got, the little it turned out to be," she said
sarcastically, "fruit of the forbidden tree and Mr. Collins, fine
upstanding turd that he is, walks."

"When is this happening?" Jackson asked. "At least let us
talk to him first."

"What would be the point of that? Before you got him back to Seattle, his lawyer was already filing motions. He's never going to talk to you without him and you won't get anything anyway. Besides, the Chief wants neither of you anywhere near him."

"Burke isn't going to fight it?" Owens asked.

"She'll do whatever she can but with the allegations of excessive force leveled against you in particular Dave, I don't think the judge will let it hold up. Looks like we lost this one." Jackson and Owens looked at each other in disgust, they didn't reply, Jackson just shook his head. "Well, since you two have just attained more complaints than most cops get in their entire careers and that was just from fellow government agencies, plus that thing last year." That was how Knox had taken to referring to the terrorist attacks, as "that thing last year." "The Chief thinks it would be a good idea for you two to take a break from all this."

"What do you mean?" Jackson asked, visibly worried.

"He thinks that you two are overexposed, I can't disagree, so we're taking you out of narcotics, at least for a little while."

"What about my teams?" Jackson asked.

"Squads two and three will assist vice and be under their own squad leaders, I'm putting N.S.1. on criminal intelligence duty. They can't do any harm there, they'll just be collecting information and handing it off."

"What about us?" Owens asked.

"Well I wanted to put you in the records room, that way I

could be sure that you can't blow anything up but the Chief likes you and we have a homicide problem."

"Oh no, not the corpse patrol." Owens said.

"As you know, we have had more homicides in the city already this year than in the last two years combined and the homicide division is severely overworked. So that's where I'm putting you two." Knox took a folder off her desk and opened it. "I have a good one for you, it's a nice simple murder that you two will have no problem working, hopefully for a long long time. Two months ago a sixty-two year old accountant named Randy Taylor was shotgunned to death out by Seward Park. He had his ten year old granddaughter with him, she was also shot."

"I take it she didn't die?" Jackson asked.

"No, apparently something startled the suspect and he fled before he could finish the job. Another fisherman found her wandering around with a gunshot wound to her chest and shotgun spray in her back. She spent over a week in critical condition but she pulled through." Knox handed Jackson the file. "Homicide didn't get a grasp on it because of the girl's condition. Since they're booked solid, I thought you two could do something with it."

"This case is cold." Jackson scanned through the file.

"Yes and no." Knox replied. "The initial investigation yielded no leads so it was put in the to-do stack. The little girl recovered and went home. Three days ago, the mother called us and told us that she believes she has some information that can help us.

So its not exactly cold, just slightly chilled. When the Chief mentioned, in an outdoor voice, that you two should lay low, I thought this would be perfect for you."

"In other words, you're shuffling us off into the backroom so we can't bother you anymore?" Jackson translated.

"That *is* my sincerest hope, yes." Knox replied. "This wasn't random, he wasn't robbed or anything like that, so it was probably someone he knew or had dealings with of some sort. It's a nice little homicide that you won't have to blow anything up to solve. I shouldn't have to tell you that I don't want to see you in this office again until you've got something solid and are ready to make an arrest. Please, can I have a couple of weeks without anything happening involving the two of you? That's all I ask."

3

"C.I.P.A."

The sun rose up over the beautiful Seattle skyline in the embrace of a baby blue sky. Even before daylight broke on the busy metropolis people began moving about in their daily routines. Under cover of the pre-dawn morning, traffic heightened, car lights could be seen scurrying about on the roads and highways, shopkeepers prepared their storefronts for opening, cooks readied the ingredients to their patron's favorite breakfast dishes and coffee was brewed. As alarm clock/radio/coffee makers all over the Northwestern seaboard struck 6:00 A.M., the aroma of hot java permeated the city streets. Within an hour the city was aglow with the morning's light, its citizenry moving about their routines.

The highways, interstates, main roads, secondary roads, one-way thoroughfares all jammed with activity. School buses, trams, taxicabs, public buses, privately owned vehicles, and carpools swam through the endless sea of traffic that was the normal reaction to the sun's ominous glow. On Second Avenue, a black Mustang Shelby GT-500 parked itself next to the street. The vehicle's two occupants got out and put some change in the meter before beginning the two block walk to their favorite coffee shop.

"So why didn't you ask her to stay?" Jackson asked, continuing their conversation while they walked.

"I don't know, I just couldn't, I liked her but she wanted too much." Owens replied, slightly appalled at his own behavior.

"I don't get you man." Jackson told him. "There you have Jill, who's a great girl, who cares about you and you're turning her away."

"It's not about how great she is. She's annoying, she snores somethin' fierce."

"Oh who cares." Jackson said, brushing off his excuse.

"I just don't want to have half my stuff tied to her when she realizes what we do for a living."

"No, you don't want to have half your stuff tied to her at all." Jackson told him.

"Yeah that too, there's something to be said for being a bachelor." Owens remarked.

"There's something alright, sleepless nights, never knowing when your going to laid again. Yeah there's something." Jackson said.

"Look, I just don't wanna be tied down alright?" Owens asked his partner's permission.

"Hey, live your life the way you want, but trust me, you'd be much happier if you didn't constantly push away good things." Jackson told him before taking a few steps to think and finally asking what was on his mind. "What is it you're so scared of?"

"Clowns, I hate clowns, they're evil." Owens joked.

"C'mon." Jackson ordered.

"Alright." Owens relented as he opened the door to the coffee shop and they entered. "You really wanna know? I'll tell you."

"Yeah, I wanna know. What makes you act like an ass all the time?" Jackson said, getting in line.

"Ok, I was in love once. It was right after high school, in my first year of college." Owens confided.

"Junior College doesn't qualify as real college." Jackson laughed.

"Community college and we were poor, don't knock it. Not everybody could go to the University of Washington on a football scholarship you know."

"Ok, tell me about her." Jackson pushed.

"It was the most painful experience of my life and I aint never doing that again."

"Awe, did my lil' partner get burned?" Jackson said in a

childish voice.

"That's great, make fun of my pain." Owens returned. They finally reached the counter.

"What can I get for you today sirs?" The barista asked. Owens turned his attention to the menu.

"Yeah, I'll have a..." Owens read the menu. "Café Con Leche, short and dry, quad, venti, double cupped with wings and room."

"Good choice sir, and you sir?" The barista turned to Jackson.

"Drip." Jackson answered without having to think.

"How would you like that sir?"

"Black." He replied.

"Right." The barista answered, a little put off by Jackson's lack of enthusiasm. The two cops paid for their coffee's and moved to the waiting area.

"So, what's so special about this one girl?" Jackson asked.

"Nothin' special about her, just I never really wanted anybody else is all." Owens replied.

"That's it?" Jackson was now surprised.

"Dave, you know how when you met Marcy, you knew immediately that she was the only one for you?" Owens asked.

"I was drunk at a frat party, she turned me down and slapped me, twice. Yeah I knew I was in love." Jackson reminisced.

"Well that's how it was for me. I've never wanted anybody

else. Nobody before or since has ever made me feel like that. I decided that since I wasn't going to get the woman I wanted, I don't want anybody."

"That's pretty narrow minded don't you think?" Jackson said. Their drinks were served.

"One Café Con Leche, short and dry, quad, venti, double cupped with wings and room, and one house coffee, black. Here you go. Have a nice day and come back and see us gentlemen."

"Thanks." They both replied simultaneously before taking their coffees and stepping back out onto the street.

"So what happened?" Jackson asked after they started back to the car.

"I really don't wanna talk about it."

"Come on, what happened?" Jackson asked again.

"It's too painful."

"Out with it." Jackson prodded.

"Well, she died." Owens said, stopping and looking at the ground, a sad expression on his face. "She was on her way home from my place and there was this drunk driver..."

"Oh, man," Jackson touched his partner's arm in sympathy, "I'm sorry."

"Nah, I'm just screwing with you." Owens said, returning his expression back to normal. "She ran off with some football player."

"You prick." Jackson said sarcastically and started walking

again.

"Still, though, she was all I ever wanted." Owens strode beside Jackson again.

"What about a family, don't you want that?" Jackson asked after a moment's reflection.

"Hell no. A family? Let me see...the world of anniversaries, birthdays, babysitters, doctor's visits, diapers, crying, giant purple dinosaurs, nagging wives and three a.m. runs to the store for baby formula...that kind of family? Screw that!" Owens replied.

"People say that before they have kids but later they realize how important they are. You just don't realize the joy they can bring to your life." Jackson said, getting into the car.

"They're loud, smelly, annoying and needy. I can be all those things all by my lonesome and I don't even have to change diapers. I got all I need thank you very much." Owens stated confidently.

"Ah the ignorance of youth." Jackson dismissed. The car pulled out of the parking space and the two detectives continued to chat about the woman that Owens had never gotten over. They headed north, past the University district to find the house they were looking for.

The house was located in Phinney Ridge, a neighborhood named after a real estate developer who was influential in the area. The homes in this old Seattle neighborhood were characterized mostly by the hilly terrain and the ridge that they sat upon. They were mostly larger homes, the majority of them sitting atop small hills with steps leading up to them from the road. The lots that they sat on were small, barely large enough to hold the houses themselves which packed the homes in very close together.

Some of the homes were over 75 years old, though several had been restored and had additions built onto them, mostly second floors. They were made of wood, with aluminum siding of different colors. They were also swamped by trees and bushes that grew in their extremely small yards.

Jackson and Owens quickly found the residence they were looking for. It was a large home, sitting atop a hill with a large front porch that didn't seem so from the road because it wasn't rectangular, instead it was circular and wrapped around the front door. It was two stories, with unique arching dining room windows that looked out at the street. It's white window paneling contrasted beautifully with the dark blue aluminum siding that was so common to the area.

The narrow driveway ran up the short hill to the house, and because one car was already present, Jackson's Mustang barely fit when he parked it. Jackson and Owens each finished off their coffee before exiting the vehicle. Both looked at the house in admiration, each wishing they could live in such a home.

"Bring the files." Jackson ordered, Owens reached into the back seat and picked out the files that related the case.

"You think traffic is bad here?" Owens asked, more out of

curiosity than anything else while they walked up the steps to the home.

"Probably not. I'm wondering how much it costs?" Jackson returned.

"More than we make, that's for sure." Owens said when they reached the porch and Jackson rang the bell. They waited several seconds before hearing someone moving around inside, a few seconds later the door slowly opened to reveal a pudgy brunette with a soft face, wet hair, sparkling blue eyes and moderately pale skin wearing jeans and a white blouse that accentuated her curvy torso.

"Good morning, I'm Lieutenant David Jackson, this is Detective Owens, Seattle P.D.." Jackson showed the woman his identification. Owens, having forgotten to take out his I.D., fumbled with the files for a moment before producing it. "We're looking for Courtney Taylor."

"Yes, that's me," the woman said in a soft voice, "this is about my father?"

"Yes ma'am." Jackson answered. "Can we come inside?"

"Oh," Courtney hadn't thought about inviting them in. "Of course." The trio went directly to the living room, where a ten year old girl was laying on the sofa, watching a soap opera, her right arm in a sling and secured with duct tape to her body. Jackson and Owens' eyes shot to the duct tape, which generated confused expressions.

"Kaylee turn off the television, these two men are with the

police." Courtney told her daughter.

"But James is about to walk in on Trish and Neil in bed!" Kaylee exclaimed. The two cops stared at the tape. Instead of turning off the television completely, Kaylee muted it, that way she could be a part of the conversation without missing the excitement. Courtney noticed the stares and felt momentarily uncomfortable.

"I'm sorry, Kaylee's wound hasn't healed completely yet and she insists on moving her arm, so we had to tape it to her." Courtney told them. Jackson and Owens didn't reply.

"I'm going back to the Doctor tomorrow. If he says it's alright, we can take it off." Kaylee told them.

"Kaylee, sit up." Courtney told her daughter, who complied while keeping one eye on the television.

"You said you found something that could help us?" Jackson asked the woman, getting straight to business.

"Yes, we were cleaning out some of my father's things the other day and we found this picture." Courtney took a photograph out of a drawer. "It's not old maybe a year, Kaylee says that this man here is the man who shot her." Courtney pointed to one of four men in the photo. The men were gathered in front of a fishing boat, each holding fish. One of the men was Randy Taylor. Jackson took the photograph from the woman and stared at it.

"Do you have the negatives?" He asked, studying the man she had pointed to.

"I'm afraid not, all we found was that one picture, we looked for others with that man but didn't find any."

"Have you ever met him before?" Owens asked, sitting the files down on a table.

"No, I don't recall ever seeing him before." Courtney answered.

"How about you?" Owens asked Kaylee.

"Yeah he shot me." She replied sarcastically.

"I asked for that." Owens smiled.

"I'm sorry Detective..." Courtney paused. "I didn't get your name?"

"Owens."

"Detective Owens, Kaylee has an odd sense of humor," Courtney turned to her daughter, "and doesn't always mind her manners." Kaylee glanced back at the television to see that the man who was about to catch his wife cheating had gotten a phone call and left before he went in the bedroom.

"Because of the circumstances, the initial detectives didn't get a chance to talk to Kaylee." Jackson told Courtney. "Is it alright if we ask her a few questions?"

"Sure, go ahead."

"Do you know what scared this man away after he shot you and your grandfather?" Jackson asked the little girl. They all sat.

"She did." Courtney answered for her daughter.

"She did?" Owens asked.

"He didn't know about Kaylee and she scared him, when he

saw her, he ran off." Courtney replied, Jackson and Owens looked at the little girl with puzzlement.

"Mommy says that I wasn't thinking right because I got shot. I just got up and started yelling."

"I'm sorry..." Jackson said, looking at the report he'd brought with him. "This says you were shot with a .357 Magnum?"

"You mean you don't know?" Courtney asked them. "We told the first detectives about her condition but we didn't know exactly what happened until later, when Kaylee had come out of the intensive care ward and could tell us."

"Know what?" Jackson asked. Kaylee started making faces at Owens, who smiled at her.

"Kaylee's special." Courtney told him. Kaylee stuck her tongue out at Owens who noticed that the tip of it was missing and winced slightly.

"I have CIPA." Kaylee informed.

"CIPA what's that?" Jackson asked. Courtney leaned forward in her chair, she'd given this lesson many times and practically had the textbook memorized.

"It stands for Congenital Insensitivity to Pain with Anhidrosis." Courtney began. "But Kaylee doesn't have Anhidrosis..."

"I'm sorry, Anhidraxis?" Owens asked.

"Anhidrosis, that's where you don't sweat, Kaylee doesn't have that part but most people with the condition do."

"What exactly is this condition?" Jackson asked.

"Kaylee doesn't feel any pain, she never has." Courtney answered.

"Oh, cool." Owens interjected.

"No, it's not." Courtney said, a little annoyed at being interrupted. "Pain is a vital part of us, its much more than simply a feeling or an emotion, physical pain is your body telling you that something is wrong. Say for instance, you step on a rusty nail. When the nail punctures your skin, the nerves in your foot tell your brain to stop whatever its doing with that foot. Your brain understands that and you stop pressing your foot down on the nail, you take it out and go and get a tetanus shot. Kaylee can step on a rusty nail and because pain is the only sensation she would feel from that...She might not know that the nail is in her foot for quite some time, maybe even days. If Kaylee slips a disk in her back, she might not ever know. She would continue using her back normally until it just gives out."

"I see." Jackson said somberly.

"When she was less than a year old, she scratched the cornea of her eye, we didn't know it until it got infected and the entire area swelled up. When she was three, she put her hand on a red hot stove burner, I had only turned around for a few seconds to get something out of the cupboard but by the time I saw it, well, she'll have scars on her hand for the rest of her life. We have to check her every night for cuts or scratches she may have gotten during the day without her knowledge because if we don't they could become horribly infected within days. So no detective it's not cool."

"I'm sorry, I didn't mean it like that." Owens said sincerely. His apology caused Courtney to realize how harsh she sounded.

"It's my fault detective, with my father's death and everything that's happened and until now the police haven't seemed very interested in our case." Courtney said, realizing that she'd put Owens on the spot and hadn't meant to.

"I've never heard of this disease, how did she get it?" Jackson asked.

"It's not really a disease." Courtney replied. "It's a genetic mutation. Point mutations in my DNA and her father's were passed down to her, you see the point mutation has to occur on a specific gene in the reproductive cells, then it has to be passed on to Kaylee. Because the specific gene is recessive, her father also had to have the same point mutation on the same gene for Kaylee to develop the condition. That's why its so rare, there are only between thirty to thirty-five cases in the U.S. and it's thought that there aren't more than one hundred in the world."

"Can she feel things?" Owens asked.

"She can feel anything but pain, the texture of the sofa, the taste and feel of foods, my touch. She has some trouble with temperature, she can feel hot and cold, that is to say that she can distinguish between the two but she can't really feel how hot or how cold."

"There's no way to treat it?" Jackson asked.

"It's as much who she is as her accent or eye color, she's taken medication but nothing has ever seemed to help and I'm sorry to say that because it's so rare, there isn't very much research for it."

"We didn't know." Jackson apologized. "It wasn't included in the report that we got."

"That's alright detective, we're used to explaining it to people." Courtney told him before turning to her daughter. "Aren't we babygirl?"

"You forgot the part about my blood." Kaylee reminded her mother.

"I know, I got distracted." Courtney told her before turning back to Jackson and Owens. "When Kaylee began teething, she also started chewing on everything around her, besides biting the tip of her tongue off, she also chewed her fingers almost to the bone. Since then, we've..." Courtney stopped a moment and thought of her father, "we taught her to recognize the sight of her blood, that helps out a lot."

"Red means stop." Kaylee stated the rehearsed the line.

"Anytime she sees her own blood she knows to stop whatever she's doing and ask for help."

"Yep," Kaylee told her mother and held her hand in the air. "That about covers it."

Courtney saw that her daughter's hand was raised and high fived it. "It's a game we play." She told the detectives.

"We'd like to go over some of the particulars and get Kaylee's official statement," Jackson said, getting back to business, "even if this man in the picture can be identified, we'll have a long road to building a case."

"Sure, we'll help in any way we can" Courtney told them.

Damon's bright strawberry blonde hair contrasted with his black suit. He was standing in the small room of the King County Correctional Facility in Seattle. Since the city of Seattle contracted out to have its inmates housed by King County, most of them ended up in this large facility, though some were sometimes sent to others Seattle had contracted with, such as Yakima County or the city of Renton, a suburb of Seattle.

Waiting with the man standing next to him leaning over a counter filling out paperwork, Damon unwrapped a piece of hard candy and slipped it in his mouth before rubbing the hair of his goatee. He was in an uncharacteristically bad mood, which was evidenced from his scowl. His glowing green eyes scanned the room, which contained one iron barred window that led to another room where a Sheriff's deputy was filling out paperwork of his own.

Damon's wait had been a long one but he knew to expect that, he'd seen the inside of this jail several times before and each time he'd detested its statically white walls and buffed tile floors decorated so delicately with seas of thick black bars. He hated the fact that he had to be back in this place because the last time he'd left it he'd sworn to himself that he'd never return.

"I need you to sign at the x Mr. Collins." The bail bondsman turned to him. Damon took the paper, looked it over very quickly, it was a standard promise that Damon would guarantee that the inmate would appear for his court appearances and silently signed it. Soon the fat metal door to the inside of the jail opened. Eddie emerged, clothed in the same clothes he'd been wearing when he was arrested, handcuffed with his hands in front of him. Eddie's garb had only minutes before been an orange jumpsuit; he had been given his clothes by the jailers when they were told to release him. Damon's stare stuck upon the large bruises that covered Eddie's face.

"Do you have his things?" Damon asked the deputy inside the window.

"Just what was on him, everything else, the Seattle P.D. kept." The jailer said. He emptied a manilla envelope onto the counter in front of the window and pushed the items through the large hole in the bars. Damon sifted through the items until he saw that the piece of paper he was looking for wasn't among them. "Thank you." He told the deputy while he stared at his brother. The deputy that brought Eddie out took his handcuffs off and went back through the door, closing and locking it behind him. Eddie hugged his brother. Damon didn't hug back.

"When did you get in?" Eddie asked, seeing his brother's

anger.

"This morning." Damon replied apathetically.

"You know that most of the charges against you have been dismissed," the bail bondsman told the two brothers, "but you still have to appear on the resisting arrest, fleeing from the police and leaving the scene of an accident charges. I need you to sign this promise to appear." Eddie took the paper and signed. "It's good to see you again Mr. Collins." The bail bondsman extended his hand.

"Good to see you too, give my best to your wife." Damon smiled and shook the man's hand. Damon and Eddie left the jail right behind the bail bondsman. They got into Damon's Mercedes Benz ML350 SUV. The tension inside the vehicle permeated the air around the two brothers. Both sat silently. They headed north to Edmonds, another suburb where Damon had purchased a modest home for his brother.

"Stay here." Damon pulled into the driveway. Damon got out, put a code into the electronic panel outside the garage door because he didn't have an automatic opener in his car. He then pulled the SUV into the garage. Shutting the vehicle off, he sat back in his seat and thought in silence. Eddie wanted to speak but knew that his brother wasn't pleased with him. He looked over at his brother just in time to see Damon swing the back of his fist from the steering wheel to his face. Eddie let out a squeal.

Damon got out of the vehicle, slammed the button to close the garage door, then picked Eddie out of the SUV and slammed him against a tool box in the corner of the garage. Eddie didn't resist. Damon smacked him several times with a closed fist.

"I'm sorry, I'm sorry." Eddie cried, the sound of which made Damon hit him a few more times. When finished, he grabbed his brother's red hair and lifted his head up to look at him.

"What did I tell you?" Damon slapped Eddie's face, this time with an open hand.

"I know, I know."

"What did I tell you?" Damon slapped his brother a few more times. "You can buy, you can sell! You never make, you never ever make!"

"I know, I'm sorry." Eddie cowered.

"How many times have I told you that people who make take all the risks? How many times?" Damon screamed at him.

"I thought I had it covered. I didn't think man, I'm so so sorry."

"Quit it!" Damon grabbed his brother's face and lifted it up. "You sound like a bitch." Eddie worked at regaining his composure.

"I screwed up bro, I just screwed up."

"No shit you screwed up." Damon was now calm. "What happened to it?"

"What?" Eddie asked, which got him slapped again.

"You know what!" Damon told him. "Where is it?" Eddie's anxiety maxed out when he realized what Damon was talking about, he'd forgotten all about it.

"It...it was in the glove box, the cops must have it." Eddie stammered, before flinching for the slap he knew was coming.

"You couldn't have delivered it first?" Damon asked in anger. He smacked the back of his younger brother's head several times. "You couldn't deliver one piece of paper before doing your own thing?" Damon continued to hit his brother. "Jesus Christ!" He yelled, taking a step back, picking up a wrench and throwing it against the wall. "Do you know how much money you just cost me? Huh? Do you? What? Are you trying to get us caught? Is that it?" He yelled at Eddie.

"I'm sorry man, I'm so sorry." Eddie cried. Damon slammed his fist into the toolbox.

"Alright, alright." Damon said after about a minute of trying to calm himself down. Reluctantly, he took Eddie in his arms and held him tightly against his body while his brother cried. "You can't be doing this." Damon spoke in a soothing tone. "We're all we have man, we have to do this right, you can't make the mistakes that I made."

"I know, I know." Eddie said, his head on Damon's shoulders.

4

"Cold Case"

ackson spent the morning looking over the evidence again. There wasn't much. The forensic investigators had gone over the scene with their usual diligence but given the location; a rocky, sandy beach, not much was found. Only about three clear bootprints were discovered in the area. There was minor trace evidence but it didn't seem to lead anywhere and there were only two witnesses of value: Kaylee Taylor, and the fisherman who found her. Jackson also had the coroner's report but that didn't seem to contain anything of significance either.

The bootprints were the most valuable evidence that was collected. One belonged to the fisherman who found the scene, another belonged to the victim, and the third set belonged to the suspect. Forensics had already matched the type and size of boot to a Danner Battalion, a quasi-expensive hiking boot that ran for about 275 dollars. The size was a ten and a half. A microscopic analysis of the print revealed no unique qualities, which could be interpreted as the boot being new. Both the type and size were extremely common for the area and even if the suspect owned a pair, it would be circumstantial evidence at best.

The trace evidence was equally inconclusive. This meant that the killer left nothing of himself behind or at least nothing that was found. Since the weapons used to shoot Randy and Kaylee Taylor hadn't been recovered and the bullet that went through Kaylee had never been found, it would be virtually impossible to match a weapon to the crime. The investigator's report stated that the shotgun blast that killed Randy Taylor had been at extremely close range and Jackson made a notation to check any suspected shotgun he found for biological matter. All the blood evidence recovered from the scene had been virtually useless, it had been determined to be the same type as Randy and Kaylee's. In such a situation, it would have been unlikely that the suspect would have cut himself, however everything that could have been tested, had been.

Kaylee's firsthand account of the incident had been a little jumbled, there were parts that she didn't remember, either because of the loss of blood or because she had repressed the memories. Either way, her testimony could be useful but would definitely be suspect. She had remembered the first shot knocking her out of her chair and seeing the suspect standing on her grandfather, talking to him but hadn't heard anything useful. She remembered being shot the second time but didn't actually see the suspect shoot her grandfather, which may benefit her later on. She had missed the most gruesome aspect of the traumatic incident and perhaps that would help her mind recover.

The fisherman that found her was useless as far as testimony was concerned. He had been fishing about two hundred yards away when he heard the shots. Though he immediately proceeded to the scene, there was a lot of vegetation to obstruct his line of sight and by the time he was in a position to see anything at all, the suspect had already fled and Kaylee was wandering around senseless because of her blood loss. It had actually been his quick thinking and his shirt, which he ripped in two and used to cover both sides of her through and through gunshot wound, that saved her.

One of the reasons that Jackson wasn't a full time homicide detective, besides the lack of action, which there was plenty of in narcotics, was the macabre focus of the job. Homicide detectives had to deal with death on a daily basis. Unlike on the television, the cops who worked homicides had to contend with the most ghastly crime scenes one could ever imagine. As a matter of routine they had to investigate bodies found weeks after death, mutilated corpses, decomposing cadavers and elderly accountants who had had most of their heads ripped violently from the rest of their bodies by the force of more than half a dozen shotgun pellets smashing through it at well over 1,500 feet per second. It was the crime scene photographs of the latter that made even an experienced police officer cringe.

The coroner's report on Randy Taylor was pretty straight forward, cause of death was due to massive trauma to the head. Specifically, a shotgun blast at close range to the face. The report also stated that had he gotten medical attention immediately after the first shot, he most likely would have died anyway. In the first shot that hit both him and his granddaughter, Randy had taken the majority of the pellets. Two of the pellets had entered his lung and one had punched through a major artery.

The initial detectives' cursory investigation into Randy Taylor's financial and entrepreneurial adventures likewise yielded no leads. He had been an accountant for over thirty-five years and according to the report at least, he was well liked in the circles he traveled. He had the usual number of clientele, not all of which had been interviewed but the three clients that had been had nothing but good things to say about him and his work. The majority of his clients were private citizens who were wealthy. He had a couple of businesses as clients, mostly smaller locally owned businesses, where he handled specific aspects of accounting, such as taxes or payroll deductions. Occasionally he worked as a consultant for Microsoft but the record indicated that his last project for them hadn't been for quite some time.

Even more astounding, to Jackson anyway, was Taylor's

past. He'd lived his whole life in Seattle, attaining no traffic citations, no arrests, a home mortgage that had been payed off, several car loans that had also been paid in full. He had married at age eighteen and after forty-two years of marriage his wife died of cancer. One daughter, Courtney, age thirty-two. He wasn't known to abuse drugs, alcohol or cigarettes. He had no known vices whatsoever. He liked to fish and play golf, which was part of his networking to find new clients.

Jackson put the files on his desk, leaned back in his chair and yawned. The tiny black letters were beginning to blur together for him and he decided he needed to take a walk and think for a few minutes. He got up from his chair, left his small, fully enclosed cubicle, which he called "the closet," a perk that had been given to him with his Lieutenant rank. He sauntered out his office door where the Narcotics division was whisking around like an ant colony.

Even though they were working on a homicide, Jackson and Owens could not be bothered to move their things over to the homicide office, besides, they'd soon return to leading the narcotics teams. Owens had his own desk, which until Jackson had been promoted and given his cubicle, had faced Jackson's. Now his desk faced Sergeant Casteel's, who was in charge of Narcotics Squad One.

Owens had spent the day trying to ascertain who the man was in the picture that they'd been given. He was currently on the telephone repeating names and places and writing them down on a note pad. Owens had finally tracked down the boat that the men were standing in front of in the photograph and the two detectives left to interview the owner.

The owner of the boat was Jason Godesky, a real estate developer and client of Taylor's who turned out to be one of the men in the picture. In the interview, Godesky identified the two unidentified men, one was a friend of Godesky's who came along on the all day fishing trip at the end of which the picture was taken. The other man was Richard Olsen, a small time printing press operator.

It turned out that Olsen was one of Randy Taylor's clients too, Taylor had worked for Shoreline Printing–Olsen's business–as a management accountant pretty regularly for nearly a year. His purpose was to analyze the budget and find ways to cut the overhead costs of the company. Though there didn't seem to be anything unusual about the practice of hiring an outsider to do this type of work, Jackson and Owens' suspicions deepened when they got Olsen's arrest record.

Olsen had only been arrested once when he was twenty years old for stealing a car and taking it on a joyride while on a cocaine trip but he'd been implicated by several others for a variety of white collar crimes. He looked like a standard white collar criminal who had never been caught. Now in his early forties, he'd held a multitude of entry position jobs, most for no longer than six months, that is until he'd gone into the printing business two years ago. The two investigators found that fact very interesting because he'd never had any experience in publishing before suddenly starting up Shoreline Printing. An even more enigmatic question was about his finances, though they'd need a warrant to get his financial records, they could tell from his large listing of jobs that he could not have had the capital to start an expensive business such as that.

A quick check on Google revealed a newspaper article from the Shoreline Gazette which featured the grand opening of Shoreline Printing, a printing company that specialized in contracts with businesses to provide advertisements, flyers, labels and other materials used for marketing products. The article accompanied a picture of Olsen standing with the mayor of the small town just north of Seattle, shaking hands. It also stated that Olsen was a lifelong resident of Shoreline, something Jackson and Owens new wasn't true because he had grown up in Tacoma Washington and that he had received several tax breaks and funding from "the community" to open the business which was supposed to employ around thirty people. Jackson laughed when he read the last part.

"What?" Owens asked.

"Funding from the community?" Jackson asked rhetorically.

"So?"

"So, I don't buy that." Jackson said. "Shoreline's been growing for years, they've got several large businesses moving in there, why would they want a ditsy, dirty, printing press?"

"Yeah, this guy couldn't have been rich, his file has him listed as living all around town, mostly in ghettos." Owens said, agreeing with Jackson.

"He barely has enough money to eat with and all of a sudden he's got his own business and an expensive one at that. Why?" Jackson asked, more to himself than his partner. "Community funding has to be a silent partner, there's no way any community would give this chump any cash."

"Lets drag him down here and ask him?" Owens suggested.

"Not yet, we need to know more."

"Then what?"

"Let's hit up Taylor's records, I bet he's got some that we didn't find, guys like that, they always keep backups somewhere." Jackson speculated. "And I want that kid to pick Olsen out of a photo lineup, we need to make sure her I.D. is airtight." Sensing someone outside, Jackson looked up to see Casteel knock on his office door. "Come in."

"Hey, we got something strange here, I thought you'd wanna see it." Casteel entered the tiny cubicle with a small evidence bag. Jackson looked at the bag's contents.

"What the hell is Cozaar?" Jackson asked.

"A blood pressure medication, those papers have the complete recipe on them. We collected it from Eddie's van." Casteel informed, which made Jackson look up at him.

"Is he making legit drugs now?" Owens asked. "How do

you do that anyway, go from illegal narcotics to legal narcotics, there can't be any money in that."

"You couldn't sell them. They would have to be inspected and selling this on the street wouldn't even cover the cost of making it." Casteel answered.

"This has Merck's factory label on it." Jackson observed. "He could be lifting it, then selling it off to Merck's competitors?"

"I don't think so." Casteel told them. "They already know how to make the stuff, that's how we can buy generic versions of drugs."

"Did Eddie get out?" Jackson asked.

"Yesterday." Casteel replied.

"Get on him, I wanna know what he's up to." Jackson asked.

"Like flies on shit."

"I thought the chief said we weren't allowed anywhere near Eddie?" Owens asked.

"Yeah us but Knox put N.S.1. on criminal intelligence duty and that's what they're going to be doing, the chief didn't say anything about them watching Eddie." Jackson answered.

"Oh, it's you." Kaylee said when she answered the door and saw the two cops standing in front of her. "Mommy! The pigs are back!" She yelled to her mother in the kitchen. Jackson's smile spread from ear to ear and Owens' jaw dropped. "Come on in."

"Thanks." Jackson tried to hold in his laughter while hey stepped into the house.

"Kaylee, it isn't nice to call them that." Courtney said, she was drying her hands with a dish towel.

"But that's what Grampa used to call them." Kaylee replied.

"Grampa didn't mean for them to hear that." Courtney scolded, mildly embarrassed.

"Ms. Taylor," Jackson began, "you said yesterday that your father did some work out of his office here. If you don't mind we'd like to have a look at it."

"Sure."

"I'd also like to show Kaylee some pictures." Owens added.

"Mugshots?" Kaylee asked gleefully.

"Yeah." Owens replied. "Kinda."

"Well lets go." She said excitedly to Owens bewilderment.

"She watches a lot of TV, she loves cop shows, she's talked about nothing but the two of you since yesterday." Courtney told them. "Let me show you my father's office."

"I'll be right back." Owens said, putting the books full of mugshots down on a coffee table. Kaylee frowned and watched Courtney lead them up a flight of stairs and down a hallway. She took a key from atop the door frame and unlocked the office door.

"I gave you guys everything we could find yesterday, I don't think there's anything left in here." She said as they entered. The room was small, beige wallpaper, a hanging light and a small sofa in the back of the room, under the window. Randy Taylor's computer was sitting on a desk next to the door and Jackson immediately rifled through the drawers. "May I ask what you're looking for detective?" Courtney asked.

"We think your father may have kept some backup records." Owens told her.

"He did." Jackson said, producing a small memory stick and handing it to Courtney. It was rectangular and gray and bore the words "B Drive" labeled in white background and black lettering. "May we use your computer here to look at it?" Jackson asked.

"Sure." Courtney told him, amazed that she hadn't found it before. "Just boot it up." Jackson hit the button and the computer started cycling through its startup process. "I'll be downstairs in the kitchen if you need anything." She told them before leaving the room.

"What if this guy isn't Mr. Clean?" Owens asked, glancing over at a bookcase.

"So what," Jackson replied, "nobody's perfect and besides, whatever he was into, he didn't deserve to get killed and his granddaughter surely didn't deserve to get shot."

"That's why I hate homicide." Owens told him. "You always find out that seemingly normal, good people are into some bad shit, it's depressing."

"Way of the world whitey, we all got skeletons in our

closets."

"At least in narco we know we're chasing scumbags."
Owens returned. The computer signaled that it was up and running.
Jackson slipped the memory stick into the USB port on the front of
the tower and pulled up the "my computer" screen before clicking on
the device. A new screen emerged, this one prompting for a
password.

"It's protected." Jackson said.

"Ms. Taylor might know the password, I'll go ask." Owens
started out.

"Hold on, let me try." Jackson typed something in, only to
get a repeat of the prompt.

"Oh, you're a hacker now?" Owens asked.

"I dabble." Jackson put in a new word but only got the
prompt again.

"You'll be here all night, I'll go ask." Owens said. A second
later "******" granted Jackson access. "How'd you do that?"
Owens asked.

"I figured it might be Kaylee." Jackson answered. "I just
can't spell for shit."

"I don't know why, it's only been on a dozen reports we've
read. That's those Washington schools." Owens said, moving to the
door.

"Like the schools in Tennessee are any better." Jackson
retorted, looking at the computer screen and moving the mouse

around.

"Better than here." Owens stepped through the doorway. "I'm gonna go get that I.D."

"Really, how do you spell it then?"

"K-e-y...You know what, screw you." Owens turned to go down the hallway. "Asshole."

"Hillbilly." Jackson said just before his partner left earshot, he knew Owens heard him and smiled at the interchange. Those types of conversations were common to the two and both knew the other enjoyed it.

Owens found Kaylee sitting on the sofa, mugshot book in her lap, glancing over the pictures. Sitting down next to her and taking half the book in his lap, he found that she'd already passed the page where he'd inserted Olsen's picture.

"See anyone you recognize?" He asked the little girl.

"This one looks like Tim Robbins." She said pointing to a white collar criminal.

"How do you know who Tim Robbins is?" Owens asked sarcastically.

"He's that political guy who also does movies, Grampa used to make fun of him." She replied seriously, not noticing Owens' caustic remark.

"I bet you miss your Grandpa don't you?" Owens asked.

"Yeah, Mommy said that he's still with us but I wish I could talk to him." She confided.

"You know, I lost my Grandpa when I was about your age too." He told her.

"It's hard." She looked up at him. "I miss sitting and watching the news with him the most. After he got home from work we would watch Jeopardy then the news." She said before giggling at her memories. Looking up at him, she noticed the large scar on his throat. "What's that?" She pointed.

"Oh, yeah, you know, I got shot once, just like you." He replied, feeling the scar with two of his fingers.

"Did it hurt?" She asked, genuinely curious.

"Why don't we look at the pictures to try to find the man you saw." Owens tried to change the subject.

"He was on the third page, halfway down, you didn't do a good job putting his picture in, it was crooked." She replied without pause, still staring at his scar. "What did it feel like?"

"It felt hot, like fire, it burned and then it felt wet, after that I passed out, I don't know. When I woke up I was in the hospital." He confided.

"I don't know what it feels like, I've never felt fire." She said, her disappointment obvious.

It took Jackson a little more than twenty minutes but he finally found something worthwhile. Hidden inside one of the spreadsheets was a note and when Jackson clicked on it he found that Randy Taylor had left a message to remind himself to bring up a minor discrepancy of twenty-five hundred dollars in the next meeting he had with Olsen. The specifics were on Drive A. It wasn't much but Jackson had seen people killed for lesser amounts of money. His gut told him that this wasn't it though, it didn't seem right. Why would Taylor leave a note to himself to ask about a sum of money if he had taken it?

There was also another cryptic clue at the end of the note, it read: "file in Drive A in case of emergency." What did this mean? What type of emergency was Taylor referring to? Was it some sort of financial or legal emergency he was preparing for, or was it something else? After cross checking the other files in the Shoreline Printing folder, Jackson indeed found a discrepancy of twenty-five hundred dollars.

"If he was skimming money off this business, maybe he was doing it with the others." Jackson said aloud. He clicked out of the Shoreline Printing folder and into another folder. It was empty. He clicked out and into another. That too was empty. He tried another folder then another and another but they were all empty, all except the Shoreline Printing folder. He checked the creation dates on all the folders, they were all the same. "Maybe he intended to make backups of all his material, but didn't have time?" Jackson surmised, but the question still plagued him; "why would he remind himself to bring up a discrepancy if he caused it?"

Jackson clicked out of the external hard drive and removed it from the USB port. He slipped the memory stick in his pocket and looked in the desk for another but came up empty. Undeterred, he started a methodical search of the room.

He divided the room into quadrants. Starting at the door he worked his way around the walls, searching the computer desk, the bookcases, the sofa, window sill, end tables. He made his way through the room in a spiral. After spiraling toward the center of the small home office, Jackson found himself standing in the middle of the room empty handed. "Damn," he said, "wherever it is, it isn't here."

Jackson quickly made his way down the stairs and saw Owens sitting on the sofa, sharing the book of mugshots with Kaylee, both laughing and giggling and making jokes with each other. He had to stop himself and watch them. A little less than a year ago, Jesse Owens didn't want to watch a three year old for two minutes because in his words "they have no souls" now Jackson was watching him sit and laugh with a child. He couldn't believe it.

"What about this one?" Owens asked the little girl.

"Nah, he looks like Ted Kennedy." She replied, which made Owens laugh.

"Remember, if asks you if you need a ride home, just say no." Owens joked.

"Did she make the I.D.?" Jackson asked when he overcame his astonishment at the scene and started down the stairs again.

"Yeah, just fine, come here man, you gotta see this, she can tell you exactly which celebrity each of these guys looks like." Owens informed.

"Well, I happen to like Teddy." Jackson quipped at the bottom of the stairs. "Where's Ms. Taylor?"

"She's in the kitchen making us some hot tea." Kaylee replied.

"Thanks." Jackson remarked before turning toward the kitchen.

"Never mind him, he's always like that. What about this guy?" Owens asked.

"Definitely Katie Couric." She replied.

Jackson found Courtney dropping tea bags into three cups of hot water. Her gaze continuously shifting from her work to her daughter and her new friend. She noticed Jackson and turned back to her task.

"Find anything?" She asked, checking the cups. "Would you like some tea?"

"Sure." Jackson replied and Courtney grabbed another cup. "I did find a minor note about some missing money but I don't know what to make of it, if anything." He watched her drop another tea bag into the hot water she'd just poured into a new cup.

"Do you think my father was into something illegal?" She asked, scared at what his answer might be.

"I've got no reason to believe that yet." Jackson replied, he saw the relief on Courtney's face. "Do you mind if we keep this for a little while?" He held up the USB drive.

"Sure, anything that might help."

"I think there is another one like this one somewhere, if you find it, please let us know." Jackson didn't want to make his statement sound like an order but it did anyway.

"Sure." She reached into the freezer, picked out four or five ice cubes and dropped them into one of the cups, stirring to make them melt faster. "They're for Kaylee." She said, noticing Jackson watching her. "If we don't cool the tea for her, she'll gulp it down and burn the inside of her mouth."

"It must be tough adjusting to this kind of routine, I'd have never thought of that." Jackson told her.

"Dad and I did just fine, it was worth it for her. I can't work because someone has to watch after her full time but Dad always took care of us." She said, adding one more ice cube to the cup.

"What are you going to do now?"

"I don't know, right now we're making it off Dad's savings and soon we'll get his life insurance but when that runs out, I don't know what we'll do." Courtney looked out into the living room at her daughter laughing. "She likes him, I haven't seen her laugh like that since Dad passed."

"I'm glad somebody does." Jackson didn't mean to make the sarcastic remark in front of Courtney and quickly changed the subject. "Do you mind if I ask you a personal question?" Courtney nodded. "Where's Kaylee's father?"

"We were together but never really wanted to get married. My parents were furious but he stayed with me after Kaylee came. We didn't find out about her condition until she was almost a year old and when we did," Courtney shrugged, "he just changed. Then one day he just didn't come back for a few weeks and when he did he got his stuff and left. He never gave a reason but I know, he never looked at her the same after we found out." She let slip a small smile. "We just thought she was a good baby, she never cried, she never seemed to get temperamental, we thought everything was fine. Then she tried climbing out of her playpen one day and fell on her head and got a concussion. We took her to the doctor and we knew something was wrong because her brain had been bruised and she didn't seem phased. We went to a specialist, he suggested the test and that's when everything changed. Anyway, not long after he left, we moved in here."

"Did she take her grandfather's death hard?" Jackson asked.

"She likes to play tough, she never cried but I know she's hurt on the inside, she just doesn't know how to say it. They were very close, he's the closest thing she's ever had to a father." Courtney placed the cups on a tray and took them out to Owens and Kaylee. Jackson stayed in the kitchen sipping his tea and thinking, he felt uncomfortable with this entire case, he couldn't put his finger on it, but something was bothering him.

5

"Eye To Eye Again"

E ddie took Interstate 5 to downtown Seattle. He got off at the Mercer Street exit but since Mercer was a one way street going the opposite way that Eddie wanted, he hopped on Broad Street then Roy Street to get past Seattle Center. He turned down Queen Anne Avenue and with another left was finally on Mercer again. He parked his SUV in a parking garage and proceeded to walk to the club that was his destination.

The Lion's Gate club was one of Seattle's best kept secrets. That suited its patrons they didn't want tourists or out-of-towners in their club. It was underground, as many clubs in Seattle were. The dark, damp mood enhancing its experience. Its patrons were from all over Seattle and its suburbs, they ranged in age from early twenties to early sixties with the majority being in their forties. Their clothing ranged from black leather and dog collars to suits, ties, and Sunday dresses. Their occupations were equally varied; trash men frequented the club, as did mechanics, hotel managers, computer engineers, programmers, corporate executives, and housewives.

The club itself was neither hidden nor illegal. Anyone passing on the street could hear the loud music vibrating through the concrete. The line to get into the club extended out onto the street with several signs strategically located with subtle messages to warn off newcomers that didn't know what the club was for. It wasn't for everyone, The Lion's Gate club had a very unique clientele, almost all of which were married.

Half a block east of the club, parked on the side of the street was the unmarked Seattle Police Department's Criminal Intelligence van, currently manned by members of the Narcotics Squad One.

In the early 1990's, the idea of individual police departments collecting detailed information on criminals became popular. This information could later be used to obtain warrants and make arrests. Seattle Police Department had initially bought into this idea with enthusiasm and purchased several millions of dollars worth of high-tech surveillance equipment. Soon the costs of operating and maintaining the unit overcame the worth of the information it generated and the unit became defunct. Now the department assigned officers to Criminal Intelligence duty only when the need arose.

Inside the van were several television monitors along with some antiquated listening devices and a countless array of cameras, both still and video. Casteel and Johnson were currently in the back of the van watching one of the monitors. They had sent Holloman out to the area of the club with a pair of what was affectionately referred to as B.C.G.'s by the detectives. B.C. G.'s or Birth Control Glasses were a very large, thick black pair of eyeglasses, which looked like they came straight out of the 1940's. They were called Birth Control Glasses because the assumption was that anyone wearing them had absolutely no hope of having sexual contact with a woman. The reason that Detective Marcus Holloman wore them tonight was because contained in the thick black very unattractive frame was a miniature camera and radio transmitter, which sent everything the glasses saw directly to the Criminal Intelligence van.

Outside the van, Ari Rothstein and Kimberly Mason crossed the street and headed into the van through its back door. Rothstein and Mason sat down and made themselves at home.

"Eddie just went into the Lion's Gate club." Casteel told them before picking up his radio and speaking into it. "Marcus, go in and see if you can't find him."

"I'm on it." The reply came through the radio.

"We shouldn't send him in alone." Johnson remarked.

"I agree." Casteel said turning to Rothstein and Mason.

"Why does it always have to be us?" Rothstein asked.

"Because you two look the most normal." Casteel answered which made the two cops look each other over and wonder.

"C'mon, do you know what they do in there?" Rothstein objected.

"Don't tell me you've never been to a Swinger's club before?" Johnson chimed.

"Just get in there and back Marcus up, Ok?" Casteel finally ordered. Rothstein and Mason reluctantly placed tiny radios on their belts and put cordless earpieces in. After testing the radios they emptied the van and strolled down the block and into the club.

Inside the club, they were flooded with the luminescent colors of the rotating lights around the dance floor. Blue, red, yellow, purple and white lights were spinning slowly around the club contrasting perfectly with the dark black background of the walls and ceiling. The music was a combination of modern hits along with other retro styles, all of which was made to flow through the basement by a DJ in the corner of the large room. In the back was a series of smaller rooms, which were windowless but didn't have doors, just long sheets of thick black cloth split all the way up several times. Rothstein didn't want to think about what those rooms were used for, he wanted to concentrate on his objective.

On the dance floor were two or three dozen middle aged couples and one couple in their sixties, all gyrating to the music with their respective partners. Each pair hung on each other as though they were the only people in the club, they routinely grabbed parts of their partner's anatomy and one couple was completely topless, with the male fondling the woman's breasts. Occasionally, two couples would switch partners, then after a few minutes of fondling and other gratuitous gestures, they would switch back.

Holloman watched as two couples left the dance floor and went into one of the back rooms after switching partners several times. He then turned his attention to the elderly couple, where the woman had slowly danced her way down to her knees and was licking her partner's clothed crotch.

"What the hell is he watching?" Johnson said, looking into the van's monitor. Casteel was inching forward toward the monitor also trying to see what had caught Holloman's attention.

"Is she unzipping his pants?" He asked, not really to Johnson. Suddenly both men shrieked.

"Oh, gross!" They both proclaimed in unison. Casteel hastily grabbed his radio.

"Marcus! Quit watching that old timer get a hummer, you pervert!" He yelled.

"Sorry, it's like watching a train wreck." Holloman replied.

"Hey, does anybody have Eddie?" Rothstein spat into the radio, perturbed that they were screwing around while he had to be in the club.

"No, I lost him when he came in." Holloman replied, back to business.

"I got him." Mason radioed. "Ari, get some drinks, I got a

table with a view." The drinks weren't for fun, they didn't want
Eddie to notice them so they had to blend in. Rothstein was already
at the bar, he ordered two club sodas and took them to Mason who
was sitting at a table that indeed had a good view of Eddie, who was
currently sitting alone.

Fifteen minutes went by, then twenty, Rothstein and Mason
talked to each other in short spurts integrated with long periods of
silence. Their conversations were the usual sort for them, mostly
complaining about how they always had to do this work. Eddie sat
at his table with a beer, he watched the dance floor mostly, but
occasionally looked at his watch.

"You see that?" Mason asked her companion. A young
Asian man approached Eddie and shook hands before sitting down.

"That's Jimmy Nguyen." Rothstein said, watching the two
men sit and talk.

"Aren't they competitors?" Mason asked.

"Yeah, last year they went to war for a couple of months."
Rothstein told her. "Hey, you getting this?" He pushed the speak
button on his belt radio.

"We're getting it." Casteel answered, watching the monitor.
Holloman had positioned himself next to a wall and had a good view
of Eddie. They watched Eddie slip a thick envelope under the table
to Nguyen, who stuck it in his back pocket. Eddie and Jimmy
Nguyen shook hands again and Jimmy Nguyen left. Eddie remained
behind for a few minutes before also leaving the club. Holloman

stayed on him. Rothstein and Mason made their way back to the van, both visibly relieved to be out of the club.

"What the hell's going on?" Rothstein asked, Johnson helping him into the van.

"I don't know but Jimmy Nguyen is one of the biggest dealers in the city. If he's in it with Eddie, its got to be something big." Casteel surmised.

The next morning, Jackson and Owens took a trip to Shoreline. It was a simple drive, they took Interstate 5 and were in the northern portion of Seattle in not less than fifteen minutes. Jackson's Mustang took some time negotiating traffic on the side streets but soon they'd found a suitable parking space and were getting out.

"I told you I'd be there." Owens told Jackson, shutting his door.

"Damn right you'll be there." Jackson returned. They started down the street to Shoreline Printers. "It's at three o'clock tomorrow and we'll go straight from work."

"I don't see why you get so excited over a soccer game anyway?" Owens asked.

"C'mon man, it's Tonya's first game starting. When you have kids, you'll understand." Jackson replied.

"I'll understand that my kid won't have a problem passing. It's a miracle they're starting her at all. What'd she do, pull a Tonya Harding on the starter?" Owens commented, which made Jackson stop walking and turn to him.

"No and she does not have a problem passing." Jackson stated seriously.

"She kicked the ball into her teammate's head last game, I'd call that a problem passing."

"She got hit as she went for it. It wasn't her fault."

"She got anxious and beaned a Persian girl, that's a problem passing man."

"She doesn't have a problem passing, you just like to criticize my kids."

"She nailed that Abu chick then kicked the other team's wingback in the balls, she's got a temper problem as well as a passing problem. Not unlike her old man I might add."

"She got fouled, and it was an accident, besides it's an all-girl team, the wingback didn't have balls."

"She didn't get fouled, she folded under pressure, and that chick had balls, I swear." Owens answered.

"Fine, let it go but you're gonna be there tomorrow." Jackson ordered.

"Okay. I wasn't doing nothing no way." Owens said when they reached the building.

The lobby was a light gray color with several chairs in the

waiting area and a forty-something secretary sitting in the back of the room guarding the door to Olsen's office. Jackson and Owens confidently strode over to the woman and took out their I.D.'s.

"Seattle Police, I'm Lieutenant Jackson, this is Detective Owens, we need to speak with Mr. Richard Olsen." Jackson said in a very professional tone.

The secretary looked up at them from her computer screen, complete contempt on her face. "He's in a meeting." Her tone stating that she didn't care who they were. "He'll be out in a minute, you can wait over there." She went back to her screen. The two cops put their I.D.'s away and sat down in the waiting area. They could play her game for a little while. Both refused to talk to one another and picked up magazines that were laid out on a foot table.

"It's a passing problem." Owens said after a few minutes.

"Shut up." Jackson retorted. "Are you playing that girl to get to her mother?"

"What?"

"You know what I mean?" Jackson replied.

"That's insulting." Owens said in a disgusted tone, Jackson held out his hand for Owens to lower his voice. "I can't believe that you would make that suggestion." Owens whispered. "I would never use that little girl's illness like that and I resent the implication."

"Really what about Theresa?" Jackson asked.

"I really liked Theresa."

"She didn't have any legs and you told her you were going to school to design prosthetic limbs."

"Yeah but I really liked her."

"Ah, ok." Jackson said sarcastically. "That's why when you broke up with her you said that it was because you two couldn't jog together."

"You know what, just don't talk to me right now ok?" Owens went back to reading his magazine.

"She doesn't have a problem passing." Jackson told him.

Thirty minutes fell off the clock. Finally, Jackson put down his magazine and looked at his watch. The secretary was still typing on her computer, she hadn't moved since they'd come in, not even to answer the phone.

"If she doesn't produce that guy in sixty seconds, I'm breaking down his door." Jackson told his partner, his agitation visible.

"That would be subtle." Owens whispered back. "You're always talking about being professional, how about you let me work my charm on her?"

"You think that will work? Go right ahead." Jackson picked up the magazine again. Owens ran his fingers through his hair and touched it up a little before standing and straightening his clothing. He confidently strolled to the secretary with his best James Dean walk. The secretary ignored him for a few seconds before glancing at him with a look that was saying: *what do you want?* Owens batted his eyes at her and smiled his best smile. His next move was a military style left face; he marched right past her desk, slammed the office door open and entered Olsen's office.

"Wait!" The secretary yelled at him. "You can't go in there!"

"Be quiet." Jackson told her, quickly passing her desk.

"What's going on here!" Olsen stood up from behind his desk to face the intruder. The man sitting in front of the desk, who was examining sample prints, sat motionless, stunned at the situation.

"I wanna talk to you!" Owens told him before turning to the other man in the office. "You, frog" he pointed, "hop off."

"You don't get any points for subtle." Jackson said, stopping next to him and taking out his badge. "Lieutenant Jackson, Detective Owens, Seattle Police, we'd like to ask you a few questions Mr. Olsen." Jackson then turned to the other man. "Didn't you hear him? Hop." The man looked at Olsen, who nodded.

"You should make a complaint." The man said in parting.

"What can I do for you officers?" Olsen asked, his voice kind and businesslike.

"We'd like to ask you about Randy Taylor." Jackson replied.

"Such a horrible tragedy. Did the child survive? The news didn't cover it." Olsen replied, motioning them to sit down. Jackson and Owens didn't move.

"He worked for you, didn't he?" Jackson purposefully didn't answer Olsen's question.

"Yes he did, we had a very good working relationship." Olsen sat down anyway, allowing the detectives to look down on him. "He was one of the best in his field."

"Did he find that twenty-five hundred dollars was missing from your accounts?" Owens asked.

"He did, we found that the money was taken out of our supply account to pay for what we call social networking. All that means is that we purchased a trip for a perspective client to come and see our operation here. Do you have any suspects?" Olsen's new question also went ignored.

"Where were you on the morning of March twenty-second?" Jackson asked.

"What? I'm not a suspect am I?" Olsen asked with a smile.

"We'd like to establish your whereabouts on that morning." Owens told him.

"You barge into my office and start treating me like a criminal? What is this?"

"Sir." Jackson said with a forceful tone. "Where were you on the morning of March twenty-second, if I have to ask you again, I'll be doing it at my office."

"He was with me. Sergeant David Jackson." Damon Collins echoed through the door to the office. Jackson whipped his head around at the sound of the voice and the expression on his face was that of a man who thought he was looking at a ghost. "We had breakfast together, then caught up on some extra work for a few hours." Damon used his surprise to step into the office and maneuver himself in front of Olsen's desk. Jackson and Damon stared at each other a moment before Jackson spoke.

"It's Lieutenant now." Jackson told him, his voice deadly serious.

"My mistake." Damon returned casually. "I haven't kept up, I've been out of town. Is this the new partner?" Damon looked Owens over. "He doesn't have Rent's panache."

"He can hold his own." Jackson replied, his hateful ire apparent in each of his words.

"Too bad about Rent, I heard that after he got out of jail, he went and got himself killed." Damon continued with a sarcastic smirk. "I never got the chance to thank him for getting me acquitted. Planting evidence wasn't it?"

"So you're the silent partner?" Jackson asked, already knowing the answer. Damon didn't trouble himself with the question, instead he turned his head to talk to Olsen.

"You see Lieutenant" Damon accentuated the word "Jackson and his former partner tried to frame me up for a murder a while back. I can't say that I blame them, after all, they were after me for years," Damon slowly turned to Jackson as though he intended to hit him in the face with the words, "and they never could get the cuffs on me, at least they couldn't make them stick anyway." Damon was now flaunting his victory.

"That's why I love life, it always gives second chances."
Jackson gave a wry smile, one that told Damon the exact meaning of
his words.

"I doubt that." Damon told him. "Besides, I've come a long
way from the guy I was three years ago. I'm honest now. Legit."

"Right." Jackson laughed.

"It's hard to change his opinions." Damon told Owens. "As
much as I enjoyed seeing you again, we do run a business here, so if
you're not picking up my associate and you don't have a warrant, I'll
thank you to get off our property." Damon told them.

"You want a warrant, I'll get you one." Jackson grinned and
nodded before turning to leave with Owens right behind him.

"You do that." Damon replied, his tone no longer kind.

"It was good seeing you again Damon." Jackson said at the
office door. His tone flattened. "I hope our paths cross again real
soon."

Damon watched them cross the lobby and exit the door
before turning back to Olsen, whose face showed a look of
confusion.

"They know." Damon told him.

"They don't have anything."

"They have an eyewitness, you were sloppy."

"There's something wrong with that girl, something isn't
right about her." Olsen said.

"She's a little girl, you can clean that up can't you?" Damon picked a piece of hard candy out of his pocket and unwrapped it.

"Of course."

"Good, because if you can't clean your messes, I'll clean mine." Damon told him, popping the candy into his mouth.

"There is absolutely no way I would ever get you a warrant with that amount of evidence." Assistant District Attorney Vanessa Burke told Jackson and Owens while she stood next to Knox's desk. Burke had been a lawyer for almost eight years but she'd only worked in the District Attorney's office for a little over one.

She was Thirty-six and still maintained much of her younger beauty, her striking blonde hair rolled down onto her shoulders naturally and her face was still virtually void of wrinkles or blemishes. Knox wondered how she did it.

She came over to the District Attorney's office after several years in private practice, her civic mindedness overriding her greed. She replaced an Assistant District Attorney that had worked for over twenty years, though he wasn't especially effective. He was notorious for making strategic mistakes that eventually embarrassed the District Attorney's office enough to get rid of him.

"There's simply no way I can move forward without more." She told them.

"Why? We have the little girl, a fake alibi and the monetary discrepancy." Jackson asked.

"Kaylee Taylor's account won't hold up very well. She was experiencing extreme trauma and she had two months to find that picture and memorize that guy's face." Burke told him. "You can't prove the alibi is false, from what Bethany told me, nobody has seen this guy Damon Collins for over two years, which means that nobody can establish his whereabouts at the time of the murder. The monetary discrepancy is even more confusing than it is circumstantial. So I'm sorry, I just can't take that to a judge. I'll get eaten alive, I need more boys."

"Do you have anything besides the little girl to connect Olsen to the murder directly?" Knox asked from behind her desk.

"No." Jackson replied uneasily.

"Well Damon Collins doesn't sanction a murder over twenty-five hundred dollars. He had to have a better reason." Knox returned.

"I'm not familiar with Damon Collins, what's his story?" Burke asked.

"It was before you came onboard." Jackson told the story of his former partner. "Carey Rent was a no holds barred cop, we'd gone through the academy together and went to narc together. He was sent up for planting evidence, then after he got out he got mixed up in the middle of that terrorist attack last year and was killed. I'm sure you know about that.

"Anyway, Rent and I had been after Damon for years. He was Seattle's premiere goto guy for narcotics. He had it all down and he was good at it." Jackson told her, much to Knox's chagrin, lately, she became uneasy anytime Rent's name was mentioned. "See Damon was a subcontractor, that's what made him so hard to catch. He contracted everything out, nothing led to back to him, not the drugs, not the money, nothing. We could never get a handle on him because every time we hit his operation, it would lead to a dead end.

"Then we got lucky. One of Damon's dealers got popped for domestic assault, the responding officers found enough smack in his place to put him away for fifteen flat. He had a good looking wife and two kids, which weren't going to wait for him, so he cut a deal with us. In exchange for a reduced sentence, he'd get us Damon. It worked good for a while and we started building a solid case but at some point Damon figured it out and we found the dealer face down in his house, along with the rest of his family.

"I don't think anyone had any doubts that Damon did it. At the scene we found a partial fingerprint that preliminarily matched Damon. We finally had him but the print was smeared and we weren't sure if we could get a conclusive I.D. from it. Not one that would stand up in court anyway. So one night, Rent went into the evidence locker and switched the partial with a better one we had on file from Damon. You know the rest, the forensics guys found a discrepancy in the paperwork, Internal Affairs came in and caught

Rent on camera making the switch and he was sent up."

"And Damon walked?" Burke asked.

"The department screwed Rent on the whole thing, didn't support him at all," Jackson shot Knox a dirty look, then turned back to Burke "your predecessor offered Rent a deal, eighteen months, out in three. The problem was that the moron forced the deal down Rent's throat and did it before Damon went to trial. Damon's defense convinced the jury that if one piece of evidence was suspect, all of it was and he used Rent's conviction to do it. After they acquitted him, Damon dropped off the face of the earth, nobody knows where he went or what he did, not until now that is."

"The bottom line is that if Damon's back in town, he has a reason for it." Knox added.

"Okay, get me what I need to win the case, then I'll get your warrants." Burke ordered. "Have a good evening." She picked up her briefcase and strolled out, leaving Jackson and Owens with Knox's menacing glare.

6

"School Bully"

Kaylee's day began like any other ordinary ten year old's but with a few modifications. At seven o'clock Courtney woke Kaylee for school. The studious mother made her daughter a light breakfast of cereal, Cocoa Pebbles was Kaylee's favorite, but they'd emptied the box the previous morning so today it was Cheerios. After devouring the morning meal, Kaylee was sent upstairs to bathe under Courtney's watchful eye of course.

Kaylee had argued vehemently to her independence in the matter but her mother was deathly afraid that the little girl would fall entering or exiting the tub–Kaylee's klutziness was well documented–so a compromise had been reached. Kaylee would leave the bathroom door open at all times and Courtney would find some excuse to be in the upstairs hallway during her bath. Kaylee wasn't privy to the finer details of the compromise but she enjoyed the comfort of knowing that her mother wasn't far away.

Upon finishing her bath, Kaylee told her mother that she was finished and her mother came into the bathroom and checked her for cuts or bruises, this was done at least twice daily, sometimes more often depending on the vigorousness of the day. Cuts and scratches were very important to Kaylee because she almost never noticed that she had them and they could become infected very quickly. Recently, after her grandfather's death, Kaylee had started scratching herself in her sleep. The scratches weren't bad but they worried her mother.

"I already checked Mommy." Courtney was told during the morning check.

"Ok but I can see places you can't." Courtney told her daughter. "Look...you did it again babygurl." Courtney informed that she found several scratches overlapping on the little girl's left arm. "I don't know why you keep doing this."

"I had another bad dream last night." Kaylee confided.

"I know, I heard you. Don't you remember me waking you up?" Courtney took some rubbing alcohol, put it on a cotton ball and applied it to the wound. Kaylee answered her mother's question by shaking her head. "What was it about?" Courtney inquired.

"Me and Grampa was fishing again." Kaylee replied.

"Did you feel it again too?" Courtney asked, Kaylee nodded.

"What did it feel like, can you describe it?"

"It was hot, very very hot and something else, I think it hurt, I didn't like it." Since her return from the hospital, Kaylee had been having nightmares. The doctors told Courtney to expect that. Kaylee had been through a very traumatic experience but there was something that stood out in the dreams in which Kaylee relived the shooting; she could feel the pain. The doctors couldn't explain it but didn't think it was a bad sign either.

"Ok," Courtney said, sitting the cotton balls down and picking up a pair of nail cutters, "give me your hand."

"But you said I could grow them out and get them done." Kaylee objected.

"You weren't putting scratches all over yourself then." Courtney told her. Kaylee slowly complied.

"When is Jesse and the other man coming back?" Kaylee asked while her mother cut her fingernails.

"Owens and Jackson?" Courtney stopped cutting and stared into her daughter's eyes.

"Yeah, I like Jesse, he's funny." Kaylee replied.

"I don't know babygurl," Courtney said, cutting the last nail, "but they don't come here to play, they have a job to do."

"I know." Kaylee replied, her voice telling her mother everything.

Kaylee went to school year round, her schedule was three weeks on, one week off but she had missed the majority of the last two weeks because of various doctors visits. Courtney steadfastly picked up her assigned lessons though and forced her, virtually at gunpoint, to complete the work everyday at home.

Kaylee didn't enjoy staying home from school, anything that got her out of the house made her happy and the friends she had at school were the only people she had contact with except for her mother and grandfather. Now that it was just her and her mother, she had come to feel incredibly lonely.

Most of her emotional state was because of her extraverted personality, which was probably her grandfather's little contribution to her genetic soup. Randy Taylor was very outspoken and made friends easily, his daughter didn't. Courtney had friends and they occasionally visited but her daughter had been her life for so long that the rest of the world seemed like it had slipped into a bottomless void. It was her grandfather that kept Kaylee anchored to the Earth. He would take Kaylee out and meet his friends. He would sit and watch television or movies with his granddaughter and most important of all–at least to Kaylee–he would joke and play with her.

She enjoyed laughing and making others laugh. Because her mother was so serious most of the time, it was her grandfather's ability to make her laugh that had kept her in such high spirits.

Courtney made sure Kaylee dressed appropriately for school–the little girl didn't always want to wear garments that were to Courtney's standards–packed her lunch, loaded her homework in her backpack and set off.

"You don't have to walk me in, I know the way." Kaylee said when Courtney pulled the car into the crowded circle in front of the school where parents typically dropped off their young ones.

"I really think I should walk you in babygurl." Courtney told her.

"It makes me look weird." Kaylee shook her head. "Nobody else's Mother walks them in."

"I don't know." Courtney told her. Kaylee was reaching an age where she wanted to demonstrate her independence, Courtney had been dreading this time and particularly disliked that it was happening right now. "Alright but I'll pick you up at the door this afternoon." Courtney conceded, letting her daughter win this round. Kaylee looked at her mother with a sarcastic look.

"I can walk out to the car just fine." Kaylee proclaimed. Courtney thought about it, looked around at all the children walking from their parent's cars into the school and caved again.

"Alright, you've got my cell number, promise me you'll call if you need anything at all."

"I promise." Kaylee gleamed, leaning in to give her mother a kiss, then jumped out of the car and hurried inside the school, with her mother worrying all the way.

Jackson and Owens' day started with the same regularity that

Kaylee's had. Jackson was roused by his wife with his usual scuffling. Marcy Jackson believed in hot breakfasts to get the kids going and they had oatmeal with English muffins. Once the kids were sent off to class, Marcy embarked on her trip to the daycare to drop Trevor off and finally on to the doctor's office at which she worked.

Jackson took his Mustang and picked up Owens, who had to carpool because his truck had broken down and he was saving money to get it fixed. They conversed their way to their favorite coffee shop. After a quick stop at a pornographic video store in which they bought a VHS tape for $4.99–it was on sale and they didn't want to spend very much–which was packaged in a thin brown paper bag that barely covered the video, they headed to Seattle Police Department's North Precinct. Upon walking into the squad room, Sgt. Casteel ran into them.

"Hey, I got something." Casteel stated. "Jimmy Nguyen leased a cargo ship at Harbor Island about three months ago."

"What does he need with a cargo ship?" Jackson asked.

"You got me but its not an active ship, its one of those that gets leased out for storage because the engine is out or something. Cheaper than warehouse space and the owners can make some money off it." Casteel informed, reciting the new information mostly because he hadn't known that they did that sort of thing. "Get this? The lease expires next week."

"Then that's when Damon plans to do whatever it is he's

going to do. We have to work fast. Let me know what else you find." Jackson ordered.

"Is that it?" Casteel asked, subtly glancing at the brown paper bag Owens was holding.

"Yeah." Owens replied. Casteel nodded approval before going back to work.

"Get me Damon and Eddie Collins' files, let's try to cross reference them and Olsen, see if we come up with anything." Jackson told Owens who started to walk over to his desk. "Jesse," Jackson said after Owens took a few steps, "I need that."

"Oh yeah." Owens said, handing the bag over to Jackson. Jackson took the bag into his cubicle/office and placed it in the top drawer of his desk. A few minutes later, Owens brought in the files and they began working through similarities.

Thirty minutes into his work, Jackson stood at the door and called for Holloman to come into his office. Holloman complied. Looking around and seeing that everyone else was paying attention to their work, he didn't think anything of the request.

"What's up?" Holloman came into his boss's cubicle/office.

"Sit down Marcus." Jackson ordered from behind his desk. "How are you?"

"I'm good, why?" Holloman said while looking around confusingly. Jackson didn't typically call people into his office to chitchat, even though a lot of that took place there.

"We haven't talked in a while, I thought we could catch up."

Jackson replied. "You didn't seem yourself out in Northbend and I'm just wondering how things are at home."

"I don't think I was any different on the raid," Holloman was quickly growing suspicious of the conversation. "Things are fine at home. Why do you ask Dave?"

"Ok, Marcus," Jackson said leaning forward, putting his elbows on his desk, "to be honest, some of the guys are getting a little worried, they've been telling me about some strange behavior, comments you're making, what-not." Owens, Casteel, Johnson, Rothstein, and Mason had now slid silently out of their swivel chairs onto their hands and knees and were crawling to Jackson's cubicle, careful to avoid the door, which was still open and the large windows that were at waist height.

"What kinds of comments and who's saying this?" Holloman asked.

"Nobody's accusing you of anything." Jackson backed up. "It's just that they think something might be wrong and they're a little worried."

"Who is they?" Holloman asked, becoming perturbed at the conversation. The other members of N.S.1. were now right next to the cubicle, listening intently.

"It's not important. I will tell you that it's not anybody in the unit but I've spoken to them too." Jackson told him.

"About what?" Holloman asked, a little loudly.

"I'm not all that worried but if there's anything you want to talk about, you know I'm here for you right? Or anybody else in the unit, we take care of our own." Jackson told him.

"No, there's nothing I want to discuss Ok?" Holloman told him.

"Ok, how's the wife and kid?"

"Fine, Dave, they're all fine, what's this about?"

"I just want to make sure is all. You're getting a little defensive about this?" Jackson told him. Mason had to put her hand over her mouth to keep from laughing out loud.

"Dave, you've known me for years, let me tell you straight, absolutely nothing is wrong, got it?" Holloman stood and proclaimed.

"I'm just looking out for you. I just needed to check."

"Well thanks Dave." Holloman turned to walk out.

"But." Jackson stopped him. Everyone eagerly waited outside. "Just me, let me tell you, I've had some problems that I don't necessarily like to discuss with others and there was something that kind of pulled me through. Now I'm not saying you have any problems but just in case you do, this really helped me out."

Standing on all fours next to the cubicle wall, Owens was turning red trying to hold back his laughter.

Jackson reached into his desk drawer and pulled out the brown paper bag, stood, and handed it to Holloman. "That's just in case you need it." Holloman looked at it, not knowing what was inside but having the creeping feeling that his cohorts were just outside the cubicle listening. He reached into the bag and took out the video cassette, first noticing its title: *Social Security blowjobs #43.*

An embarrassed grin came over Holloman's face and within seconds the entire squad was in the cubicle laughing. Rothstein was rolling around in the floor holding his stomach and Casteel had to sit down. Johnson was pointing out the elderly woman on the cover and asking if she looked familiar. Mason wiped her eyes with a tissue, she'd laughed so hard she'd teared up.

"We thought that since you're always complaining about not getting any at home, a little granny-porn might help." Owens barely got the words out without laughing.

"You seem to be into that." Casteel said, breaking up.

"This really helped me out." Owens quoted, putting his head into his partner's shoulder, laughing.

Kaylee was in the fourth grade. Her day started out with a spelling test, which Kaylee aced. She'd always been an excellent speller, that was due to her mother, who insisted that she spell large words at home. Courtney was a big believer in Kaylee's education, she knew that since Kaylee could never do physical work, her best chance for a successful career would be in academics.

Kaylee's math skills were not so good and when the class

began studying math, she preferred complaining and giving up on it as opposed to working the problems out. Frustrating her more was that they were practicing fractions today and of all the math that Kaylee disliked, fractions were at the top of the list. She muttered through the problems anyway and did not shy away when the teacher, Mrs. Bell, asked her to do one of the problems on the board. Kaylee enjoyed the attention of being in front of the class, all eyes on her. She enjoyed the feeling she got when the teacher praised her work. She almost expected applause from the class and always felt a tiny bit disappointed when she didn't get it.

Science wasn't nearly as difficult for Kaylee as math. Kaylee found it interesting to talk about evolutionary adaptation and constellations. She was particularly interested in astronomy, the stars, space, other worlds. Mostly, this interest came from television, which she watched almost all the time when she was stuck at home because of doctor's appointment or infected cuts, bug bites, and other ailments that worried her mother enough to keep her home from school. Courtney didn't always keep Kaylee home because she was particularly worried about her, much of the time she was kept home was because Courtney distressed more about being away from her daughter than it disturbed Kaylee to be away from her mother. Courtney's life wasn't filled with many people, the friends she did have were distant at best so whenever either Kaylee or her father were absent, Courtney battled a lonely void. Under a guise of a tick bite, Courtney could have conversation all day long. That appealed to her.

Lunch was Kaylee's favorite part of the school day, besides group activities, Kaylee found it rare to interact with her peers. Though she would sometimes have friends come over and play at her house, she couldn't get enough of the social contact that she lacked for so much of her life. At lunch she was allowed to sit and converse with the other girls and boys in her class. She enjoyed getting to know them, joking with them and discussing the important topics of their time. Like who was stronger, Pokiemon or Picachu. Occasionally talk would turn to boys and everyone would always be surprised that Kaylee liked the quiet nerdy little boys who wore glasses. She thought that glasses were cute on boys but not girls, they always made girls look smart and mean, whereas in Kaylee's mind, girls were supposed to be pretty, caring, and gentle. Kaylee couldn't see any point in a girl being nerdy, that was a boy's job.

In the culture of fourth graders, the top rung of love was "going with someone." If two kids were "going together" they were practically married. There was a definitive procedure to this social practice; first a boy or girl had to find someone of the opposite gender that they "liked." Then they had to set up a way to communicate out of the school environment–even fourth graders hesitated to mix business with pleasure–this was accomplished 99% of the time over the phone. Last, they had to make it official, announce it to the world. This was usually done with flirtatious rumor starting by the kid in question's friends. Sometimes notes were involved that contained little boxes that read "Do you want to go with me? Chek yes or no." But that was optional.

Kaylee had never "gone" with a boy but she'd wanted to. In third grade, there was a very attractive four eyed, black haired boy with big ears that just drove Kaylee insane with love. They had graduated to the second step but one day he told her that he just wanted to be friends and Kaylee's little heart had been broken for the very first time. The next day she found Bobby, whose glasses were slightly thinner than the previous boy's and more streamlined. Kaylee's love for Bobby remained unrequited for quite some time, until he moved away after last Christmas.

If Kaylee had one complaint about lunch, it would be ice. Mrs. Bell, who had been thoroughly briefed by Courtney, inspected every last piece of food that Kaylee obtained from the old, very overweight, rather grumpy lunch lady. Kaylee's informed and strident teacher insisted on putting ice on everything even remotely warm that Kaylee ate and it was a standard gripe to her mother, so much so that Courtney had taken to packaging meals for Kaylee to eat in a lunch box.

After lunch was recess, the part of the day that Kaylee detested. Apparently, Mrs. Bell believed that since Kaylee couldn't feel pain, she was also porcelain. Kaylee wasn't allowed to swing with the other children or run or seesaw and the monkey bars were treated like the anti-Christ. Kaylee was to sit on a very nice rug on the concrete and watch the other children have fun. Mrs. Bell didn't understand the torture she was putting Kaylee through when she required this however, Kaylee in her usual optimistic fashion, made the best of the situation and was the loudest, most annoying child on the playground. The other children tolerated her mostly humorous, sometimes sarcastic comments while they played basketball or jumped rope.

Library time came late in the day. Here the children learned important things like the Dewey Decimal system and computer databases. Computers were now household items as such the curriculum of elementary schools were straining to keep up. During their library time, which came on Monday's, Wednesday's, and Friday's with physical education lumped in the off days, the students were separated into two groups, one half would work with the standard library systems, the other would learn how to work the computer.

Kaylee found the entire adventure useless and boring, she had little time for books at home when she could more easily entertain herself with a television and she had already learned to work a computer. For her eighth birthday, her grandfather purchased her a child's computer. The computer itself was a regular desktop, her grandfather however had installed a massive series of security features which effectively prevented Kaylee from viewing inappropriate content when she searched the internet. These features were so effective that Kaylee felt restrained by them, even to the point where she could not visit some of the children's sites that she would have wanted to. For this reason, her computer was used mostly for school work and playing games that her mother or grandfather bought for her.

Kaylee was as smart if not smarter than most of the other children. She'd learned proper library etiquette with the other children but she neglected to abide by it. She was a talker and being inside a library and being a talker didn't mix. Being inside an elementary school classroom and being a talker didn't mix either. Kaylee usually ended up spending most of her library time in a corner staring at a map of the United States with the objective of learning the capitals of all fifty states.

This type of punishment was common with Kaylee. She could recite all fifty states with perfect clarity by the end of the second grade and all the states of Mexico, Canada, and the countries of Europe and South America by the end of the third grade. Being stubborn like she was it was difficult to get her to attend to a task that she didn't care about. Instead she usually joked or talked to the other students, both activities she never tired of. Suffice it to say, she spent a good deal of her day in corners looking at maps or doing math problems.

The Seattle Public School System had eliminated corporal punishment in the 1990's but Kaylee made the faculty regret that decision even though they knew it wouldn't have an effect on her. When she set her mind to misbehaving, there was little anyone could do to stop her, a fact her mother could testify to ad nauseam.

Courtney found that the most effective way of punishing Kaylee was by taking away her television privileges. Kaylee watched entirely too much television. This was a byproduct of her mother's overprotectiveness, which had eased slightly in the last couple of years but was still a major barrier between the world and Kaylee's drive to experience new activities. By taking away her television privileges, Kaylee seemed to get the message that she wasn't in charge. Though this punishment only lasted until her grandfather came home and restored them. Something that Kaylee had seen her two guardians fight about on multiple occasions.

The last class of the day was Social Studies. Fortunately Kaylee was usually very prepared for her lessons, at least geographically. Today they were studying the civil war, the reasons why the war occurred and the key figures involved. Kaylee had always been interested in history, American history in particular. Her grandfather instilled a sense of patriotism in her at an early age. He always told her how lucky she was to live in a country where she could say anything she wanted about anyone she wanted and she quoted him often about that same subject, though it was usually to her teachers and it never kept her out of the corner looking at maps.

Even through their annoyance at some of her more flamboyant qualities, the faculty knew and loved Kaylee, she didn't always cause problems and they could all see what a sweet girl she was. Mrs. Bell was especially impressed with her intellect. After years of watching period piece movies and shows with her grandfather, she had developed ideas and logic, particularly about history, that was well beyond her time. She was never afraid to ask questions when she didn't understand something and no matter how many times she failed at an assignment, she never gave up.

Whenever Mrs. Bell asked questions of the class, Kaylee's hand was always the first to smack the air. This behavior was bittersweet for Mrs. Bell who couldn't call on Kaylee to answer every question but enjoyed the knowledge that Kaylee usually had a correct answer. Kaylee didn't see Mrs. Bell's lack of acknowledgment as giving the other children a chance to answer the questions, she saw it as a personal rejection of her delightful anecdotes. Therefore when another student answered a question wrong, Kaylee would occasionally have something to say, which she instinctively blurted. These comments weren't always funny and caused her to frequent a corner of the room that she rather disliked.

Class let out at exactly 3:20 in the afternoon. Twenty minutes before, Tonya's soccer game had started, which Jackson and Owens were attending.

Starting around three o'clock, cars began lining up in the parking lot around the school. The more impatient parents liked to walk up to the school and mingle with each other while they waited for their children. Courtney had been in her father's lawyer's office discussing some issues when she noticed the time. She hurried out to the school but all the good parking spaces were already taken and Courtney had to wait on the street in her car. She was typically the first car in line each day that Kaylee was in school and was worried that Kaylee wouldn't see her car all the way past the courtyard on the street. She considered going up to the doors and waiting with the other parents even though Kaylee had asked her not to but decided that she needed to respect her daughter's wishes for once.

Courtney had been wrestling with her overprotectiveness for quite some time. Because of Kaylee's frequent mishaps as a toddler, Courtney had settled into a routine of never taking her eyes off her daughter. The only time she ever felt that Kaylee was safe was when she was with her grandfather and that schema had now been completely shattered. She was constantly reminded of the worst day of her life two months ago when the police officer came to her house and informed her of the tragedy. She knew that the danger had passed but she had to fight the overwhelming urge to wrap her arms around her daughter and never ever let go. Kaylee was all she had left in the world.

Courtney knew that her mental anguish and her drive to protect her daughter was becoming a problem with Kaylee's development and forced herself to hold back. The front yard of the school was filling with parents and soon, students. She saw Calvin Patterson, the School Resource Officer, a uniformed Seattle Police Corporal that she'd known for several years, standing at the crosswalk of the road, looking around for anything suspicious and told herself that she need not overreact. She picked up a magazine that she'd bought earlier in the day for Kaylee in an attempt to get her to read more and began burrowing through it.

With its usual regularity, the dam that was the front doors of the school suddenly overflowed with first through fifth graders ready to begin an evening of family life and playtime. Courtney looked up at the flood of children and tried to spy Kaylee, a single snowflake in the avalanche of children but couldn't. In keeping with her work at not being overprotective she forced herself to return to her magazine.

Kaylee was being admonished by Mrs. Bell for a few minutes for her behavior in Social Studies class. Mrs. Bell was attempting to explain to the little girl that it was mean to make fun of her fellow classmates because they gave the wrong answer and that it made them feel bad. Kaylee understood what her teacher was telling her and dutifully apologized. She hadn't thought about the comment before she said it and she regretted that.

Surprised that her mother wasn't at the door to meet her, Mrs. Bell pointed out Courtney's car to Kaylee to make sure that she saw it and released the little girl out the front doors. At the same time Kaylee went through the doors, Mrs. Ottman released her fifth grade class. A new wave of students flooded into the courtyard. Courtney again looked up from the magazine but Kaylee had already been lost in the sea of the older children. Calvin Patterson was watching a group of children cross the street to a church parking lot where many of the children's parents liked to wait.

Kaylee was glad to see that her mother wasn't at the door,

she enjoyed the semi-normalcy that it provided her to walk across the maze of sidewalks and parking circle's to get to the street. She was being particularly careful when stepping on and off the pavement because she knew that if she had an accident at this important juncture in time, her mother would be at the door every day for the rest of her life. She was watching her feet when stepping up on a sidewalk when she felt a man's hand on her shoulder.

"Come with me quietly or I'll kill your mother." Olsen whispered into her ear. Kaylee's stomach sank, she began shaking and fear engulfed her. She stared straight ahead while Olsen led her down a different sidewalk, on their way to his car.

7

"Scared"

Courtney was reading an article about arts and crafts that Kaylee could easily make at home when she looked up to see if she could find her daughter. She scanned the courtyard looking for Kaylee but could not differentiate between all the children. Then she saw Kaylee's backpack, it was on Kaylee but she wasn't coming to the car. Instead she was accompanied by a strange man and heading off on one of the other sidewalks. Courtney squealed a terrified gasp when she realized who the man was. She jumped from her car and yelled for help.

Many of the students and parents turned to look at Courtney, who was pointing and yelling, running to try and save her daughter. Olsen heard her and knew that he'd been discovered. He grabbed

Kaylee by the hair and drug her along the ground, dashing for his car.

Calvin Patterson, the School Resource Officer, who was standing at the crosswalk, saw the situation and also began running in Olsen's direction. Kaylee's fear had paralyzed her. She allowed Olsen to drag her limp body along the concrete by the hair and didn't try to move. She was scared for her mother most of all and herself second. She didn't know what to do, not that she could have really done anything. Olsen continued running, dragging Kaylee, the concrete scrapping skin off her legs by layers, until he reached his car.

Courtney reached the car at the same time and attacked Olsen. Several children and parents screamed. Olsen whipped his fist around into Courtney's face, sending her into a patch of grass. Olsen, whose planning skills were not very efficient, had to get the keys out of his pocket to unlock the passenger side door of his car. He threw Kaylee in like she were a doll and rushed to the driver's side.

Igniting the engine, Olsen realized another problem in his plan, cars had arrived behind him to wait in line and he was blocked in. He yanked the gear shift to reverse and slammed the gas, colliding with the car behind him in an attempt to push it back so that he could leave. He threw it in drive and smacked the car in front of him while turning the wheel but he didn't create enough room to free himself so he repeated both steps.

Patterson had already screamed into his radio for backup when he reached the car that was still trying to punch its way out of the gridlock. He saw Kaylee in the passenger side seat and jumped over the hood to get to the driver's side. Taking out his extendable baton, he broke the driver's side window into tiny shards of glass. Olsen reached under his seat and pulled out his gun. Patterson saw his suspect reach down, dropped his baton and drew his weapon.

Kaylee's eyes widened when she saw the guns. Without thinking, she yanked the handle of the door and it opened. She fell onto the concrete sidewalk just before Olsen hit the car behind him one more time.

"Drop it!" Patterson yelled to Olsen, neither of which knew that Kaylee had fallen out of the door, their attention was completely on each other. In one swift motion Olsen dropped the gun in the floor next to his feet and with his newly freed hand, slammed the car into drive. Patterson didn't want to fire into the vehicle because he still thought Kaylee was inside, instead he aimed for Olsen's front tire.

At the moment Patterson discharged his weapon, Olsen hit the gas and the tire lunged forward. The bullet slammed straight through the hubcap and redirected off of the wheel. The hubcap shot off the tire and into the air, landing on another car. Olsen stomped his foot and the car spun off into the street with Patterson radioing in its license plate numbers.

Courtney grabbed Kaylee, securing her with arms. Kaylee

didn't speak or cry, she returned her mother's embrace and stared straight ahead.

Ten minutes later, Marcy Jackson had her face in her hands while she watched her husband arguing with her daughter's soccer coach. What made the situation even more embarrassing was that Owens had gone down to the field in an attempt to take up for the coach and now there was a three-way shouting match between them. The disturbance had become so loud that the game had to be temporarily stopped and the game officials surrounded them.

Jackson was almost finished with his rant when his cell phone rang, he picked it off his belt and plugged his opposite ear to listen. After he few moments he waved his hand at Marcy to come down. She shook her head no but he waved again and she came.

"We gotta go." He told her after she pushed her way through the crowd to him. "You make sure he puts Tonya back in." Marcy cast him an odd look.

"She doesn't deserve to go back in, she passed to the referee!" Owens objected.

"We gotta go, something's happened to Kaylee Taylor." Jackson ignored him. "C'mon."

Jackson's Mustang pulled into the school, where a patrolman on traffic duty recognized him and let him in. Most of the children and parents had already left the school but several were still there being interviewed by patrolmen. The remainder of the large crowd around the school were now police, bystanders who always gathered to see what was happening, two ambulances and no less than three news crews from local networks. CNN, FOX, and MSNBC were piping their live video feeds from local reporters on the scene.

The courtyard in front of the doors to the school had been cleared and all that remained were ambulances and fire department trucks. Kaylee and her mother had been taken into the school to have the paramedics look at them. Several witnesses that were close to the action were also inside the school talking to the police. The Crime Scene Investigators that Jackson requested over the phone were on their way but hadn't arrived yet. Most of the teachers stayed on the grounds and were outside the school discussing the incident with each other and a few reporters. The Patrol Watch Commander was taking some information from the principle.

Jackson and Owens first approached an ambulance in the courtyard where they saw Calvin Patterson being treated by the paramedics for a scrape to his arm that he attained jumping over the hood of Olsen's car. He looked shaken and worried, nodding and listening to the paramedics whenever they spoke to him. They were warning him about his blood pressure but he knew that he would be fine. He still had yet to come off the adrenaline that the experience caused to surge through his body.

"How you doing?" Jackson asked..

"I'm good, I'm fine." Patterson replied, his nerves evident in his voice.

"Well, for what its worth, good job out here today." Jackson told him.

"Thanks." Patterson said somberly. Jackson turned and began walking to the Watch Commander.

"Let me ask you a question." Owens said to Patterson before following Jackson. "Did you intend to kill the hubcap or just maim it?"

"You know what Owens, screw you." Patterson replied.

"Touchy aint ya," Owens said, walking backwards, away from Patterson, "one little ricochet and you be getting all hot." He finished then turned around and walked normally.

"Lay off him will you?" Jackson told him. "He thought he lost that kid."

"But he didn't, therefore, I can make fun of him."

"Just don't forget that he's the reason she's still alive." Jackson told him.

"Ok." Owens felt a dash of embarrassment at his behavior. "I'm gonna see how they're doing." Owens broke off and headed into the school. Jackson continued to the Watch Commander who informed him that ADA Burke was on her way to the scene and that the school had an extensive camera system that they believed caught most of the event.

On the outskirts of the crime scene, the five members of N.S.1. had to duck under the police tape to get into the courtyard. They all nodded to the Officer in the light blue uniform that held the tape so that they could walk under it. The five of them looked more like miscreants than cops, wearing the usual rundown clothing they used when working narcotics, with their badges hanging casually on chains around their necks.

"Would you look at all this?" Casteel was saying.

"Yeah," Mason responded, "anytime somebody stubs their toe at a school, this happens."

"Any excuse for a circus." Holloman said.

"I wonder if the news people sit at home waiting for crap like this?" Rothstein thought aloud.

"This and disasters." Johnson answered. "The occasional celebrity DUI."

"Hey, Casteel, Johnson!" One of the patrolmen working the crowd turned and yelled. "You guys better be careful, I think a lady over there has a poodle and there aren't any trees for you to climb." Casteel thought about flipping him a bird but with all the news cameras around, decided against it. Instead he shrugged it off and approached Jackson and the watch commander.

"Don't you just love it when this happens?" Casteel said to Jackson when they got close enough.

"Don't you know it, just makes my day." Jackson replied. "Anything on Olsen's car?"

"Nobody's picked it up yet." Casteel told him. "It's been thirty minutes, he could be halfway to Walla Walla by now."

"Hang out here a bit, I'm gonna look at the security tapes." Jackson told them.

"Where's the vic?" Owens asked the patrolman just inside the doors of the school. The uniform pointed to the principle's office, which was decorated with firemen and paramedics. Owens practically had to push his way through the outer office to get to the principle's personal office. Stepping into the door, he saw Kaylee holding onto her mother tightly and being looked over by a paramedic. The little girl looked up to see him, jumped off her mother's lap and wrapped her arms tightly around his stomach, repeating his name over and over. Courtney watched the situation with a sense of surprise.

"You ok?" He rubbed her head, not expecting her reaction either.

"I thought he was going to hurt Mommy." She exclaimed, trying to explain herself to him.

"Don't worry, you're safe now." He comforted. "How is she?" He asked the paramedic checking her out.

"Some scrapes and bruises, nothing bad, I'm going to take her to the hospital for some x-rays." Courtney replied. She was worried but didn't want to let it show.

"You'll come with us, won't you?" Kaylee smiled up at Owens but her question unnerved her mother.

"Of course." Owens couldn't say no.

When Assistant District Attorney Burke arrived, she went straight in to view the security tapes with Jackson. Since the incident was already on the news, Burke knew it was important to get to the scene quickly and begin gathering the evidence she was going to use in court.

The security tapes showed mostly Olsen's back when he came up behind Kaylee and only the profile of his face could be seen when they shifted direction to his car. Since the car and most of the action happened out on the street, the school's camera didn't pick it up but Jackson had the principle pause the tape on what he thought was the best view of Olsen.

"Do you think he was acting by himself?" Burke asked.

"Not in a million years." Jackson replied. "He's too stupid to come after her without orders."

"Now we just have to prove that Damon Collins gave that order." Burke told him.

"That's not going to happen. I know him, he wouldn't say anything in front of anyone else. It may be possible to flip Olsen if we can grab him though." Jackson told her.

"If Damon gave the order to kill the little girl, why would he let Olsen muddle it like he has?" Burke asked.

"Damon rarely does this type of thing himself, he prefers not to be connected, so whatever orders he gives, he expects his people to do the rest. You can reasonably bet that Olsen was completely on his own with every part of this, except the idea to kill her in the first place."

"Then the only way we could get Collins for this is if Olsen testifies against him. If that's my only evidence, I'll never get a jury to buy it." Burke's disappointment evident.

"That's why he uses this strategy, he knows he can beat the rap. More important than getting Damon right now, is getting Olsen. You don't screw up this badly and live if you work for Damon Collins." Jackson informed. "He's going to try again."

"What are you doing to get him?" Burke asked.

"We've got a BOLO out on him and his car. We've sent it out to every department in the Northwest. I just ordered patrols to check his house and business, he doesn't have any family so we can't check there but I don't think he'll leave Seattle. He has some friends, we're going to look at them, see what we can get. When we do get him, we need to keep him. That's your domain."

"I can take this tape to a judge, with Kaylee Taylor's ID and this tape, I should get a warrant for both this and Randy Taylor's homicide. You should pick him up as soon as you find him but I prefer to have the warrant in hand first, it will give us more leverage with the warrants for his business and home and anything we try to put on Damon or Eddie Collins." Burke said.

"That's swell but we can't wait a week for it. We need to pick him up ASAP." Jackson told her.

"Our main concern is the girl's safety, find him, pick him up. I'll worry about the warrant." Burke promised.

"I want protection for her too." Jackson said.

"You got it, I'll call Knox." Burke said, picking her cell phone out of her pocket and dialing a number. Jackson excused himself from the room and headed to the principle's office where he found Kaylee still with her arms around Owens. He stepped into the outer office and passed several paramedics who had just cleaned up their gear and were leaving, an angry look on their faces from comments that Owens made to them.

"What's up?" Owens asked. Jackson waved N.S.1. to enter, once they were in, he started giving his orders.

"I want one of you with her around the clock." Jackson pointed to Kaylee, then to Owens. "You take the first shift since you're joined at the hip. Casteel work out a roster, then I want you to get back to the office and take N.S.2. off whatever Knox has them working on and have them canvas Olsen's known associates, the list is on my desk. Have them start now and keep looking until they find him but make sure they don't move on him until I say so."

Kaylee's trip to the hospital was uneventful, though she insisted on either her mother or Owens remaining with her at all times, she was uncharacteristically quiet. Owens didn't know what to say, he'd never been in a situation quite like this one before, he'd never had a child drawn to him in this way. He tried making a few jokes and even got Kaylee to smile once or twice but not laugh. She also didn't make any jokes in return, which wasn't like her.

At the hospital, Kaylee went through a battery of x-rays, CaT scans, and MRI's. Kaylee's personal physician came in to check on her, his worries rested in possible trauma that wasn't exhibited by outside symptoms. He was particularly concerned about whether or not she'd hit her head. Since she wouldn't be able to feel any type of concussion or skull fracture, the doctor took great pains in ascertaining her physical condition.

Kaylee was accustomed to these types of tests and though she usually complained about them, she didn't this particular evening. Kaylee'd come to think of the hospital as a second home, all the nurses knew her and almost immediately after coming in, she found herself showered with her favorite hospital delicacy–If there was one–Jell-O. Kaylee was partial to the green kind, she didn't know the flavor, she also liked the red and yellow and she dealt well with the chocolate pudding they always had on hand but didn't care for the vanilla. Having heard of the incident at the school on the news and after being called by Kaylee's doctor to prepare the necessary tests, the nurses felt obliged to welcome their cutest patron with a cheer-me-up.

They didn't get home until almost ten o'clock in the evening and Kaylee was more than worn out. Her fear was slowly but surely subsiding and she was talking more. Mostly she was asking Owens questions about his southern accent and his hometown of Unionville Tennessee. His voice seemed to comfort her while she laid in her mother's lap on the sofa. Courtney didn't know what she could do for her daughter, she would have thought that holding her was enough but Kaylee seemed to need more right now.

The conversation mostly focused on Owens' history, Kaylee chimed in every once in a while but mostly she wanted to hear Owens and her mother talk. When Courtney decided to make Owens a cup of coffee, she left Kaylee alone on the sofa. The moment her mother got up, Kaylee crawled up in the chair that Owens was sitting in. She hadn't asked, she simply got up and sat down next to him. Her sudden move caught Owens off guard. He'd always felt uncomfortable with children, he was a little scared of them. She laid in the chair, silent, wrapping her arms around him. Owens couldn't help the uncomfortable feeling while he told her about his family, his church back home, his brothers and sisters and why he'd come out to Seattle to be a cop.

"Do you ever worry that something's going to happen to them while you're not there?" She finally asked when Owens began talking about his parents.

"I do." He looked down into her sad eyes. "But sometimes I have to have faith that everything is going to work out."

"What if that man comes back?" She asked him, for the first time mentioning Olsen or even what happened.

"Then I'll be here or another pig who won't let him hurt anybody. So don't worry." He slipped in the joke to see if he could get a smile or giggle. He didn't.

"He said he was going to hurt Mommy." She told him.

"I know." He said. "But your Mom is very brave and she knows that I won't let that happen. She's not scared and you shouldn't be either."

"Mommy said once that she worried about me because I'm never scared." Kaylee said, her eyes tearing up. "But I was scared today. I was so scared!" The dam broke. Kaylee tucked her head into Owens' chest. Her cries wailed through the house as if on a loudspeaker.

In just a few minutes, Kaylee cried ten years of tears. All the pain she'd felt in her life, from breaking her first doll, to her last moments with her grandfather, to watching Olsen smack her mother free flowed from her eyes. Every time she'd been made fun of at school, all those awful afternoons sitting on a rug watching the other children run around and have fun. Every ice cube or MRI or x-ray, every moment of her life that she'd been reminded that she was not normal; that she was a freak, a genetic anomaly, an outcast. Every last thing that she couldn't do or that someone had to do for her because she was different, it all exploded in a firestorm of tears and bellowing.

"Why did he have to kill Grampa? Why does he want to hurt us?" She was practically screaming. Owens didn't know what to do. He had no idea what to say. He froze, he didn't even move his head to look down. He tried to formulate something but his words couldn't come out. He started to put his arms around her but hesitated, something inside him didn't want to. He didn't want to become connected to a her like this, he didn't want to be attached to her at all. Owens enjoyed that he wasn't attached to anyone or anything but here was this horrified little girl who had chosen him to break down to and though he thought she was a cute kid, he'd always intended to finish the case and move on. If he put his arms around her, he knew he wouldn't be able to.

"It's going to be alright." He finally decided. He held her close now, closer than he'd ever let himself get to anyone. "I'm here." He told himself. "Let it all out, I'm here little sister, I'm here."

Courtney watched from the kitchen door. She wasn't surprised, she was hurt. Kaylee'd chosen a stranger, someone she'd only known for barely three days to confide to, not her mother. She stood silent, motionless, her tears thick raindrops inching down her face. She loved her daughter more than she loved herself, more than she loved anything but now she felt rejected in Kaylee's time of need. Courtney needed to cry on Kaylee's shoulder just as much as she needed Kaylee to cry on hers.

Kaylee cried for what seemed like an eternity to Owens. Over time, the cries gradually faded to silence. Owens looked down to see the little girl sleeping peacefully, still holding him tightly. He slowly and carefully took the child in his arms and carried her to her room. Sitting her on the bed and covering her with a thick bedspread, he brushed the hair from her face. He knew that Courtney was right when she told him that Kaylee was special, but it wasn't because she couldn't feel pain, it was because she hid it so well. He leaned down and kissed her forehead.

"I'm not going to let anything happen to you little sister. I swear to God." He whispered.

Downstairs, Courtney placed Owens' coffee on the table and was taking out a blanket and pillow from a closet when he rounded the stairs. She didn't say anything to him, she laid the blanket out on the sofa and propped the pillow on the armrest. Owens moved to the window and looked out through the beige drapes.

"I'm going to sleep with Kaylee tonight." Courtney finally broke the silence. "I want you to make yourself at home." She said with a disappointed tone. Owens looked over at the sofa and noticed what she was doing.

"I won't need that." He told her. "I won't be sleeping, another officer is going to relieve me at midnight."

"Alright." Courtney said, apathy in her voice.

"My relief's name is Kimberly Mason, you'll like her, she'll be here through the morning. She's very good." He said, looking back out the window and down the street for anything suspicious. Courtney nodded, a minute of uncomfortable silence passing between them.

"I'm not looking for a man." Courtney blurted. Owens turned his head to her, the statement didn't offend him, he figured he probably deserved it.

"I know." Was the only reply he could think of.

"I'm not looking for a father for my daughter either." That statement did hurt Owens' feelings, he didn't know why but he took offense to it.

"Look," he said, "if I've made you feel uncomfortable, I'm sorry. I can wait outside." He started for the door.

"No." Courtney said without much volume. "It's alright, please," she frowned, knowing that he didn't deserve her anger, "make yourself at home and the other officer too when she gets here." Courtney didn't know what else to say. She turned away from him and went upstairs to hold her daughter.

8

"Takedown"

The warrant was issued at 4:48 a.m. the next morning. ADA Burke spent the entire night going over the evidence that had been collected from the Randy Taylor homicide along with the attempted abduction of Kaylee Taylor at her school. She prepared the warrant with special emphasis on the investigation continuing to be ongoing bound with the accusation that Richard Olsen was a danger to Kaylee Taylor. Great care was taken to word the warrant in such a way that Damon and/or Eddie Collins could be implicated in both the homicide and kidnaping attempt if new evidence was found. This way of preparing the warrant would hopefully give the District attorney's office more leverage in gaining search warrants for Olsen's home, business and possibly further warrants for the homes of Damon and Eddie Collins.

Once ADA Burke finished the warrant, it was painstakingly proofread by two separate law clerks and finally read and approved by the District Attorney of King County. It was unusual that a D.A. would insist on approving a warrant draft, however the high profile of the case demanded special attention. With the warrant approved, ADA Burke hand delivered it to the house of the Magistrate Judge who read and signed the warrant at 4:48 a.m..

The warrant was then taken to the Magistrate Court of King County and filed. Three copies were made, one for the District Attorney's office, another for the Seattle Police Department, and the last for the suspect. ADA Burke supervised the process and delivered last two copies into Jackson's waiting hands at the North Precinct. Jackson took the Police Department's copy to the records division where it would be filed and entered into the National Crime Information System, a gigantic database of warrants and records that was networked across the country. The other copy Jackson kept, his hope, to deliver it to Olsen personally, along with an escort to jail.

Olsen spent the night at an old friend's house. He'd dropped his car in an alleyway in the downtown area and taken a bus to the house. He hadn't told his friend why he needed to stay the night but only that he'd been having his home fumigated at the last minute because of termites. He also asked to borrow his friend's car the next morning, which his friend obliged to allow.

Olsen needed to think, he knew that the police would be looking for him now and didn't know what Damon Collins would do when he found out that he had screwed up in such a visible way. He knew that he needed to make contact with Damon, to work things out with him, that if Damon understood the circumstances, Damon might be able to provide him at least some assistance in solving his newly developed legal problems. Olsen had seen Damon beat many raps and began thinking that Damon was the best person to go to for this problem. That was if Damon didn't kill him on sight.

That was the danger that Olsen was truly scared of, Damon Collins didn't play around. He was a hardcore criminal who never had any compunction or remorse at taking another human life, even an innocent one, which Olsen knew he wasn't. Olsen battled with his three options the entire night, he could talk to Damon, plead for forgiveness and his help and hope that Damon didn't kill him. He could turn himself into the police, try to cut a deal and hope that Damon didn't kill him or he could take the car and run, in which case both Damon and the police would hunt for him mercilessly. When he was finally caught and he knew that he eventually would be, he'd be back to his second option, the prospects of which were not appealing. He knew that if he was in police custody, whether he cut a deal or not, Damon could and would have him killed without batting an eye.

In the early morning hours, Olsen came to the conclusion that his only hope to live through this ordeal was to throw himself on Damon's mercy and hope that the expression of loyalty would appeal to Damon's sense of pride and he'd be spared. Olsen's plan was to go to Damon, admit his fault and ask for help. It seemed simple enough, but Olsen knew that it wouldn't be a walk in the park. By this time, he knew that the police were scouring the city for him, so he couldn't go to Damon at Shoreline Printing, the police would definitely be watching that. Damon and Eddie's upscale home would be under surveillance also. Luckily, Olsen knew that Damon and Eddie had plans for this morning.

This day was special to Seattle for two reasons, the first of which was because it was the first day of boating. Boating season had no official beginning or end, however boating was a staple of Seattle's culture and as such, one of the yearly festivities that Seattlites enjoyed was an unofficial festival known as the opening day of boating. Sponsored by the Seattle Yacht Club, the festivities carried on for almost a week, which was the usual length of time for such things in Seattle, a city which loved parties.

The biggest day of the festivities was the first Saturday in May, during which Seattle's boaters got together to have a Mardi Gras style party with a boating theme. The festivities were held annually on the west side of Union Bay, just south of the University of Washington campus. In the very early morning hours, the boaters congregated at two giant log booms on either side of the canal leading out into the Puget Sound. The booms were over a mile long each and extended east into Union Bay. There, they tied their boats to the booms and each other, creating a mile long parade route with the space of the canal between the log booms. Since space was limited and there were always more boats than room, each boat anchored itself to the bottom of the bay and also to the log boom then tied themselves to the boats on their respective right and left.

Between the log booms a parade of boats, several crew races, an official U.S. Navy concert, a dragon boat exhibition race, and a commissioning ceremony for a U.S. Navy ship among other common sights of a parade ensued. Along with the official festivities came the usual Seattle revelries of drinking, barbecues, socializing, and dancing. The boaters of Seattle held the opening day of boating as a celebration of their lifelong love of water recreation and it was taken with such sanctity.

The second important occurrence of this day was completely unknown to all but a handful of Seattle's residents. With the massive amount of people converging on the Lake Washington Ship Canal area for the opening day of boating, Damon Collins intended on using the commotion to hide the transportation of a special type of goods that he intended to sell. Having carefully worked out the schedule for his newest venture, Damon leased a warehouse just off of San Juan Road, which ran parallel to the canal.

Today was the day he planned to move his items to another location. One where they would be appropriately packaged and prepared for distribution. There would be massive confusion around the area, so much so that Damon knew that no one would notice his moving out of the warehouse. For this task he'd hired six tractor trailers and over two dozen men, none of which knew exactly what kind of merchandise they would be moving.

Besides the merchandise itself, Damon had to quietly dispose of a large amount of equipment that he'd brought in to create the merchandise. Damon knew that it was essential that this equipment never be located and only trusted his certain trustworthy men to deal with it. While the other dozen and a half of workers and truck drivers were in the warehouse preparing and moving the merchandise, Damon's trusted men hid the equipment. It would be removed via a hastily built underground tunnel that led half a mile north and came out in the boiler room of the University of Washington's medical center. In the boiler room, all of the equipment would be destroyed and Damon's men would be able to leave the area undetected.

Damon's plan was for the operation to begin in the early morning hours, with the merchandise being sealed in boxes then the hired help would come in around 8:00 a.m., pallet the boxes and move them with fork lifts to the trucks.

Upon deciding to plead to Damon for help, Olsen decided

that the best place and time to come to Damon would be at the warehouse shortly after eight, Olsen knew that Damon wouldn't kill him in front of the hired help and that the police wouldn't be watching the warehouse. What Olsen didn't know was that the police had already found him.

After the incident at the school, the detectives of Jackson's entire narcotics unit were reassigned to bringing Olsen to justice. The teams of N.S.1, N.S.2, and N.S.3 began a low profile manhunt for Olsen which consisted of them contacting every person on the list of known associates that Jackson had given them. Most of Olsen's associates were either active or retired petty criminals and because there is little honor among thieves, they willingly gave the detectives as much information as was thought might get the detectives off their backs and out of their lives.

Though the teams tracked down every lead they could get, only one would pay off. An ex-con who had done time with Olsen and was currently spending three months in the King County jail for parole violation informed a detective from the N.S.3 team about a friend of Olsen's parents who had always had a soft spot for him. Though he wasn't involved in criminal activity that the associate was aware of, he was trusted by Olsen. N.S.3 sent two detectives to the home and on a cursory evaluation of the outside of the premises, found that the man had male houseguest. Because they had only seen the houseguest through a draped window they couldn't tell that it was Olsen and because Jackson had given explicit orders not to move on Olsen unless absolutely necessary, they set up surveillance.

Shortly after 1:00 in the morning, Olsen's bad habit of pacing in front of a window enabled a detective with a cheap pair of binoculars to positively identify his suspect. Jackson was immediately informed, he then contacted ADA Burke, and Knox who both agreed that unless they were in danger of losing contact with Olsen, the takedown should be put off until the morning.

Once the warrant was signed and delivered to Jackson, he notified the members of N.S.1 of the impending arrest. N.S.1 reported to the north precinct at 6:00 a.m. and the briefing commenced. Jackson and Owens would take Olsen directly, with Casteel as their backup, Ari Rothstein and Marcus Holloman would take the back of the house, in case Olsen was quick and tried to escape, Joel Johnson would remain on a perimeter, ready to backup anyone who might need it. Kimberly Mason would stay with Kaylee Taylor at least until Olsen was taken into custody, then the need for a personal protection detail for the little girl would be reevaluated.

At 6:45 a.m., the members of N.S.1 relieved N.S.3 from their surveillance. Taking up the same positions that their predecessors had been in, N.S.1 continued to watch the house while Jackson made the last minute arrangements for the arrest. Desiring a by-the-book takedown, Jackson contacted the local hospital and put an ambulance on standby. He also contacted the police precinct in the area and informed them of what was about to take place and requested additional patrols to be in the area and ready to move in when the raid went down. Once everything was in place, N.S.1 geared up with their bulletproof vests and readied their weapons. Rothstein and Holloman closed in on the house from the back, Johnson took up a position around the side of an adjacent home and Jackson, Owens, and Casteel prepared to approach the house in Casteel's unmarked police cruiser from a parallel street.

"Standby all." Johnson said into his radio just before Jackson gave the go order. One of Johnson's jobs was to watch the house while the team got into position. "Target is exiting the building." Johnson soon informed.

"All units standby." Jackson reiterated on the radio. He knew that Olsen would only go outside if he was leaving, he wouldn't expose himself more than he had to.

"Target is getting into the car in the driveway." Johnson told them a moment later. Jackson knew that this was an opportunity he couldn't pass up.

"All units abort the takedown, I say again, all units abort." Jackson said into his radio which caused Owens to shoot him a worried look.

"What if he's going back after Kaylee?" Owens asked from the back seat.

"Not this soon, no, he's going to Collins." Jackson replied.

"All units resume surveillance." He said into his radio from the passenger seat before turning back to Owens. "We can get them both at the same time."

"Vehicle is heading to you, N.S.Actual." Johnson radioed, watching Olsen back the newer model Nissan out of the driveway.

"N.S.1.5 back mobile." Holloman radioed Jackson after he and Rothstein got back in their unmarked cruiser.

"Roger that, Actual will take the first leg, prepare to conduct a rotating tail," Jackson told them, his car following Olsen, "looks like he's heading for the interstate. 1.5, pick him up there."

Holloman acknowledged when they picked up Johnson and moved out. Holloman's team picked Olsen's car up on the interstate. When Olsen got off, Jackson's vehicle picked him up again for a few blocks until relieved by a member of N.S.2. who had been nearby, on his way home. He tailed Olsen for several blocks, radioing in his position every few minutes or anytime Olsen made a turn, then was relieved by 1.5 again. 1.5 followed Olsen until he turned onto San Juan road, where Jackson resumed the tail.

Olsen parked at the end of San Juan road, and walked to Damon's leased warehouse space, which was located in the ground floor of a much larger office building. When he saw that they would be on foot, Jackson positioned 1.5 on an adjacent street and sent Casteel back up San Juan road to cross through the warehouses and meet up with 1.5. Jackson and Owens then followed Olsen through a small concentration of Office, warehouse, and other miscellaneous buildings.

Concealing themselves with the side of another building, Jackson and Owens watched Olsen take a flight of steps down to the door that led to the basement of a fairly vacant office building.

"That's it." Jackson told his partner before speaking into his radio. "Alright, he's going to the basement of the last building on Columbia, it's the Maritime Office Complex." He informed so that every member of the team would know. "We'll follow him down the south side, 1.5 take up the north in case he tries to run. Casteel, Johnson, cover the inside entrance on ground level on the west in case he comes out there."

"1.5 roger, we're already in position." Holloman replied.

"We're moving." Casteel informed. After he was acknowledged, Jackson motioned Owens to move and the two made their way quietly down the steps through the door. The south basement door led into a small maze of hallways and corridors with many doors, mostly empty or unused offices. Shortly after they entered, both cops realized that they'd now lost Olsen. The door they entered put them directly into the middle of a long hallway that made turns in both directions.

Hoping to hear Olsen's footsteps, they listened intently for a few moments but could not discern which direction he went. Optimistic that he would get lucky, Jackson turned left and proceeded down the hallway. A few twists and turns later he realized that he had not only lost Olsen but had gotten himself lost as well.

"What's he doing here?" Eddie pointed for Damon who was supervising the hired men palleting the boxes and putting them on the trucks.

"What? Damn it." Damon said, looking at Olsen entering the main storage space of the basement. "What are you doing here?"

"I didn't have anywhere else to go." Olsen told him. "They're looking for me."

"I know that. We can't talk here. Come on." Damon turned and led Olsen and Eddie through a door and into the hallway. The trio remained silent throughout the hallway until Damon opened an office door, inside which was Damon's men packing the equipment he needed to dispose of into very large backpacks. "What the hell did you think was going to happen when you tried to take a kid from a Goddamn school?" Damon asked when they were in the room.

"I didn't think it would go down like that, look man, I need help." Olsen replied.

"No shit you need help you dumb son-of-a-bitch. You've got every cop on the west coast looking for you!" Damon tried not to lose his temper but couldn't control himself. "And then you come here! Here of all places! You could have led them right to us. Are you sure you weren't followed?"

"Yes, of course. I'm not that stupid."

"Christ." Jackson muttered under his breath when he heard his cell phone ring. He frantically picked it out of his pocket and silenced it before placing it to his ear. While Jackson spoke, Owens continued to look around, hearing loud voices he turned a corner and looked in a room that was empty before realizing that the hallway itself was echoing the voices.

"Dave, we've got a problem." Knox said into her phone as a uniformed officer handed her a piece of paper which she sat down on her desk and signed. "A federal hold has been placed on your warrant."

"What?" Jackson replied, not believing what he was hearing. "By who?"

"We don't know, we just got it ourselves, it's a cease and desist writ. All I can tell you is that it was signed by a federal appeals court judge. We're trying to find out which agency issued it but it's going to take a couple of hours. Until then I have to order you to abort your takedown."

"Bethany, we're in motion, we can't pull out now without being spotted." It was almost true. "We still have the probable cause to pick him up and he's still a danger to Kaylee Taylor."

"Alright." Knox reluctantly agreed. "Bring him in but don't

tell him about the warrant."

"Affirmative." Jackson closed his phone, put it on vibrate and placed it back in his pocket. Jackson turned the corner to see Owens slowly making his way down the hallway. Now Jackson could hear the voices also but like his partner, couldn't tell which room they were coming from. As Owens slowly and carefully looked in the offices in the hallway, Jackson passed him and peeked around a corner. He didn't notice Owens freeze suddenly.

Owens couldn't believe he'd made such a rookie mistake. He stood completely still, totally silhouetted in the doorway in which the Collins brothers and Olsen were arguing. Between them and Owens was a man who had been shoving some kind of round glass jars in a backpack. The man was staring bewildered at Owens, who only stared back, watching the man's eyes blink every few seconds.

Slowly and very deliberately, Owens reached his hand up and put it on Jackson's shoulder, slightly tugging it. The man continued to stare at Owens and blinked again. Jackson was still peeking down the other hallway and trying to make out the echoed words when he felt Owens hand. Frustrated at being robbed of his concentration he turned around to snap at his partner.

"What?" Jackson said in a loud whisper. A whisper loud enough that everyone in the office heard it. Jackson slowly turned his head to the inside of the doorway and saw the man packaging the equipment, along with Damon, Eddie, and Olsen staring back at him. "Shit!" He yelled and shoved Owens out of the doorway, pushing himself backwards at the same time and narrowly avoiding two bullets from Damon's gun.

Drawing their weapons, the two cops entered the room to find that Damon, Eddie and Olsen had fled through a back door that led into the hallway. Owens covered the men in the room while Jackson reported the shots into his radio. Leaving the men in the room, the two cops ran out the door after their suspects.

Damon, Eddie and Olsen ran down the hallway until they reached a T-intersection. Jackson and Owens followed quickly but Damon fired several more shots when they approached the turn. Jackson was able to get across the hallway and took cover around the corner with Owens on the adjacent corner. Immediately after two more bullets hit the wall at the end of the hallway, Jackson stuck his .45 into the corridor and blindly fired several shots at the suspects. Jackson started to move into the corridor, his weapon out in front of him, ready to fire but a barrage of bullets from Eddie's gun forced him back behind the corner for cover.

"I think you missed." Owens yelled at him sarcastically from behind the opposing corner. "You know what people like these days? Aim! I hear it drastically improves your chances of hitting the target!"

"Thank you very much Dick Cheney!" Jackson yelled back, flipping Owens a hand signal. Simultaneously, the two moved into the corridor to find that their suspects had turned another corner. They ran to the next corner and after a quick peek around it, ran into the hallway.

When they reached the doorway to the main warehouse space, they saw that Olsen had split off from the Collins brothers and gone into the warehouse to make his escape.

"Olsen's going out the back dock!" Jackson yelled into his radio, continuing after the Collins brothers.

"We've got him!" Holloman replied into his radio. He and Rothstein made their way toward the trucks at the dock.

Damon and Eddie Collins headed for the stairwell that led to the lobby of the office building but when they opened it, found that it was blocked by a large metal gate. Damon covered Eddie while he climbed over the gate, then fired his last round at Jackson and Owens before they rounded the corner. Once Eddie was over, Damon climbed up and over through the thin hole between the top of the gate and the ceiling. Jackson and Owens arrived at the gate just in time to see Damon and Eddie run through the door and into the lobby.

While Owens scaled the gate, Jackson informed Casteel and Johnson in the lobby that the Collins brothers were coming to them.

Olsen ran out the back dock of the building right before Holloman and Rothstein got to it. They both yelled for Olsen to stop but he ignored them and continued running down the street and into an alleyway. Holloman followed closely with a short of breath

Rothstein lagging behind.

Casteel and Johnson already had their weapons drawn when Eddie came out of the stairwell door firing. Both detectives returned fire but hit the wall behind their moving targets. To avoid Eddie's fire, Casteel jumped to the floor as though he were sliding into third base and Johnson took cover behind a pillar. Damon threw his empty weapon at his pursuers and tugged on his brother's shirt, telling him to run for the lobby doors. The room erupted in gunfire when both the police and their suspects unsuccessfully shot at each other.

A half second after Damon and Eddie hit the warm sunlight of the outdoors. Jackson and Owens burst through the door to the stairwell.

"Doors!" Casteel yelled, picking himself off the floor and all four cops hit the lobby doors running. Damon and Eddie continued east down the sidewalk slipping between two buildings with the cops fast on their shirttails. The Collins brothers quickly came to a fork in the alley, one way led east toward the docks, the other south toward the Montlake Boulevard Canal bridge. Eddie took the east route, Damon took the south.

Jackson yelled for Casteel and Johnson to go around the buildings, hopefully boxing them in while he and Owens turned down the alley. Soon they came to the fork in the alley and not knowing which route their suspects took, Jackson headed east and Owens south.

Olsen ran into the lobby of a three story medical office complex which was very busy. Seeing an open elevator, Olsen jumped in just before the doors closed and pushed the button for the top floor. Holloman, followed by Rothstein arrived in the lobby just in time to watch the elevator lift off.

"Which floor?" Holloman asked.

"Top," Rothstein replied, gasping for air, "retards always go to the top floor."

"I'll take the stairs." Holloman told him and headed through a nearby door.

The second elevator opened releasing a tidal wave of people. Rothstein jumped in and hit the button for the top floor

Jackson found Eddie heading through a small wooded park that led to the docks. Owens picked up Damon fleeing across the canal bridge. Casteel and Johnson also saw Damon on the bridge and followed Owens over.

Eddie made his way across the park and into the extremely crowded area around the docks. Pushing his way through the bystanders, he jumped onto the first boat moored at the giant log booms. The public watching the opening day of boating parade didn't seem to notice him running along the boats at first but began to panic when they saw his gun. Jackson jumped onto the boat behind Eddie, who was jumping from boat to boat to try to get away from Jackson.

After crossing the canal bridge, Owens chased Damon down Shelby street toward the second log boom. Casteel and Johnson cut through several driveways lining Shelby street in an effort to get to the southern log boom before Damon and Owens.

The elevator doors and the door to the stairwell opened at exactly the same moment, Rothstein and Holloman emerged, guns drawn and scanned the third floor quickly until a secretary walking through who had been knocked down by Olsen told them that he headed to the roof. Holloman shot back into the stairwell very quickly with Rothstein moving to the door until he was stopped by the secretary once more.

"Not that way." She informed. "He took the other stairs at the end of the hall." Rothstein reversed course and dashed to the second set of stairs, moving up them. Soon he kicked the door to the roof open. He quickly found Holloman who was also scanning the roof with his weapon and turned in a 360 degree rotation. Olsen was gone.

"Where the hell is he?" Rothstein yelled to Holloman.

"I thought you had him?" Holloman returned.

"There's nowhere for him to go!" Rothstein blustered.

"Goddamnit!" Rothstein kicked the door behind him in anger.

"Police! Show me your hands!" Casteel yelled, he and Johnson aimed their weapons at Damon. Damon could clearly see that his escape was blocked by the two cops in front of him, and Owens was quickly closing. His only chance was to take the log boom boats, which was the last place he wanted to be because he knew that he'd be trapped. Moving quickly, he ignored the police's commands, who didn't fire because he was unarmed and their distance combined with a background full of people was too risky. Damon jumped onto the first boat, knocking a woman in a bikini overboard. Taking several short steps he jumped to the second boat with Owens right behind him.

Eddie punched a man who tried to grab him when he landed on the 9th boat attached to the log boom. Jackson jumped on the boat several seconds behind Eddie but his suspect had already jumped onto the next boat when Jackson got there.

Realizing that he was boxed in, Eddie knew he had to turn around and get past Jackson to get to shore. He leaped onto the 12th boat, and found his prey, a good-looking teenage girl in a yellow bathing suit. She jumped from her chair to get away from him but he grabbed her by the hair and put his gun to her head.

Jackson saw Eddie reach out for the girl and instead of jumping on the boat directly behind Eddie, he jumped slightly to his left, holstering his weapon and using the side of the two story fishing vessel to conceal himself. Eddie reached his arm around the girl's chest and turned his hostage to where he thought Jackson would be. Eddie saw that Jackson wasn't where he thought he was and scanned nervously, trying to locate him.

When he jumped to the sixth boat, a sailboat, Damon was caught by Owens' full weight and went to the deck with his pursuer on his back.

"I got your ass now!" Owens yelled into Damon's ear, punching him in the kidneys with his right fist and grabbing Damon's left wrist with his left hand. "How's that for panache you red headed prick!" Owens repeatedly punched at Damon's kidneys. Damon struggled to break free and rolled onto his back with Owens still trying to restrain him.

Eddie was still scouring the area for his pursuer when Jackson jumped from the second story of the boat. Jackson landed behind him and grabbed Eddie's gun arm, straightening it and pulling the gun away from the girl's head. Eddie let go of his hostage and tried turning toward Jackson who slammed his hand into an aluminum railing, sending the weapon onto the deck. Eddie punched Jackson who lost his balance and fell back against the side railing.

Jackson bound up and shot two punches to Eddie's face, and two more to Eddie's stomach. An uppercut landed Eddie on his back, next to his gun.

While Damon and Owens struggled for control, Damon noticed out of the corner of his eye, Jackson and his brother fighting across the canal. Owens noticed his gaze and their struggle stopped momentarily.

Eddie rolled onto one knee and grabbed his weapon. Jackson saw Eddie's intention and reached back, drawing his weapon and having it aimed by the time Eddie had laid his hand on his gun.

"Don't move!" Jackson yelled, leveling his .45 at Eddie. Everything stopped. Eddie stopped, Jackson stopped, even the breathing of the people on the other boats watching them stopped. Eddie looked up at Jackson, hate filling his eyes. "Eddie, don't do it! It's not worth it!" Jackson warned. Eddie's stare didn't falter. "Don't!" Jackson warned again. The look in Eddie's eyes changed, indicating he'd made his decision. They became calmer.

In a very quick, swift movement, Eddie yanked the gun up, pointing it at Jackson. Jackson fired three rounds, all of which hit Eddie in the center of his chest. The instantly dead man was flung backwards into the water and landed with an eerily thunderous splash.

"Eddie!" Damon yelled, resuming his struggle with Owens. Owens worked to secure Damon's left hand but Damon reached with his right to a line holding the main sail in place. Damon tugged the line and it came loose. Without the line to hold it in place the pole to the sail rotated and smacked Owens in the face, sending him overboard and into the water.

Damon jumped to his feet and started back to shore. He'd crossed two boats when he saw Casteel and Johnson jumping boats to get to him. Knowing that his only other escape was through them, Damon jumped feet first into the water. A moment later, Casteel and Johnson arrived at the location from which Damon had jumped.

"What now?" Johnson asked.

"Johnson go in after him." Casteel ordered, which spawned an ugly look from Johnson.

"I wouldn't do that if I were you." An old man on the boat said. "That water's not but nine or ten feet deep and all these ships are anchored. It's got the bottom stirred up, you wouldn't be able to see an inch in front of you. That guy is gone."

"Damn." Casteel said, looking overboard at the water.

"We'd better go get Jesse then." Casteel surmised and they started for the spot Owens had just surfaced.

9

"Ramifications"

"Bravo team in position." The radio crackled. "Alpha team in position." Jackson listened in on the SWAT team from the command van.

Inside the Maritime Office building, Captain Manuel Carrasco, the Alpha team leader, stood, his knees slightly bent, next to the door to the warehouse space that led to the back dock area of the building. Bravo team was at the door to the office, inside which the first shots of the morning's firefight had been discharged.

"Roger that, bang and clear on my mark." The command van operator said into the radio. "Five...four...three...two...go, go, go." Simultaneously, Alpha and Bravo teams threw flashbangs, large harmless grenades that only exploded in a deafening bang and blinding flash of light into their respective rooms before rushing through the doorways, their MP-5 submachine guns ready to shoot any suspects which presented a threat.

"Clear!" The Bravo team leader yelled to his team. "Bravo is clear." He next told the command van operator.

"Clear!" The Alpha team leader yelled to his men. "Alpha is clear." He said into his radio. "You'd better get Jackson down here."

"They're asking for you Lieutenant." The operator said to Jackson.

"Tell them I'm on my way." Jackson said, leaving the command van through the back doors and picking up Owens and Casteel, who were waiting outside with N.S.1. The trio went down into the warehouse using the stairs on the side of the building and made their way through the maze of hallways, past the office that Bravo team was searching and into the warehouse space where they found Captain Carrasco. Carrasco had already taken off his Kevlar helmet and was using his free hand to pull his balaclava from his face, his MP-5 was sitting peacefully on his chest, held in place by a three-point sling.

The three narcotics detectives came into the large room looking around in wonderment. They moved in a straight line to the center of the warehouse space where Carrasco was standing, his helmet under his left elbow. They stood in front of Carrasco still gazing around the room in disbelief.

"It was here I swear it." Jackson told him a moment later. "This room was filled with boxes."

"They're gone now." Carrasco said, turning around to show Jackson the empty room.

"That's impossible." Owens remarked. "How could they move all this in two hours?"

"Not even," Casteel interjected, "we had a patrol with eyes on in thirty minutes. He didn't see anyone enter or exit the building until you guys came in."

"He did report that the trucks were gone when he got there." Jackson said. "Damn."

"Captain? I think we found something." One of the SWAT team members told Carrasco. He led the group across the room to a corner where a wadded piece of paper was laying.

"Casteel." Jackson said, staring at the paper. Casteel produced a small digital camera and took three pictures, one close up with Jackson's pen next to the paper to scale the size, another at a medium range, and the last from a wide range. When Casteel finished, Owens picked the paper up with a pair of latex gloves. Careful not to tear the paper, he unfolded it while Jackson and Carrasco stared over his shoulder.

"It's a box label for Merck." Jackson spoke of the pharmaceutical company.

"All that and this is the only evidence we have." Owens said with a frown. "Collins probably left it on purpose to tease us."

"I doubt that. He doesn't play around like some high stick-up guy who leaves his wallet at the scene. It's not his style." Jackson informed. Carrasco put his hand on his radio and spoke a few words.

"Bravo team has something, let's go." He told them before leading them through the hallway and into the office that Bravo team had cleared. They were looking at a piece of flooring that was loose, when Bravo team leader reached down to take a closer look, he found that it was easily picked up revealing a small tunnel that led down into the sewer system.

"I doubt they got those boxes out through this little thing." Jackson peered down the hole.

"Somebody took it." Carrasco replied. "Fresh footprints."

"You a tunnel rat?" Jackson asked.

"We'll follow it as far as it goes but they're long gone." Carrasco promised. "Murphy, you're on point. Lets move." Bravo team began strapping their flashlights to their weapons and two men lowered Murphy into the hole slowly.

Jackson watched the SWAT team do their thing. A second later Owens tapped him lightly on the shoulder. Jackson turned around to see Agent Wilson, and Agent Parker from the Seattle Police Department's Office of Professional Accountability walk through the doorway to the office. The Office of Professional Accountability was the politically correct name for what had previously been the Internal Affairs Division. Jackson was slightly annoyed at seeing them because he had already had a lengthy conversation with them about the shooting and because they were the same Internal Affairs agents that investigated Rent several years ago.

"You boys aren't finished yet? I thought you'd be back in your office jerking off to Serpico again by now." Jackson commented dryly. He enjoyed insulting the Internal Affairs guys, plus he knew he could get away with it. The Office of Professional Accountability wasn't named that for nothing. They were held to a much higher standard than other officers and because of such, if a person didn't particularly like them and most didn't, they could say pretty much anything they wanted to them and the agents were supposed to ignore it.

"You're on administrative leave, you're not supposed to be here." Agent Wilson reacted dryly. "Have you touched any evidence?"

"Really? I thought you boys were just blowing smoke up my ass with that business." Jackson said in a sarcastic tone.

"Hey," Owens interjected, seeing an opportunity, "is that mortician still drilling your wife or is she on the market again?"

"Any time there's an officer involved shooting, our office has to investigate it and the officer involved is put on administrative leave. You know that, it's policy, plus I officially put you on leave an hour ago when you gave your statement. You can't return to work until the board of review clears you." Wilson ordered again, completely ignoring Owens remarks.

"Rothstein shot a dog last week," Owens told him, "you didn't investigate that?"

"Maybe we should investigate why two of your detectives were up in a tree when he shot that dog?" Wilson replied.

"They thought it was your wife." Jackson responded without missing a beat.

"Or your daughter, girl's ugly as a armadillo's ass." Owens added.

"Did you touch any evidence?" Wilson asked Jackson again, trying not to become upset at their comments.

"This is my investigation." Jackson responded.

"Not anymore its not, did you touch any evidence?" Wilson repeated, raising his voice.

"No." Jackson answered.

"Good, Chief Knox wants to see the two of you in her office yesterday. I took the liberty of informing her that you were still working despite my ordering you on leave. I'd hate for you to lose your job over this."

"Gosh, that's mighty white of you." Jackson grinned sarcastically. "Casteel, take over the investigation."

"My pleasure sir." Casteel accepted, then pointed at the two agents. "Oh, that means you two turd hunters are in my crime scene, I'm going to need your shoes and detailed reports of anything you may have touched or accidentally gotten your stench on before you leave."

"Don't feel bad guys, I'm sure there's something else you two can investigate, maybe one of our horse patrols shit on the sidewalk somewhere, you can put him on administrative leave too." Jackson told them.

"Yeah," Owens added matter-of-factly, "why don't you two go down to the stables and mount each other?"

"I'll see you at the board of review." Wilson said, staring in distaste at Jackson.

Jackson and Owens dismissed themselves with a few more snide remarks, then headed to the North Precinct and to Knox's office. When they arrived, they found Knox sitting at her desk speaking to another man that neither had seen before. The man was tall, Jackson could tell even though he was sitting down and wore a cheap black suit. Jackson and Owens knocked on the door. Both she and the man rose to greet them.

"Agent Pierce, this is Lieutenant David Jackson and Detective Jesse Owens, they're our leads on the Taylor Homicide." Knox introduced. "David, this is Special Agent Ronny Pierce of the Drug Enforcement Administration. He's the one who put the cease and desist writ on Olsen."

"I've heard a lot about you Lieutenant." Pierce said congenially, shaking Jackson's hand. Jackson responded with the usual pleasantries.

"Please sit." Knox ordered her detectives. They complied

before Knox spoke again. "Agent Pierce, please tell them what you were just telling me."

"Of course." Pierce said. "The DEA has been conducting an investigation of Damon Collins. Now I can't discuss the details of this investigation but I can tell you that Richard Olsen is very much a part of it and I have to respectfully order you to abandon your homicide investigation."

"Excuse me, how can a drug related investigation take priority over a homicide?" Jackson asked.

"Like I said, I can't divulge that. What I will tell you, out of admiration for your work, is that Randy Taylor was working for us. Since he was one of ours, we'd like to bring his killers to justice."

"He was a DEA agent?" Owens asked out of surprise.

"I'm afraid not detective," Pierce answered, "he was a civilian in our employ, more than an informant but not quite an agent. You see we found Damon Collins six months ago in Couer d'Alene Idaho. He was putting together a drug related operation and needed an accountant. Randy Taylor was doing some consulting work for us at the time, off the books of course and he was the perfect candidate to place with Collins. I can also tell you, to satisfy your investigation, that Mr. Taylor's purpose was to obtain a list of Collins' associates and locations which he was using to complete this operation. Mr. Taylor was supposed to get this information the weekend that he was killed. Unfortunately we don't know if he was successful or if he was, where he put the information. Olsen could have retrieved it when he murdered Mr. Taylor. This has set our investigation back quite a bit and after what happened today, we need you to back off of both of them. We're also going to need all of your original materials regarding this case and any other that you may be building against Olsen or Collins."

"Wait a minute." Jackson said. "You placed an elderly civilian with a known criminal who has a history of not only murdering those he thinks betray him but their entire families?"

"Mr. Taylor volunteered for the assignment." Pierce answered.

"And after he was supposed to have stolen the information that could bring Collins down, he went fishing?" Knox asked. She was starting to put things together now. "Agent Pierce, did Randy Taylor know about Collins' history?" She asked. Jackson stared at Pierce from his chair.

"Chief, considering the extensive history that Collins has within the drug trade, the DEA didn't deem it necessary that Mr. Taylor know everything about his past to accomplish the assignment." Pierce answered.

"Uh-oh." Owens said to himself.

"Dave wait, don't..." but before Knox could finish her sentence, Jackson had pounced from his chair, grabbed Pierce by his suit coat and slammed him violently against the wall.

"You didn't tell him!" Jackson yelled into Pierce's face. "You didn't tell him that he was going undercover with a man capable of not only killing him but also those closest to him! You got that man killed and now his family may pay for it with their lives!"

"Collins was supposed to remain in the dark the entire time, he was never supposed to know that the information was even copied!" Pierce shouted back.

"Tell that to Randy Taylor!" Jackson replied. Several uniformed officers outside the office ran in the door. Knox held her hand up to stop them. "His blood is on your hands!" Jackson yelled.

"Don't chastise me!" Pierce yelled back and pushed himself off the wall. Jackson simply slammed him back again. "How many people has Collins killed?" Pierce asked in a calmer voice now. "How many is he going to kill? He should be in prison waiting on a syringe but he's free and that's your fault! You and Carey Rent! What? You think a state funeral and a eulogy by Senator Cale erases what Rent did? You think it erases what you let Rent do? The truth is that Randy Taylor's blood is as much on your hands as it is mine!"

"I never sent a man into danger not having been told about it!" Jackson returned.

"Spare me your righteous bullshit, that informant was working for you two years ago when Collins killed him! Do you think his family knew?" Pierce returned. "You're a hypocrite!"

"Stop!" Knox yelled at them. "That's enough. Agent Pierce I'm sure you're aware of the federal statute of disclosure regarding civilian informants. Rest assured that I will be discussing this matter with the U.S. Attorney. Until this is settled, I want any and all DEA operations conducted in the municipality of Seattle put on hold."

"You don't have the authority to do that. I have a federal mandate." Pierce told her.

"Really?" Knox replied before pointing to the uniformed officers at the door. "Show Agent Pierce the exit. You may have your mandate but if I find you're conducting operations without our knowledge or approval I'll give you a police escort, lights blaring and sirens wailing, everywhere you go. That is until I have you booked on violation of federal law regarding disclosure." The officers approached Pierce. Jackson let go and took a step back. Pierce straightened his suit and stared at Knox.

"Come with us sir." One of the officers grabbed Pierce's arm. Pierce angrily jerked it out of his hand.

"You can't charge me with that unless you have an indictment." Pierce told Knox.

"No but I can hold you for seventy-two hours while I get one." Knox replied.

"It'll never hold up."

"If you try to conduct any more operations in this town, we're going to find out. Won't we?" Knox replied, then nodded to the uniforms, both of whom grabbed Pierce forcefully by the arms and led him out of the office.

Knox turned to Owens who was standing beside his chair. "I'm assigning you to Kaylee Taylor's protective detail and only that until this is resolved."

"How long will that be?" Owens asked, wanting to assist Casteel with the investigation.

"I'll let you know." Knox told him sternly. "You're dismissed and close the door on your way out." Owens stepped out, closing the door. Knox turned to Jackson, an angry storm growing in her eyes. "What the hell was that Dave? Did you feel you haven't racked up enough trouble for yourself today?"

"I want back in Bethany, that shooting was legit." Jackson replied.

"I'm not talking about Eddie Collins. You just assaulted a federal agent, what the hell do you call that Dave?"

Jackson thought a moment at Knox's question. "I don't know...fun."

"Don't push me Dave, not now." Knox told him angrily.

"Look Bethany, that kid was going to kill me and there were two dozen witnesses. I gave him every chance."

"That's inconsequential, we have a policy to follow, you know that." Knox responded, walking around her desk. "It may have been legit but every officer who is involved in a shooting must be put on leave until he's cleared by the review board and the psychiatrist."

"You can't sideline me now, we're too close." Jackson pleaded.

"Jesus Christ Dave, I don't know if you realize this but

you're not the only policeman in this city. You have not one but three very good teams that can deal with this. They don't need you, leave it to Casteel." Jackson's stare admitted his compliance. "Now I have to ask for your shield and gun." Knox finished.

"What?" Jackson replied in surprise. "Why?"

"Because I can." Knox replied.

"That regulation hasn't been used since I've been on the job." Jackson replied regarding the regulation that an officer's immediate supervisor had the right–though it was almost never exercised–to ask for the badge and gun of any officer put on administrative leave.

"I'm using it now." Knox replied. "I know you, you won't let this go, you'll walk out of this office and go straight back to work. I can't allow that, I want your badge and gun on my desk and I don't want to see you in this building until you're cleared. I think you need to contact your union delegate too."

"You sure you're not going to pull him?" Jackson asked bitterly before taking his badge off his belt and slamming it on her desk. He took out his Smith & Wesson .45 Caliber Tactical pistol, removed the magazine and the round in the chamber and slammed that on her desk also. "It was righteous and we both know it!" He said loudly before slamming the door behind him.

Wild Waves-Enchanted Village was an amusement park just

slightly south of Seattle in the suburb of Federal Way. It was built in 1977 on just twelve acres but by the turn of the millennium had grown to over seventy. Currently it was owned by the Six Flags corporation which was refurbishing some of the older rides and adding a few new ones. Typically the park would have been open for the first Saturday in May, however the renovation had gotten behind schedule and the park couldn't be opened until at least the beginning of June. Richard Olsen didn't seem to mind.

Enchanted Village was the prearranged rally point for Damon Collins and his crew if something should go wrong. Since something had gone very wrong, Olsen waited until after midnight before showing up at the meeting point under the newly built Wildcatter ride.

The Wildcatter was a typical amusement park ride, though technically a rollercoaster, it wasn't in a traditional sense. It was designed to take riders, who had been placed sitting down on their backs in a cart that held four, straight up ten stories and then drop them into a freefall for a few seconds before the ride came to an end.

After getting into the park the usual way–both nighttime security guards were on Damon's payroll–Olsen made his way to the bottom of the large metal ride. Since he was satisfied that he was alone, he sat on a nearby bench for a few minutes. Soon, he was wandering the park again.

Standing in front of the Timberhawk – the largest wooden rollercoaster in the Pacific Northwest – he was caught in the back of the head by the butt of Damon's gun. Olsen fell to the ground and Damon began kicking him in the chest and face. After releasing some anger on Olsen, Damon dragged him by the hair into one of the small, square, concrete buildings which housed an over-priced eatery common to so many theme parks. Throwing Olsen into several boxes of frozen hamburgers, Damon readied his newly acquired Desert Eagle .50 Caliber pistol to deal with the man who'd led police to him and his brother.

"Wait, Damon, wait, please!" Olsen yelled. Damon closed the door to the concession building. "I didn't do it, I didn't lead them there! I swear!"

"You showed up, then they did." Damon replied in an eerily calm voice.

"I know but I didn't lead them. I swear to God, they tried to get me too."

"They did get Eddie." Damon informed.

"They caught him?" Olsen asked.

"They killed him." Damon said, stepping slowly toward Olsen.

"Oh God, I'm so so sorry! Please, you gotta believe me, I didn't have nothing to do with it. No, Damon, please don't." Olsen pleaded, tears rolling down his face. Damon came slowly closer. "Listen, they could have known, we never got the information back from Taylor, maybe they found it, maybe that's how they knew. For Christ's sake man, you can't kill me!"

"That's exactly what I plan to do." Damon grabbed his throat and put the .50 Caliber pistol to his left eye. "Then I'm going to kill that bastard who shot Eddie. I'm going to kill him, his partner, his family and every piece-of-shit he ever cared about."

"Wait, I can help you, I can help, look, you can't get to cops they protect each other." Olsen begged. "But I know some guys. What if we can do it all, what if we can get the money, get your stuff out, kill the girl, the cops, the whole thing? I know how!"

"You don't know how to tie your own shoelaces." Damon told him.

"I know some guys, they can help you, they work cheap and they just got out of the pen, they're good for it, they need the money." While Olsen pleaded, Damon started to think that Olsen could still be useful to him. "I'm with you man, you know that, they want me the same as you, we need the same things, I can help you!" A few guys wouldn't hurt but Damon didn't yet know how he was going to collect the money he'd hidden around town, without which he couldn't pay any muscle.

"How can I trust you?" Damon asked, already knowing the answer, if Olsen had been turned by the cops, he would have led them straight to him and he'd already be in custody. Damon also knew that the close brush with the law that his other men had at the warehouse had caused them to abandon him and leave town. Facing a bad situation, Damon decided he didn't need to lose another man right now. Olsen would pay his part for Eddie's death but right now he needed him.

"You think I'd come here by myself if I was with the cops?" Olsen asked.

"I don't put that much faith in you being that smart...but?" Damon removed the muzzle from Olsen's eye and smacked him hard against the face with the butt of the gun.

10

"Reinforcements"

Everyone watched Sunday pass, waiting to see if Olsen or Collins would be found by the police. The two wanted men had gone underground and even though there was a state wide All Points Bulletin out for both of them, they were nowhere to be found. Jackson spent Sunday with his family, attending church and then a small barbecue hosted by one of their fellow parishioners. His wife and children knew about the shooting, it wasn't Jackson's first and they were always supportive. He ended up spending most of his off time working on his house, catching up on maintenance that he typically didn't have time to do.

Casteel worked out a schedule for Kaylee's protective detail, giving the majority of the time spent with the little girl to Owens (upon his request), with most of the overnight details going to either Mason or Johnson. The rest of the team worked tirelessly to locate Olsen and Collins, conducting interviews, canvassing areas where they were known to frequent and conducting surveillance on Shoreline Printing.

On Monday morning, ADA Burke handed Casteel a search warrant for Shoreline Printing but when the team arrived to execute the warrant, they found that the DEA was already inside the building, conducting their own search. After a few angry words exchanged between Special Agent Pierce and Casteel, the DEA finally got their way and N.S.1. left the scene.

Having exhausted their leads, N.S.1.'s next step was to cover Eddie Collins' funeral which was to take place on Tuesday afternoon. Casteel knew that if they were lucky Damon might try to pay his respects.

Owens took Sunday off but arrived at Kaylee's house around noon on Monday afternoon to relieve Holloman who'd been there since midnight. Owens had been told by Mason that the little girl was slightly distressed because Olsen hadn't been caught and he thought he might cheer her up with a walk in the park.

"Who's that?" Kaylee asked when she saw Owens walk in the door.

"That's my new partner." Owens exclaimed to the little girl. Owens nodded to Holloman that he could leave. The tired officer stretched and yawned before stepping around Owens and his new partner to get out the front door.

"He's not a pig?" Kaylee joked.

"He's pretty close." Owens returned.

"Can I pet him?" She asked, Owens nodded and she approached the gruff looking bulldog that was restrained by a leash Owens held.

"Kaylee," Courtney yelped to get her daughter's attention, "don't touch that dog, you don't know where it's been." She ordered.

"It's alright, it's my dog." Owens informed.

"Like I said, you don't know where it's been." Courtney reiterated sarcastically. Kaylee ignored her order.

"What's his name?" Kaylee looked up at Owens.

"Ugly." He replied. She smiled.

"No it's not." She argued.

"I swear, cross my heart." Owens made the sign over his chest. The child laughed and played with the friendly animal. "I thought we could head down to the park and take him for a walk."

"Are you sure about that, with those two still out there?" Courtney asked.

"Please Mommy, I haven't left the house all weekend, I'm going crazy here." Kaylee pleaded.

"It'll be fine, we can all go, I asked one of the patrols to hang out at the park for a while today, it's perfectly safe." Owens assured.

"I don't know." Courtney frowned, not liking the idea.

Owens bent down to Kaylee and made a humorous face.

"Why don't you tell your Mommy to stop being such a grinch." Owens told the little girl, Kaylee smiled and then looked up at her mother with big overly dramatized puppy dog eyes. Facing such a fierce strategy, Courtney caved and gave permission. Within twenty minutes the trio set out down the street toward Woodland park.

When they arrived at the park, Owens gave Kaylee the leash and the excited bulldog led the little girl around the path, always with Owens and Courtney not far behind. About half-way through the path, Ugly led Kaylee off into a mowed field, both the girl and the animal ran around happily. Mother and detective watched them from the gravel path.

"I said some mean things to you the other night." Courtney broke the silence after a few minutes. "I need to apologize, I didn't want to make you feel bad, I just wanted to protect Kaylee."

"I know." Owens returned. "You don't have to protect her from me."

"I really think I do." Courtney told him. "I don't mean to be rude again but she likes you. She's happy around you and she's not going to understand when you leave."

"Well maybe when this is done, I can come and see her?" Owens asked.

"I'd really rather you not." Courtney replied.

"Why not?"

"I have a favor I need to ask of you." Courtney said, completely ignoring Owens' question. "I want you to tell her that you won't be back after this is over." Owens stared at Courtney, he didn't know what to say, he felt his heart drop and knew that if Kaylee's mother didn't want him to see her, then he couldn't. "It'll be easier for her that way. At least she'll know."

"But I want to stick around. Why can't she have friends?" Owens objected.

"Because you're thirty going on twelve." Courtney answered bluntly. "She does have friends but she's just a new fad to you. I've seen guys like you come and go and I won't let you break her little heart. Kaylee needs someone who won't leave and when you find another fad to occupy your time...well...I don't want to have to tell her why you won't come and see her anymore. You want to do something good for her, tell her that you won't be coming back after you catch Olsen." Courtney looked out at the field, making sure that she didn't make eye contact with Owens. "If you don't tell her, I'm going to call your supervisor and ask that you be reassigned."

"Don't you think that's a little extreme?" Owens asked, hoping that she'd reconsider.

"I'm sorry, but I have to look out for my daughter." Courtney replied. "Will you tell her?"

"Yeah, I'll tell her." Owens grudgingly answered.

"Let me be perfectly clear here." Special Agent Roy Gillespie of the DEA told Assistant Chief Knox and Chief Tibbs. The three sat in Chief Tibbs' office. "The DEA in no way, shape, or form, takes the federal statutes regarding disclosure of information to informants lightly. We are taking steps right now to discipline Agent Pierce for his actions and most likely he'll receive a formal reprimand that will go in his permanent record. I also want to apologize for not informing you of our conducting clandestine operations in your jurisdiction. It was my responsibility as Chief of Station and it was miscommunicated through one of our other agents. I am sorry."

"Thank you." Chief Tibbs returned. "And I also apologize for our actions, sometimes individual agents and detectives don't always realize that we're on the same side, working toward the same goals. I hope that this incident hasn't jeopardized the cooperation that our two agencies have shared in the past?"

"Of course not Chief." Gillespie replied. "And thank you about being so gracious about this...situation."

"Like I said, we're all on the same side here." The Chief returned.

"I have to ask that you're department leave Collins to us. I know you understand." Gillespie told them.

"Of course." Chief Tibbs replied. "I've already given permission for your men to take all of the physical evidence we have, I just ordered that all surveillance needs to stop and Chief

Knox here has the complete file we have on Collins, including all the copies that we've made." Knox handed over the thick file to Gillespie which, along with the evidence that would be handed over, completely satisfied the subpoena that Gillespie had faxed to Chief Tibbs an hour before the meeting.

"Thank you for your understanding in this matter, we will of course, keep you advised on all developments." Gillespie politely told them.

"Of course." Tibbs replied.

"There is one more matter that I wish to discuss, the officer that assaulted Agent Pierce?" Gillespie asked.

"Yes, what about him?" Tibbs politely returned the question.

"I have to ask that he be given a formal reprimand in conjunction with the one we have given Agent Pierce." Gillespie stated. "I'm sure we can both agree that both parties acted unprofessionally."

"Of course," Tibbs started his answer, "and the day that I sit in your office and tell you how to discipline your people, I'll take that under advisement." He said with a smile. Gillespie's smile vanished.

"Well," Gillespie stated. Tibbs and Knox followed Gillespie to his feet. "I think that's all. I must make sure there is no mistake. You are obligated by court order to leave Collins to us."

"No, absolutely no mistake. This department, nor anyone from it will take any action against Damon Collins or Richard

Olsen." Chief Tibbs reiterated, shaking Gillespie's hand.

"Thank you." Gillespie said and shook hands with Knox also, then left, closing the door behind him.

"I wonder what they know that we don't?" Knox speculated.

"Nothing." Chief Tibbs replied. "They'd have thrown us a bone if they did, that's how the game's played. Most likely that file you gave him will tell him a few things he didn't know." Tibbs moved from around his desk to the refrigerator in the corner of his office. "Drink?"

"What do you have?"

"Vanilla Coke, bottled water, and Diet Sprite."

"Sprite." Knox replied. Tibbs took a can of Diet Sprite out of the fridge and tossed it to his subordinate before taking a Vanilla Coke for himself.

"It's funny, when I was Chief in Vegas, they barely let me have a desk in my office, you guys gave me a fridge, fully stocked. I love this town." Tibbs remarked. They both opened their soft drinks. "What about Jackson?" He inquired, sitting down in the comfortable chair that Gillespie had sat in and putting his feet on his desk.

"I've got the report from Professional Accountability. It's a clean shooting." Knox answered. "The review board won't get to it for two weeks."

"Put him back on duty the day he's cleared." Tibbs ordered.

"What about his assaulting Pierce?" Knox asked.

"I don't suppose we can give him a commendation for it?" Tibbs laughed. "Forget about it, I'd have probably done something similar in his place."

"Yes sir." Knox replied, a little disappointed.

"You need to lighten up a little." Tibbs sipped his Coke. "In my experience, the mark of a good officer is his passion for the job. David Jackson's one of those guys that works the streets because it's in his blood. Really, that's the best place for him." Tibbs turned serious again, stood, and stepped behind his desk. "I want our guys to stay clear of the DEA for now, we've got a little bit of leverage on them but that won't last long." He said, opening a drawer, taking out a copy of the Collins file and handing it to Knox.

"We'll collect information only but what if we spot Collins or Olsen?" Knox asked.

"The DEA won't let us pick them up, just watch them for now." Tibbs replied. "I'm not going to let the biggest dealer this city has ever known simply slip through our fingers because the DEA is playing bullshit political games."

Eddie Collins' funeral was held the next day at Lake View Cemetery in North Seattle. The service was held indoors because of rain but afterwards the dozen attendees made their way outside using umbrellas to block the thick raindrops from their suits and dresses.

They stood at the plot where Eddie's casket was lowered into the ground and bowed their heads with the minister to pray.

Eddie's mother paid for the funeral, which she cried all the way through. Most of those in attendance were extended family members such as aunts, uncles, and cousins. Eddie's only brother was Damon and neither he nor Damon had ever known their respective fathers, nor any of their families. Several of the mourners were friends and subsequent business associates of the slain criminal but two, Ari Rothstein and Kimberly Mason were from the Seattle Police Department. Their purpose at the service was to identify Eddie's friends and if luck were in their favor, find Damon in the area. Other members of N.S.1. were around also; Holloman was writing down the license plates on the cars of the attendees and Casteel and Johnson were scouring the cemetery grounds for Damon.

Damon stood on a hill in Volunteer Park which overlooked the cemetery, safe from police detection. He didn't use an umbrella and watched his only brother interred to the earth from a distance. Damon stared at the far-away sight with his heart aflame. The heavy raindrops being pulled by gravity off his red goatee, his expression was that of murderous anger.

Having been alienated from the rest of his family since his early teen years, Damon felt that his little brother was the only person he'd ever had a connection with his entire life. During their formative years Damon had taken the responsibility of raising his brother. Their mother had been an honest woman but as a waitress, a maid, and a cashier at a fast food restaurant, she had little time to spend with the two sons that she still could not make enough money to support. For years, Damon and Eddie learned to fend for themselves in the ghettos of Seattle's International District. It had been on the streets that Damon made his first money as a runner for a local drug dealer. That was where he'd learned the business, where he'd seen the mistakes that others made and where he'd learned how not to get caught. Damon expected to take his brother to the top with him, to go legitimate, maybe open up their own business, something that could make them honest money. Where they could live out their lives without the fear of being caught, killed or incarcerated. All that was gone now, each drop of rain reminded Damon of that.

After Eddie was laid to rest, Damon went to the abandoned church he'd decided would be his new base of operations in Shoreline. Damon needed a place that he could spend time to think things through, a place where the police could not find him, that was until he wanted them to anyway. The Lutheran Church of Christ off 172nd Street in Shoreline provided just that. Two years ago, when the church moved to a much larger facility several blocks away, they kept the property that the old church was on with the intent of developing it into a mission. Because of a decline in attendance and falling revenues, the venture never materialized and the church building sat unused.

Damon and Eddie's mother took them to this very church during their childhood in the hopes that they would learn morality and virtue. Damon felt safe in the church, which was one of over two dozen "safe" places that Damon kept on tap in Seattle.

At fourteen years old, Damon had seen a fellow runner and friend shot down by police. The boy had been targeted by narcotics officers because he worked for the same drug dealer that Damon worked for. They trapped the boy in an alley and when the boy reached for a .380 he kept in his pants, they shot him dead. That incident taught Damon the value of preplanning. Had the boy planned out an escape route, he would never have been cornered like that. Since that day, all of Damon's emphasis went to planning. Damon planned for every imaginable contingency, he'd always had an escape route and never ever allowed himself to go into a situation where he might be cornered. Each time he set out to do a job, he meticulously preplanned every aspect. This was the main reason that the police always had such a difficult time pinning anything on him.

That is until now. On the last, very unlucky Saturday, Lieutenant David Jackson and his team of miscreants had finally caught Damon off guard. His escape plan had been foiled and he had seen Jackson shoot his only brother.

Damon sat in the third row of empty pews and stared at the empty alter of the rundown church, his eyes fixed with hatred. He sat intently, planning his revenge, only his personal brand of justice on his mind. Within an hour Olsen entered the church through the usual back door and came into the sanctuary through a side door followed by five very gruff looking men, including one who was at least six foot six and 300 pounds of pure muscle. Damon continued to stare forward not acknowledging their presence. All five men stood in the aisle, waiting for Damon's reaction.

"What were you in for?" He asked after several seconds.

"Everything from kidnaping to manslaughter to armed robbery." Olsen replied.

"You looking to go back?" Damon asked them.

"I aint never goin' back. I'll die first." One of the men said sternly. Damon remained silent for several more seconds, still staring straight ahead.

"The job is not a simple one." Damon started in a deadly serious tone. "It will be to secure merchandise for transport, the destination of which you will never know. We will kill several cops and many more people, including women and children. For your services you will be paid one hundred thousand dollars and be given transportation to a property that I own in Mexico, there we will discuss future employment. If anyone wants out, now is the time." Each of the men, including Olsen looked at each other.

"For a hundred thousand G's, I'll kill the whole damn city." One of the men told him. Damon nodded, then, for the first time looked over at the men, sizing them up.

"Follow me." Damon said, getting up. He led them past the alter, through a narrow hallway and into the basement. He opened the padlocked basement door with a key on his key ring and motioned the men to enter. Once they were all inside, he flipped the light switch revealing an armory rivaled only by the military. AK-47's, AR-15's, MP-5's, Uzi's, M-16's and M-14's, all fully automatic plus an M-60 machine gun, which gathered the large man's attention. Lining the walls were a cache of grenades, explosives and over seven thousand rounds of ammunition. "Gentlemen, the tools of your trade. Prepare it all. We need to move it." Damon ordered before leading Olsen out the door. "I want you to retrieve my money but first go to Martin Lynch's office downtown, he was Eddie's lawyer, get him and bring him here." He ordered, out of earshot of the others. "I also want you to go to my brother's house, on the wall is a picture of he and I. Get it and bring it back here." Damon said, not really caring about the picture but knowing that if they weren't watching the places where he kept his money, the police would definitely be watching his brother's house. "Go to the house last and then come straight here. Understand?" Olsen nodded, not understanding Damon's larger plan.

"Yeah." Owens said with disappointment into his cell phone. He stood in the kitchen of Kaylee's house. Outside, rain was pouring down and the sky was a dark gray. "Ok, we'll keep a sharp eye." He said again a few seconds later. Courtney passed through the kitchen, laundry basket in hand. "Thanks." He finally told Casteel on the other end of the line before closing his phone and slipping it into his pocket. He frowned and looked over to see Courtney staring at him. "Still no sign of Collins or Olsen." He informed. Her expression matched his and she continued on to the laundry room.

He crossed through the dining room and into the living room where Kaylee was watching some television. He sat himself in a chair next to the sofa, on which Kaylee had made herself comfortable.

"Hey, little sister, I need to talk to you about something." He said when the screen turned to a commercial. Kaylee dutifully muted the television and turned her attention to Owens. "You know, when this is over..."

"We can solve something else." Kaylee interrupted. She wasn't going to make this easy for him.

"Well, you're a little young for police work aren't you?" Owens asked.

"You're going to say that when this is over you're going to go away aren't you?" Kaylee turned serious, knowing that her mother was most likely responsible for this turn of events. It wasn't the first time.

"I don't want to but I have a lot of work." He said, breaking his own heart. Kaylee jumped off the couch and onto his lap, hugging him like she had only a few nights earlier.

"I don't want you to go." She pleaded. "Everybody always leaves. Grampa, Daddy, they always leave, I don't want you to go." She cried. Owens rubbed her hair with his hand.

"I'll be like Superman," he comforted, "never far, always there when you need me."

"But why can't you just come and visit once in a while?" She begged. "Why can't you just stay?" Owens didn't know how to reply. He'd spent most of his time trying not to think about doing this, he hadn't planned it out. "What if something happens to you?" She asked. "I might never know."

"Little sister, aint nothing gonna happen to me." He assured, his southern draw showing itself more than usual.

"That's what I thought about Grampa." She replied.

"But your Grampa's in heaven. He'll always be with you now." Owens changed the subject.

"Mommy said that in heaven you go to the place where you were the happiest." Kaylee said, seeing an opportunity.

"Yeah, little sister, that's true." Owens returned, happy that the subject had been changed.

"But I don't know where Grampa went in heaven, how do I know he's with me?"

"Because he can look down from anywhere and see you." Owens smiled.

"Where would you go?" She asked. Owens deliberated for a few seconds, he'd never thought about this question before.

"I think I would go to a place called Moon Lake, where I grew up in Tennessee." He said after some thought. "I went there once with a girl that I loved."

"Really," Kaylee looked up at him, realizing that she was learning something new about him. "What was her name?"

Owens thought a moment before replying, he didn't know if he wanted to discuss this with her. Finally, after being overwhelmed by the sadness in her large brown eyes, he capitulated. "Hillary." He spoke the name that hadn't crossed his lips in quite some time.

"That's a pretty name." Kaylee remarked first. "Did she have to leave too?" He'd fallen into the little girl's manipulative trap.

"Yeah." He instantly replied. She'd gotten him, he knew it, he couldn't dare bring about even a portion of the sadness he'd felt when the only woman he'd ever loved had left him. He couldn't do it, he couldn't tell her that he wouldn't be there for her. For all his courage, he couldn't do this one little thing. It wasn't just the sadness he would cause in her though; until this moment, he'd never realized how much this one little girl, this angelic life within the prison of her own illness, had come to mean to him. He'd let her in and now he feared that he'd never be able to push her out again. For the first time in a long time, Owens felt that he was with a bonafide member of his family. The sister that he'd never knew he had.

She continued to look up at him. "I'll do what I can to come and see you when this is over." He conceded, though he knew her mother wasn't going to be happy. Kaylee didn't say anything more. She put her head against his arm and in the security blanket of his presence, faded off to sleep.

11

"Dr. Ngo"

T he devastating olfactory property of lacquer smacked Richard Olsen in the face upon entering the front door to the Royale Nails salon. The salon was full, more than a dozen tables manicuring and painting nails on various types of women, each producing the same stringent aroma that Olsen despised the industry for. All of the employees of Royale Nails were Asian, mostly Vietnamese. Some wore thick white masks over their faces to protect them from the side effects of inhaling the harsh fumes all day long, others kept the masks off because they could better give conversation and friendliness to their customers.

A very large man, probably of Samoan descent, who had been sitting in the waiting area watching the television immediately got up to greet the new patron. The man's large size was offset by the slight limp he carried. Olsen stood in the doorway watching the man approach, noticing that the man's arms contained almost as much fat as muscle but also realizing that there were massive amounts of both.

"You want your nails done?" The man asked, crossing his arms.

"I need to see Jimmy." Olsen replied.

"Jimmy has an appointment, he won't be done for a while. Come back later." The man insisted with a stern gaze.

"Damon Collins sent me."

"Wait here." The man changed his tone. He walked to the very last table and whispered something in the ear of a man wearing one of the white masks. The man nodded, presumably saying something through the mask. A moment later, the large Samoan was standing in front of Olsen again. "Come with me." The man led Olsen to the last table, pulled out an empty chair, and sat it next to the table. "Sit." He ordered.

"Jimmy..." Olsen started to say once he sat but stopped when the large Samoan interrupted.

"No talk, he will speak to you when he is ready." He was told.

"It's alright Jas." Jimmy Nguyen told the Samoan. "I'll be with you in a moment Dick."

Olsen hated it when people referred to him as Dick but he

couldn't tell Jimmy that. No one insulted Jimmy Nguyen. Jas
continued standing over Olsen, ready to pounce, which annoyed him
greatly. Olsen waited patiently for the twenty-minutes that it took
Jimmy to finish the nails of the slightly overweight, obviously
wealthy woman sitting in front of him. He listened carefully while
they talked about the woman's children, clothes and house. Jimmy
always returned her stories with friendly remarks and only slightly
humorous anecdotes of his experiences while he listened, which
seemed to please the woman. Finished with her nails, Jimmy led the
woman to a table in the back of the shop that held a rectangular
machine that the woman put her fingers in to dry her nails. Jimmy
returned to the desk, took off his mask and cleaned up.

"You disappoint me Dick, you know I don't do business
here." Jimmy told Olsen.

"This is a special occasion." Olsen replied.

"No shit Dick, I might actually let you walk out of here on
your own steam, which is unusual for people who don't obey the
rules." Olsen could hear Jas cracking his knuckles.

"Damon needs the money he left with you and he'll also be
collecting his merchandise a little early." Olsen said, getting straight
to business.

"You want something to drink, Dick?" Jimmy asked,
finishing his cleaning and sitting down in his chair. "Maybe a candy
bar, Milky Way, Three Musketeers, Dick?"

"Where can I pick up the money?" Olsen asked, at this point

very annoyed at the usage of his unofficial nickname.

"Well, there's a slight problem with that, Dick." Jimmy said, stretching his arms over his head. "See Dick, Damon isn't exactly in the same position he was before. You know, I hear that the DEA is after him now."

"DEA, I hadn't heard that."

"Oh yeah Dick, I got good gossip that tells me that if the feds don't get him, Seattle PD will. I gotta tell you Dick, things aren't looking up for our friend." Jimmy informed and opened a drawer, taking out a snack.

"All the more reason for you to sever your business ties with him then, don't you think?" Olsen tried to persuade.

"Exactly, now you're getting it, Dick." Jimmy returned. "See I figure I should cut him loose, like I never met him. That's why I've decided to keep the money. It's not like he can stick around and get it back, now can he, Dick?"

Olsen leaned in with a serious look. "You're going to cross Damon Collins?"

"Well," Jimmy replied, "I never would have before but he isn't in the same position he was before. He screwed up. He stepped on his dick...um, Dick. I'm afraid that karma has conspired against him. Eddie's dead, I've got at least some of his money, sure I know he slipped it all over town and if the others want to give you what they have fine but I'm not going to and the merchandise he left for safe keeping, well I think I should hold onto that also. Looks like he's got dick...um, Dick."

"Alright, I can see the money, its cash in your pocket." Olsen told him.

"Exactly, a donation, if you like, Dick." Jimmy smiled.

"But the merchandise, why keep that, there's nothing you can do with it?" Olsen at least wanted to salvage something from his day, the other guardians of Damon's money had refused to give their charges up also.

"Dick, Dick, Dick...Damon isn't the only guy in this city with a brain, if he can fence that worthless shit, I can find a buyer too."

"You know what Damon will do?" Olsen now pleaded.

"Screw that, he's impotent Dick, he can't do shit. He's in hiding, he can't make any moves without getting caught now. Damon's finished Dick, don't let him take you down too." Jimmy returned. "Now Dick, I have work to do, it's been nice chatting with you but I think it's time for you to go. Have a nice day, Dick." Jimmy nodded to Jas, who took a step toward Olsen. Olsen looked up at the behemoth and knowing that he was outmatched, made his way to the door.

"So, get this..." Ari Rothstein sat on his desk and spoke to the group of uniformed officers surrounding him. "The dog comes at me and I plug it right." He made a gun with his fingers. "Then I get to where I dropped the mutt and I hear something else." The officers moved closer in anticipation, they loved this part of the story. "So I look up and there's Ben and Joel, up in this tree, scared shitless because of this dog!" Laughter burst out of everyone in unison.

"Tell it again." One of the officers demanded.

"Right, I even asked them, 'why didn't you just shoot the damn dog?' You know what they said," Ari's voice turned to that of a little girl, "We can't shoot a dog." Laughter burst out again.

"I can see that you're all hard at work while I'm gone!" Jackson said sarcastically, passing Rothstein's desk. The uniformed officers disappeared like they were four years old and got caught with their hand in the cookie jar.

"Hey, I thought you were on leave?" Ben Casteel got up from his desk.

"Yeah," Holloman remarked next, "didn't the old lady say that if she caught you anywhere near this building, she'd castrate you and make you watch all the Seahawks' games?"

"Nah," Mason chimed in next, "she said she'd make him her chocolate love machine!"

"Ah, a fate worse than death." Casteel commented.

"Funny." Jackson nodded sarcastically and turned around to face his team. "Gather aro..." His announcement was halted by Johnson yelling into his phone.

"Why don't you call me back when you remember that we're

on the same side you dag-gummed jerk!" Johnson finished and slammed the phone on the receiver.

"Joel, somebody really ought to teach you the finer points of chewing somebody's ass." Casteel commented.

"I don't want to burn any bridges." Johnson replied.

"Pity the thought." Jackson said. "That wasn't the mayor I hope?"

"IRS, we've been trying to get Damon Collins' records, maybe it'll help us figure out where he's been the last two years. Apparently, they're not being forthcoming." Casteel informed.

"I'm just glad somebody's working." Jackson returned. "Everyone gather around." The five members of N.S.1. waited patiently for what their defunct boss had to say. "Jessie with the girl?"

"Yeah." Casteel nodded.

"Alright, the IRS isn't going to help us, what we really need to know is why Collins had Jimmy Nguyen, a rival, lease a cargo ship for him."

"Obviously he wants to hide something there." Johnson blurted.

"You're a rocket scientist you know that? Of course but what?" Mason returned.

"That's what we need to know, once we know what's on that ship, we'll be able to connect the dots." Jackson hypothesized.

"Well how do we find that out, they don't have to register it with anyone?" Holloman thought aloud.

"C'mon guys," Jackson chided, "police work 101, we have to get eyes on."

"The ship?" Johnson asked.

"No, the Goddamn Kremlin you retard." Rothstein chimed.

"We need more than that, we need to get inside." Jackson told them. "We gotta be sure of what's in there and if it is drugs, we need some to test."

"Ok but how do we do that? I know, we'll show up and ask them to give us a tour, they'll be so happy to play host to a squad of narcs, they'll invite us right on in." Casteel interjected.

"I was thinking something slightly more clandestine but we can go with that." Jackson replied playfully.

"Wait, I think I know a way." Johnson added. "My brother-in-law works out at the docks."

"It has to be legit, if we force our way in, it's entrapment." Casteel informed.

"It is, every ship has to be inspected, as long as this one is due for inspection it's perfectly legal. He says they're backlogged for like two years." Johnson told him.

"That's fine and good but Jimmy Nguyen's guys are notorious for spotting cops, they'll see us coming a mile away." Holloman told them.

"He's right, we have cop written all over us." Casteel agreed.

"Not all of us." Jackson smirked, turning to Casteel, who turned his stare to Johnson, who turned to Holloman, who turned to look at Mason and Rothstein.

"Not again." Mason whispered to herself. Rothstein, who wasn't really paying attention, looked up to see everyone glaring at him.

"Aw hell no!" Rothstein declared. "Not this time! No...no...NO!"

"He's got a point," Casteel told Rothstein, "nobody ever believes you two are cops. Ari, your parents still don't believe it."

"No!" Rothstein loudly proclaimed. "Look at me!" He almost shouted.

"Ari, we are looking at you." Jackson replied cynically.

"Look at me." He said again. "Look at my eyes." He pointed to his eyes. "Especially, you, the big black one in back. And listen good! No way, no how, never...get somebody else...forget about it...not in a million years! End of story! End of conversation!"

"I'm Ari Rothstein, this is Kimberly Mason, Seattle Port Authority." Rothstein told Jimmy Nguyen's guard watching the boarding plank to the cargo ship. Rothstein's accent was that of a sloppy New Yorker which was made even more intolerable by the gargantuan wad of chewing gum that he was slapping against his teeth. The two were dressed head to toe in large overalls and hats from the Port Authority. "This ship has to be inspected for chemical toxin byproducts."

"What's a chemical toxin byproduct?" The guard, a Vietnamese man in his early twenties wearing blue jeans, a white button up shirt and sunglasses replied.

"Look, when a ship sits in the water for long enough, it starts giving off byproducts of the materials used in its construction." Rothstein slapped his gum. "The port requires that all ships moored for an extended period of time be inspected to make sure the proper mechanisms are in place to prevent spillage into the bay."

"I've never heard of that." The guard replied.

"What a surprise." Rothstein sarcastically commented. "Look, bro, whether you heard of it or not, we gotta check. I aint never heard of Snoop Dogg til my kid started listening to him, that don't mean he aint out there."

"Is there a problem." Another guard, similarly dressed, walked down the plank. The two guards conversed for a moment in Vietnamese before the new guard turned to Rothstein and spoke. "I'm Tong Ngo, I'm in charge here, I can't let you come aboard, this ship is privately leased."

"No? Like the movie, Dr. No? I seen it." Rothstein said, purposely to annoy Ngo. "Good flick but I gotta tell ya, you aint got much of a choice in the matter. According to your lease, we got the right to inspect once a year for toxins."

"I said no." Ngo patiently replied. The other guard was watching Mason, admiring her muscular physique inside the thick overalls she was wearing.

"You act like that's your name." Rothstein said, Mason suddenly felt the urge to slap him in the back of the head but didn't. "This is how it is," Rothstein looked at his watch, "it's almost quitting time, I need to get home to my kids, my little girl has a soccer game tonight...and she sucks! So I gotta cheer her on. Don't keep me from doing that." Rothstein stared momentarily at the unflinching Ngo. "Are you aware that the entry of toxins into the local water supply has been deemed a matter of national security? I tell you what, you don't want to let us inspect, fine. I'll have ten federal Marshals down here in thirty minutes and they'll be all over your shitty little ship and up your ass with a microscope so powerful they'll see amoeba on Uranus watching Star Trek." Rothstein increased his stare. "Or you can let us do our check for some toxins that will take ten Goddamn minutes to do! It's up to you bro?"

"Get me a copy of our lease. And call Jimmy." Ngo ordered the other guard. Within a few minutes the guard returned, lease in hand. The two conversed in Vietnamese again for several minutes, apparently there was a provision in the lease allowing for such inspections. "Alright, ten minutes, then you're off."

"Thank you." Rothstein walked around the two men and up the plank, followed by Mason. Ngo and the guard followed closely behind as Rothstein quickly checked the deck, marking off items on his clipboard.

"Just a couple questions." Rothstein said, preparing to read the clipboard. "When was the last time the exterior of the hull was cleaned?"

"I don't know." Ngo replied angrily. "Why clean it at all?"

"Oh, c'mon." Rothstein threw his arms outward. "Do you know what can grow on the hull of a ship?"

"No, what?" Ngo replied, which caught Rothstein off guard, he hadn't expected that response.

"Well...I imagine there's some pretty nasty shit that grows down there." Rothstein stammered. Mason rolled her eyes. "Get that done alright, I'll do you a favor and give you a pass on it." When finished marking off the items, he briskly proceeded to the hatch leading below deck.

"Why do you need to go down there?" Ngo asked, positioning himself between the hatch and Rothstein.

"Because this is an inspection." Rothstein replied like he was talking to a child. "I have to check for rust and holes and shit."

"We don't have any holes."

"How do you know that?"

"Because we haven't sunk." Ngo replied.

"Mason." Rothstein yelled.

"I'm right next to you." She told him with some annoyance.

"Good, call the office, tell them they better get the Marshals down here, I got another squirrelly one."

"You got it." Mason took out her cell phone.

"Alright." Ngo held up his hand and stepped aside. Rothstein slipped into the hatch and down the stairs, moving straight for the cargo hold. Rothstein stopped in his tracks when he entered the hatch to the hold. It was filled with large brown cardboard boxes, loaded onto specially designed pallets that were made for use by the ship's crane. Each box contained the label of a large pharmaceutical manufacturing company, and most had inventory lists and invoices attached to them, all looked 100% authentic.

Rothstein muttered a prayer in Hebrew when he saw the pallet filled hold. He didn't waste any time stepping inside to the cellophane covered pallets and inspecting the labels on the boxes, despite Ngo's objections. The first pallet's labels said that each box contained a drug called Singulair, an asthma medication. The second contained boxes of Lipitor, used for lowering cholesterol. The third contained a drug that everyone had heard of. When he saw this, Rothstein regained his composure.

"Oh shit, you got some Viagra." Rothstein slapped his gum. "Damn, this is some wicked ass shit?"

"Just continue your inspection." Ngo ordered.

"Who do you work for Dr. Ngo?" Mason asked.

"Not that it's any of your business but this ship is leased by a distribution company, these drugs are waiting to be shipped out." Ngo replied angrily.

"You know the girlfriend wanted me to take some of this shit, just to see how I'd do?" Rothstein told him.

"Why don't you inspect something...please." Ngo tried to turn back to business.

"You know what this shit does," Rothstein continued, "man I was hard for a week straight, I got ahold of that bitch and ground her pelvic bone into dust. I swear, there's nothing like it." Mason's face turned beet red and her expression changed to one of disgust.

"Can we get on with this?" Ngo asked sternly.

"Sorry," Rothstein laughed, "I start thinking about the girlfriend and completely lose my mind." Mason used all of her self-discipline to keep from striking him. "We need to inspect the seams."

"This is a ship, not a polo shirt." Ngo returned. "Ships don't have seams."

"Sure they do. Ships are welded together, there's a lot of toxin seepage at the seams, we have to check them." Rothstein said before yelling behind him. "Kimbo!"

"What?" Mason grumbled right next to him through clinched teeth.

"You aint on vacation! Check the seams." He ordered. Mason stared at him in disgust for a few seconds before moving off. After she left to find a seam, followed by the other guard, Rothstein turned back to Ngo. "I just need some information from you two." Ngo reluctantly nodded his head. "Do you eat a lot of fatty foods?"

"What kind of question is that?" Ngo replied, boiling.

"If you empty your chemical toilets into the bay, it makes a lot of sense." Rothstein told him.

"We don't do that, it's illegal, we have a service that empties them." Ngo was reaching his limit.

"Alright, no need to get defensive. Do you live alone?"

"That's none of your business." Ngo almost yelled. Rothstein stared at him for a moment with an expressionless face.

"Hey look doc." Rothstein said in an even voice. "You may not take this seriously but the federal government sure as hell does, these are important national security questions and you better start cooperating."

"Fine." Ngo said in frustration. "Yes, I live alone."

"Good, got any STD's?"

"What the hell does that have to do with anything!" Ngo screamed.

Rothstein went into a tirade about the importance of biological hazards leaking into the water. With the distraction ongoing, Mason made her way to the far end of the cargo hold. Sliding between two pallets, she found a secluded seam to inspect but knew that the other guard was still watching her. She bent down to the seam, pretending to look at it closely. While she was bent over, the guard admired her rear, which unbeknownst to her, was sticking out from behind the pallet.

"What about the other guy?" Rothstein asked after several

minutes of arguing. "Does he live alone?"

"What does it matter?" Ngo replied.

"Get him over here, let's find out." Rothstein ordered.

"Alright, if it will get you out of here, fine!" Ngo yelled at him then called the other guard to where they were.

Alone at last, Mason took a pocket knife from her overalls and looked at the boxes in the pallet she was next to. They contained Wellbutrin, a well known antidepressant. Quietly, Mason cut a thin gap in the cellophane near the top of one of the bottom boxes, reached her hand through, cut the tape on the lid of the box and forced her hand in the small opening. Feeling around in the box, Mason found a small rectangular box of pills and pulled them out while she listened to the three men argue.

"No! I do not eat cat!" The guard was yelling.

Once she had the Wellbutrin in her overalls' pocket, she went to another pallet, this one containing Celebrex. She cut a similar gap in the cellophane and box tape. This time reaching in, she discovered that the drugs were in very large bottles. Intending to replace the bottle after taking a few pills she struggled to pull it out of the box.

"No more questions!" Ngo demanded and motioned for the other guard to go back to find Mason. "I want you to leave right now!"

"Ok, ok, I'm almost done, don't lose your chi." Rothstein replied.

The guard was confused that he hadn't found Mason in the same spot he'd left her and began searching. Mason was still attempting to pull the large bottle out of the box without tearing the cardboard.

The guard rounded one of the pallets and saw the edge of something sticking out behind a box and fluttering a bit. The guard felt slightly uneasy when he saw it, he was beginning to like Mason, her strong masculine form was attractive to him but now Mason definitely seemed to be into something she shouldn't have been. He opened his stride to get to it quickly but found that it was only a piece of labeling sticking out from the plastic and being blown by the steady breeze caused by the air conditioner. He turned 360 degrees, trying to get his bearings and find where Mason had gone. Hearing some rustling of cardboard, he set out again.

Mason finally ripped the bottle out just before the guard rounded the corner and saw her. Mason shot around like lightning, cupping the bottle in her palm behind her back, her pocket knife in her other hand.

"What are you doing?" The guard asked.

"That seam back there has a little rust." She stated, pointing at a seam far behind her with her knife hand. "See." She lunged forward at his face with the knife, stopping it just short. The guard flinched back slightly but once he realized she wasn't threatening him, he peered at the knife.

"I don't see any rust." He told her.

"It's there." She said, slowly slipping the bottle in her pocket. "I think it'll be ok though, it's just a little, my anal retentive boss doesn't have to know about it." She smiled.

"Thanks." The guard told her and held out his hand, a signal for them to return to the entrance.

"We're not all sexist chauvinist pigs like him." She remarked.

"I know how that is, I have to take a lot of shit from my boss too but he's not obnoxious like yours." The guard told her. He wanted her to feel like he understood her dilemma, perhaps it would ingratiate him to her. "So do you work out?" The guard asked, hoping to make more conversation with her while they mashed their way back through the pallets to the main aisle.

"Yeah." She replied.

"I hit the gym a little myself, maybe we can go together sometime?" He said, looking her over.

"You're not my type." She informed with an ironic smile right before they reached Rothstein and Ngo. "The seams look fine." She told Rothstein.

"Well doc, that wasn't so hard was it?" Rothstein said with a smile and headed back through the hatch. "Get that hull cleaned and next year we won't have any problems at all." Ngo and the other guard watched them march down the plank, one thinking he'd like to kill them, the other thinking something slightly different.

They quickly scurried to their meeting place with the rest of the team. On their way back to the office, Ari caught a right cross with his face; he wasn't sure why.

At around two o'clock in the morning, Owens was awakened by a phone call at his apartment, quickly dressing, he ran out to a cab he'd ordered and told the driver to take him to Swedish Medical Center in First Hill. He went in the emergency room doors and was told that he needed to go to the surgery area on the third floor. He took the elevator and found Courtney Taylor and Kimberly Mason when he hit the waiting room.

Mason, even though she'd spent the day undercover, was covering the midnight shift protecting Kaylee Taylor. She'd called Owens when Kaylee's mother checked on her and found that her skin and eyes had been taken with a yellowish tint. Currently, Courtney was in a corner of the room, speaking to a doctor who'd just come out the recovery room door. Owens approached them, which caused the doctor to stop talking.

"What's the matter, what's happening?" Owens asked, worry in his voice.

"It's alright Jesse, can you give us a minute?" Courtney asked.

"Where is she?"

"Jesse, she's in recovery, she's fine." Courtney told him.

"What happened?" He asked. Courtney rubbed her forehead to relieve some tension, she knew she wasn't getting him to leave.

"Doctor?" She asked, motioning for the doctor to explain to Owens what he'd been telling her.

"She has gallstones." The doctor told him. "She tried to pass one. It got stuck in her biliary tree and caused jaundice, a yellowing of the skin. Luckily, her mother noticed it and got her down here, we don't want to take out her gallbladder because there's a danger to using anaesthesia with her. Instead we used a combination of Ursodiol and Ultrasound to break up the stone that was stuck along with the others still in her gallbladder. She's sleeping in the recovery room right now."

"Jesse, I think you should know something." Courtney told him. "Doctor."

"Are you sure, that's confidential information?" The doctor asked her. Courtney nodded. Owens was becoming increasingly nervous with every word.

"Kaylee has serious medical problems." The doctor told him. "Because relatively little is known about her condition, certain patients develop specific side effects that we can't explain. With Kaylee we believe the pain signals that her brain isn't receiving is affecting her brain's other systems. We think that her brain isn't adequately regulating her body's organs. Kaylee has extremely high blood pressure, increased hormone levels and radical shifts in regulatory functioning. Simply put, her brain isn't sensing when she's sick, sleeping or even tired, it's telling her organs to work as though she's at a high level of activity all the time. Her heart, liver, respiratory system, gallbladder, kidneys are all worn out. It's only a matter of time before one or more fail completely.

"Are you saying that she's going to..." Owens couldn't finish the sentence. A massive weight had suddenly fallen on his back.

"I can't say anything for sure when it comes to Kaylee's condition." The doctor replied. "But I think you should be prepared for it." Owens couldn't respond, he stood, frozen, unable to even think.

"How...long?" He stammered after several long seconds.

"It could be tomorrow, it could be ten years, there's just no way to know." The doctor replied.

"You knew?" Owens asked Courtney who was staring at the doctor's shoes, trying to hold in her tears.

"I thought you should know." She replied without looking at him. Owens couldn't say anything else, he took a few steps backwards. Disoriented, he turned and headed, almost at a run, out the doors.

"Jesse." Mason tried to stop him but he ignored her.

12

"Connecting The Dots"

Kaylee was released from the hospital around one in the afternoon. Mason stayed with her for the drive home, even though her shift had been scheduled to end at noon. Kaylee was rambunctious and vivacious during the ride. Having slept through the night and into most of the morning, her energy level had come back with a vengeance. She joked about the people in other cars that she saw out her window and even punched Mason when she saw a VW Bug. Mason laughed but didn't want to punch her back so she waited until the little girl turned her attention back out the car window, then lightly pinched her arm. Kaylee's attention didn't falter from the window and Mason laughed at herself when she realized why Kaylee didn't notice.

"Cheater." She said, keeping Kaylee's skin between her fingers. Kaylee looked down at it and smiled her typically mischievous smile.

The moment they came into view of their house, Kaylee saw the unmarked patrol car parked on the street and became excited. She'd asked why Owens wasn't at the hospital at noon, which was his usual time to relieve Mason but hadn't gotten a suitable reply. She had so much to tell him about her hospital stay and hoped to be able to sit down and watch Jerry Springer with him. Watching the raunchy talk show had become somewhat of a routine between the little girl and her grown protector.

Kaylee's face turned from anxious anticipation to dread when she saw Marcus Holloman step out of the patrol car. Mason got out first, followed by Courtney and Kaylee; Courtney unconcerned with the change in routine, Kaylee visibly distraught by it. Mason scanned up and down the street for anything strange which was her cautious custom but came up empty.

Kaylee looked at Holloman with a disconcerting disappointment. "Where's Jesse?" Courtney turned around to listen better to his answer.

"He had to go to court today. You're stuck with me spud." Holloman informed. Courtney rolled her eyes and lightly put her hand on her daughter's shoulder.

"C'mon babygirl, let's get inside." She ordered sweetly. Kaylee looked down at the ground and went with her mother, leaving only Mason and Holloman outside the house.

"Anything?" Mason asked when the front door to the house closed.

"I checked his apartment, nothing. He's not at the precinct. We've got no idea where he is." Holloman told her.

"Does the L.T. know?"

"I don't know if Casteel told him."

"I'd better take care of that then. Keep trying to call him." Mason ordered and took the keys from Holloman.

Lieutenant David Jackson sat in a cheap chair in the lobby of Seattle Police Department's Forensic Laboratory waiting for the results of the drug tests. The technician conducting the tests was a relative newcomer to the forensic department named Jason McCall. At twenty-four years old, McCall had graduated from the University of Washington with a masters degree in chemistry and sixty-six thousand dollars of student loans to pay off. Under a work program for the government he could have Uncle Sam pay two-thirds of his debt in exchange for five years of government service.

McCall was currently testing the first of the Wellbutrin pills that Mason liberated from Jimmy Nguyen's leased cargo ship. Jackson had been trying to wait patiently but the tests had taken all night and he was becoming more and more agitated that he hadn't seen the results.

"Hey boss." Rothstein motioned, stepping out of one of the Electronic Discovery rooms. "I got something you wanna see." Happy that there was something to look at, even though it wasn't what he wanted, Jackson stepped into the computer lab. Sitting at the large mainframe in back, Ari Rothstein was putting his degree in computer programming to a rather unorthodox use.

"What's all that?" Jackson asked.

"It's Damon Collins' IRS file." Rothstein replied.

"I thought they wouldn't give it to us without a subpoena?"

"They didn't. I used the lab's network to connect to the Immigration and Naturalization system, which is connected to the Internal Revenue Service's network. Then I used a binary decryption program that a buddy of mine wrote in college to get through their first three sets of firewalls. The fourth and fifth were a little more tricky, I had to brute force one with a back door command line, it was hell figuring out what it was. The last I had to infect with a virus that isolates pockets of code then substitutes the command prefixes with ordering initiatives and here we are." He rambled, proud of his work.

"English Ari." Jackson ordered.

"I hacked it."

"And you just made me an accomplice. Thanks."

"Anything for you who puts me undercover." Rothstein laughed. "Damon had an interesting couple of years. According to the IRS, two years ago, right after Damon was acquitted and disappeared, he started up a new business in Couer d'Alene Idaho. The beauty of this business was that it was guaranteed to stay under the radar. The tax paperwork here is perfect, every I dotted, every T is crossed. Absolutely no reason to believe there's any criminal activity."

"What was it?" Jackson asked.

"The business's sole purpose was the selling of latex gloves, now the IRS doesn't ask where he got his stock from but does ask how much he paid for it. I've already cross referenced that number with some others and it looks like if he was paying base price, which he probably was because he would've wanted to avoid drawing attention, he didn't have that much stock. What's really interesting is his personal tax returns." Jackson leaned in to look when Rothstein pulled the file up on the big screen. "He listed himself as a traveling salesman and took massive work related tax breaks, for which he had to provide receipts. Here's the paperwork." Rothstein tapped the keyboard and pulled up a new file on the screen.

"It looks like in one year alone, he crisscrossed the country at least four times." Jackson observed.

"Brilliant, you must be a detective or something." Rothstein sarcastically remarked.

"Keep talking smartass, I'll have you eating breakfast with the Taliban."

"Right...Now if you look closely at the locations and the

dates, you'll find that even though he listed his permanent address in Couer d'Alene, he didn't spend any time there. He stayed mobile for an entire year. What's so cool about it is that he wrote the whole thing off as business. Goddamn, I need his accountant."

"His accountant's dead remember?" Jackson said dryly. "What about the second year?"

"The second year is pretty interesting, Collins folded the business four months into it, filed for bankruptcy but didn't owe anything, which is strange. I don't know why he wouldn't drag it on, the IRS would've let him take a loss on the business for five years."

"Because he'd finished doing what he wanted to do. He filed bankruptcy so nobody could touch it." Jackson informed. "What about after the business folded?"

"Nothing, I'll keep looking but I doubt there's anything else." Rothstein told him.

"There you are." Johnson said, skidding to a stop at the door to the computer lab. He held in his hand a digital photograph of Rothstein and Mason in their Port Authority overalls, each with sour expressions; Rothstein's middle finger in the air.

"That's great." Jackson smiled, looking at the photo. "Put it on the bulletin board."

"No prob, McCall wanted me to tell you that he's finished with the first test." Johnson replied. Jackson nodded and they filed out of the room to the toxicology lab where McCall was crushing up some pills to test.

"I thought you were on leave?" The skinny young man with professionally spiked hair asked. "Didn't Knox say that if she found you anywhere near the building, she was going chain you up in her basement and make you tell her she's beautiful while she stripped for you?"

"I thought the Geneva Convention banned torture?" Rothstein added.

"Everybody's a comedian." Jackson responded without humor. "Where are my tests?"

"You know this lab has a nine month backlog on toxicology tests, I've got at least a month backlog on homicides alone, why should I put yours first?"

"Because I know where you live."

"Good point." McCall put two sheets of paper on the table. The sheets contained graphs with lines representing the exact chemical makeups of the drug he tested and the drug it was supposed to be. "It's Wellbutrin, through and through, well almost." McCall told them while they studied the graphs. "It's a perfect replication of the Wellbutrin drug, bottom line is that if you give this drug to someone with depression, it would work on them."

"What are these other lines?" Jackson asked, pointing to several chemicals on the graph that weren't on the baseline graph.

"I'd say that's the almost. If we were looking at a Big Mac, this would be the secret sauce." All three stared at McCall, not knowing what he was talking about. "They're about half a dozen chemicals, lead, phosphate, ammonia, others that were in the pill I examined in very low concentrations."

"What is it with people and labs?" Jackson rubbed the bridge of his nose. "Everybody gets in a lab and suddenly forgets how to talk. What is it?"

"They aren't supposed to be there, they're not found in Wellbutrin and they have toxic effects in humans."

"So Collins' is trying to poison people?" Johnson asked.

"Not purposely, at least I don't think he's meaning to. If he were, it would be in much higher doses. These are what we call leftover chemicals." McCall noticed all three detectives staring at him again. "Alright," he explained, "when you make meth, crack, ecstacy, or any other drug, the chemicals that you mix together have byproducts of the chemicals that you used to make the individual electron bonds. We call them chemical leftovers, some people call them kickbacks, others call them manufacturing byproducts. I knew a guy who used to call them covalent excrement, though that wasn't exactly right, it doesn't necessarily have to be a covalent bond to produce the reaction. All it really needs is a free electron to..."

"Jason!" Jackson yelled.

"Oh, ok, whoever made the pill that I tested, they must have made it with equipment that had previously made other drugs. If this were made in an FDA certified manufacturing lab, the equipment would have to be cleaned after every batch. Judging from the wide variety of chemical leftovers, this equipment has made everything from ecstacy to crystal meth and then it wasn't cleaned afterwards. The leftovers stick to the equipment, then get picked up in trace amounts by the new drug as they're making it. I'm sure that's nothing new to you guys, happens all the time with illegal narcotics."

"Yes it does." Jackson told him. "What are the health effects?"

"The concentrations of these chemicals are very very low, if you were to take one of these, chances are you wouldn't have any harmful effects." McCall told them. Jackson sighed in relief, maybe it wasn't as bad as he feared. "Unfortunately, the type of drugs that we're dealing with aren't meant to be taken just once. They're meant to be taken daily, sometimes two or three times a day and for indefinite periods of time. That kind of exposure adds up." Jackson turned his head to see Casteel and Mason entering the room.

"We need to talk." Casteel told Jackson.

"Listen to this." Jackson ordered and turned back to McCall. "What's the worst case scenario?"

"If these pills are released to the general population in large numbers, I'd say in six months we could be seeing fatalities."

"Tell me there's a best case scenario." Rothstein ordered.

"At the very least, there would be severe negative health effects. You have to remember that the people taking these medications are already sick. If they take drugs laced with lead and ammonia, bad things are going to happen. It's that simple."

"But he can't get them out." Johnson told them, hoping to

cheer up the glum faces in the room. "There's no market for these drugs on the street. Only prescription painkillers and we didn't see any of those. He'd have to sell them to a pharmacy and we know that no pharmacy will take homemade stuff."

"If they're dirty they will." Jackson speculated.

"That's right, Collins just spent a year roving around the country, he wasn't just selling gloves." Rothstein added. "He was making contacts to buy his homemade prescription meds."

"Think about it Joel." Jackson told Johnson. "First, he finds a way to lift the exact recipes for the drugs, then he roams the country selling latex gloves to find contacts in pharmacies that will buy the drugs off him. It doesn't matter if the pharmacies are mom and pop operations or big chains, all he needs is the help of the guy in charge. He can make the drugs for almost nothing, ship them out, sell them to the pharmacy, who, all except for the manager or whoever is working with him, thinks that the drugs are legit. Remember the labels we found? Damon must be using them to fool the pharmacies into thinking that the drugs have come from the companies themselves."

"The perfect invoices mean that the only thing that's different in the pharmacies buying the drugs from him and not the manufacturer is the account number they send the payments to. Nobody would ever know." Rothstein agreed.

"Which means that if those drugs get out and we don't know where they're going, a lot of people could die." Jackson told them.

"Even worse," McCall told them, "because of the risk of lawsuits, the FDA will put a stop on any medications from being released until all the tainted drugs can be found. A lot of very ill people might not get the medicine they need."

"So," Casteel put it together, "he makes the drugs in the labs of local underground chemists, holds them in the warehouse by Union Bay until he's ready to box them up for shipping. Then puts them for safe keeping on Jimmy Nguyen's cargo ship so he can move them out and presto, by the time he gets them going, we've got no idea where they went."

"By keeping them moving, he minimizes his chances of being found with them." Rothstein surmised.

"And that means that he's going to be running them soon." Jackson picked up the two graphs and handed them to Casteel. "Get this to Knox, you have to move on this right now."

"I will but we've got another problem." Casteel told him. "We can't find Jesse." Jackson's expression became even gloomier when Mason told him about what happened at the hospital the previous night.

"Alright." Jackson told them. "I know some places to look, I'll see if I can find him. You get that to Knox."

"I'm going now." Casteel said.

McCall fished a pack of Camels from his pants pocket and proceeded out the door.

"Where the hell do you think you're going?" Jackson

pointed to McCall.

"Just taking a break, I've been here all night."

"You still have more drugs to test?" Jackson asked him.

"Yeah but..."

"Get your ass back at that table."

McCall watched Jackson leave, then had his cigarette.

Olsen entered the church through the usual side door, and dropped Martin Lynch, Eddie's former lawyer, off in one of the offices. He had no idea that the DEA had been following him since he'd left Eddie's house. He stepped into the pulpit and found Damon next to the tabernacle lighting a candle for his brother. Olsen didn't know how Damon was going to react when he told him the bad news and thus hesitated.

"Did you bring the picture?" Damon asked without looking at him.

"I couldn't find the one you asked for, so I brought another one. It's just of Eddie." Olsen hoped that the picture would spare him at least some of Damon's wrath. Damon held out his hand, which Olsen slowly approached and placed the picture in. Damon stared at the candle, his temper searing. He didn't look at the picture, only felt the thick glass under the wooden frame with his fingers.

Olsen jumped back when Damon hurled the picture across the room. It smacked the wall of the balcony then broke over the armrest of a pew before coming to rest, face up, on the red carpet. Olsen started toward the smashed picture until Damon put one hand on his shoulder.

"Leave it." He ordered.

"There's more." Olsen was unable to look Damon in the eye. Damon turned back to the candle and stared. "Nobody would give up your money. Jimmy Nguyen won't give back your merchandise either." Olsen told him, hoping he wasn't experiencing the last few minutes of his life. Damon slowly turned around. In a quick motion that made Olsen flinch, he grabbed Olsen's face with his right hand and pinched his cheek like he was a child.

"Richie?" Damon grinned. "Did you really think I hadn't anticipated something like that?" Olsen didn't reply. "Sit down." Lightly slapping Olsen's face, Damon led Olsen to the first pew and the two sat. Damon took out a piece of hard candy and began unwrapping it.

"This is what we're going to do..."

Calamity Jane's was a bar frequented by cops down the street from the East Precinct, where Owens worked when he was a fresh patrol officer. It had a moderate amount of people, some sitting at tables talking, others sitting at the bar having a beer. Walking in the door, Jackson noticed the band Kansas' tune *Dust In The Wind* playing on the jukebox. He figured that the woeful song's lyrics were the reason that although people were talking, the ambient noise in the bar remained rather low.

He looked around and spotted Owens sitting at the end of the bar, a Jack Daniels whiskey in his hands. Owens only visible sign of life was when he glanced over at Jackson sitting down on an adjacent stool. Owens turned back to his drink without talking. The two sat in silence for a few minutes, Jackson looking over at him every so often.

"I'm going to ask Knox to put me on something else." Owens stated quietly, breaking the tension.

"You can do that if you want." Jackson answered in the same tone.

"Shouldn't I?"

"That's not for me to say." Jackson answered. Olsen emptied the glass into his mouth and placed it back on the bar. The bartender dutifully refilled it with ice and whiskey before turning to Jackson.

"What can I do you for?" He asked.

"Club Soda." Jackson told him. Within a few seconds a new glass appeared and was filled with the drink. Jackson handed the barkeep a few dollars and turned back to Owens. "We all have choices to make, I just want you to be sure that you do what you really want."

"Her mother said that I had to tell her I wasn't coming back after this was over or she'd request someone else anyway. I think she's right, why should she have to tell that child why I'm not there when this is done?" Owens confided.

"Why do you have to stop being friends with her when this is done?" Jackson asked.

Owens looked at him with anger. "What am I supposed to do? Huh? I don't have the answers all the time like you."

"Who said I have all the answers?"

"You never did anything you weren't sure of." Owens told him, which caused him to roar with laughter.

"That's what you think?" Jackson said, his tone somber again. "Three years ago, I let my partner make a mistake he could never take back." He said, looking straight ahead at the wall of photos behind the bar. "I knew Rent was going to do something, I didn't know what but I knew he was going to do something. I thought about stopping him but I didn't."

"You always say that we're only responsible for our own actions." Owens told him.

"Yeah but I let my friend ruin his life. I let him take the rap and a stone cold killer walked." Jackson said. "He could never take it back. Pierce was right. What Carey Rent did before he died doesn't absolve him of what he did when he was a cop. I saw what happens to a man when he makes a mistake he can't fix. I saw it when Collins had that little girl's grandfather killed and I know that Carey Rent is turning over in his grave knowing that Collins might actually get away with it all."

"Is there a point to this?" Owens asked.

"Carey Rent did something that he regretted for the rest of his life. I don't want you to do the same." Jackson told him. "You won't have a second chance this time. And you'll regret not being there."

"What if I'm there and I regret it?" Owens' voice broke slightly. "God already took one person I loved away from me. I'm not going to let him take another." His voice was bitter.

"Is that how it works?" Jackson asked. "She can ride out a death sentence but if you wash your hands of her, it all goes away?" Jackson didn't mean to be so blunt about it but he could see the desire to run in his partner's words. He'd seen that desire many times before, mostly with romantic interests that Owens didn't want to get too attached to. Jackson knew why too. What if he did get attached? Then what if they up and left? Like that girl years ago, that he can't forget. Owens answer to that problem was to run, whenever he felt himself getting close to somebody, anybody; he would turn and run, run for his life.

"Yeah that's how it works." Owens confirmed.

"Maybe I look at it a little bit differently." Jackson argued. "Maybe I don't see loss waiting to happen. What I see is finally a person who means something to you. Somebody you can't push away. You have to realize something about life. We lose those we care about. We can't have them forever, that's why its so important to cherish the time we have with them. The time we have with those we care about is fleeting. Its not about having them forever, its about how they enrich our lives when we do have them. Not only for us but for them. Right now that little girl is heartbroken because her friend isn't there with her."

"What would you do?" Owens asked.

"I'd tell her mother to go to hell." Jackson replied. Owens let out a laugh.

"She's just looking out for her. Even I gotta admit, she hit the nail on the head with me."

"It's a pretty big nail. Hard to miss." Jackson chided. "Why don't you show her that Kaylee means more to you than she thinks?"

"What happens when the time finally comes?" Owens thought aloud, more to himself than Jackson.

"I'll be here for you."

"Isn't that like dropping a piano on you after you've fallen off a building?" Owens said, a slight humor returning to him.

"That's why you got friends. So when you lose somebody close, they can help you out." Jackson smiled. "Come on, I'll drive you home."

"Yeah, just give me a minute will you?" Owens got up and wandered, zombie-like to the restroom. Jackson downed the remainder of his soda.

"I hope you're getting him out of here?" The bartender asked.

"Yeah why?" Jackson returned. "He owe a tab or something?"

"Absolutely not," was the quick reply, "I learned that lesson on the anniversary of Dale Earnhardt's death."

"Was he getting loud, what?" Jackson asked, slightly confused. An embarrassed look crossed the bartender's face and he leaned in to Jackson.

"Ok, he put almost forty bucks in the jukebox and quite frankly I'm getting sick of listening to Kansas."

"Gotcha." Jackson grinned. Owens emerged from the restroom. "You know what they say," Jackson tapped the bar before walking to the door, "*Carry On Wayward Son.*"

13

"Recompense"

Courtney opened the front door to see Owens, a little yellow teddy bear in his hands. The two of them stared at each other for a moment, neither knowing what to say. Courtney couldn't help but feel bad for the man in front of her, the sad look on his face told his entire story. It told how much the situation was hurting him, how devastating the news that she'd given him two nights ago was. She remembered having that look on her own face the day that the doctors told her about Kaylee's condition and she suddenly took pity on him.

"I wanted to say..." Owens broke the silence, "that I'm sorry about the other night."

"You don't have to be." She honestly replied. "Do you see

now why Kaylee needs to be happy? She doesn't have any time to waste Jesse."

"I'm not going to hurt her." Owens stated.

"That remains to be seen."

"Well where I come from, we don't abandon people." He told her.

"Where you come from people eat roadkill."

"I guess I deserved that one." Owens said empathetically. "I got her something."

"Yeah," Courtney said, looking at the teddy bear, "why does it have a palm tree on it?" Owens looked down at the bear. He hadn't really thought about why a little yellow bear would have the picture of a palm tree stitched on its belly, he thought it looked cute though.

"You know, I really...um...I have no clue." He stammered. Courtney smiled slightly at his lack of reasoning.

"She's upstairs doing her homework." Courtney told him, then moved from in front of the door so that he could enter. He found Mason picking up her things to leave. She patted Courtney on the back and assured her that she'd be back at midnight then closed the door behind her. Owens found the interchange slightly odd, typically Mason never showed anyone any affection. Owens shrugged it off and made his way upstairs into Kaylee's room.

The little girl was sitting at her computer, clicking its mouse furiously. Owens silently sat on her bed, the teddy bear in hand.

Kaylee knew he was there but chose not to acknowledge him.

"How are you feeling little sister?" He asked. Kaylee looked at him for a moment then turned back to the computer in silence. "You know I'm really sorry about not being here yesterday." Kaylee kept clicking, she was trying to find the file folder that contained her English paper but wasn't having any luck.

"You're a jerk." She said, partly with frustration at not being able to locate her paper.

"Believe it or not, I've been told that." Owens conceded. "I got you something, kind of an anti-gallstone present." He said. Kaylee looked over at the bear.

"Why does it have a palm tree on it?" She asked.

"You know, I've been asking myself that question since I walked in the door."

"You do know I'm a little old for stuffed animals?" She informed.

"Nobody's too old for bears and palm trees." Owens defended, putting the bear on her pillow. "Look, I'm not good at this. The truth is that I went to the hospital to see you and I got scared. I needed some time to think." He admitted. Kaylee swivelled in her chair to face him.

"You're a jerk." She teased, then turned back to her computer.

"Yes, yes I am." He smiled, feeling her forgiveness lift a weight from his shoulders. "What are you doing?" He inquired.

"I'm looking for my homework. I can't find it." She said, clicking on a file and pulling up an Excel spreadsheet.

"That's just tax stuff." Owens glanced at the screen. "Click out of it." Kaylee closed the spreadsheet then clicked out of the folder, then out of another, then another until she got to her system screen. "There's your problem." Owens observed. "You weren't in your hard drive, you were in your USB device."

"What's a USB device?" She asked.

"Anything that hooks into that little port at the bottom there."

"I don't have anything in there." Kaylee told him. Owens looked down at the front of the computer's tower, both USB ports were empty.

"No, I guess you don't." He said. "Why would it say you do?" He thought out loud.

"You were scared over gallstones?" Kaylee changed the subject while Owens kept looking at her computer. "That's nothing. The first day of school I stabbed myself in the leg with a fork because I was mad that mommy left me there. You wanna see scared, you should've seen that kindergarten teacher."

"That's weird." Owens said, talking about the computer.

"Yeah, if you ask me, you grownups get upset about every little thing." She said. Owens started looking at the back of the computer tower.

"They usually have some USB ports around the back." He told her.

"So I had some gallstones, big deal, its not the worst thing I ever had, yet anytime something happens to little Kaylee, everybody freaks..." She began ranting. He reached his hand back between the plentiful wires until he found the familiar shape of a memory stick. He pulled the memory stick out from behind the computer and read the word "Drive A" on it.

"...I think that you guys should all just chill out." Kaylee was continuing her rant. Giving up on doing her homework, she got out of her chair and headed out the door. "Between everybody going nuts at the least little thing..." Owens stared at the memory stick, knowing what it was. "And me not being able to do anything, I'm going crazy. Not to mention that no matter what happens I always have more homework to do. That's the only normal part of my life. Are you listening?" She asked from the hallway.

"Of course, no freaking out, homework normal, got it." Owens gave her a thumbs up and picked his cell phone out of his pocket.

"When is everybody going to realize that I'm completely normal!" Kaylee blustered at him playfully, then turned her voice to the stairs. "Mom!" She yelled. "I'm coming down the stairs now."

Courtney positioned herself at the bottom of the stairs to ensure Kaylee didn't fall. "Hold on babygirl." Courtney yelled back. "Ok, come on."

"I'm completely normal." Kaylee grabbed the handrail and carefully made her way down. Owens looked at the memory stick and put the phone to his ear.

"What the hell is this?" Rothstein put the memory stick into the USB port of the mainframe. "I asked for extra cheese, there isn't any cheese at all!"

"No," Johnson replied, "I got it right here." He unfolded a sheet of paper detailing everyone's orders. "See, it says no cheese for you."

"I asked for no cheese." Holloman stated. "There's extra cheese on mine. I can't eat all this cheese, I'm on a diet." Jackson rolled his eyes and bit a chunk out of his hoagie.

"It says right here that you wanted extra cheese." Johnson defended.

"How many times have I asked for cheese Joel?" Holloman argued.

"Hey, why don't you just give your cheese to Ari and be done with it?" Casteel asked, unwrapping his sub.

"It has low-fat mayo all over it, I can't eat that, it tastes like shit." Rothstein objected.

"I don't know why not, you could use it. Ben you want this cheese?" Holloman returned.

"Quit it with the damn cheese!" Jackson finally ordered. "What's on that thing."

"It looks like some tax returns." Rothstein said, his mouth full of bread, ham, salami, pepperoni, turkey, roast beef, lettuce, tomato, onions, mushrooms, green peppers, olives, pickles, salt, pepper, oil, vinegar, but no cheese. "It's pretty normal stuff really. Thanks Joel, I could've had a good lunch."

"Damon wouldn't have had him killed for that, there's got to be more." Jackson said after swallowing a bite. "It's ok Joel, as long as you got my order right."

"Let me search for hidden files." Rothstein hit a few buttons on the keyboard and clicked the mouse a few times between bites of his sandwich, the lack of cheese causing him disdain. "Here's one." He pulled up a file of five addresses with corresponding numbers which looked like dollar amounts and some other numbers.

"I know these addresses." Casteel leaned in. "All these places are hot."

"What's that mean?" McCall asked from the back, surprising everyone with his presence.

"Why aren't you in there testing?" Jackson asked, annoyed.

"The first test of the Celebrex didn't come out right, I have to retest, it'll take a little while longer, it's in the centrifuge now. What's hot mean?" McCall replied.

"They're known drug labs, we've been collecting evidence on them." Johnson informed.

"Yeah, we've been after two of these for about six months now. Haven't been able to get a warrant yet." Casteel added.

"These must be the labs he used to make the drugs." Rothstein told them. "These last numbers might be how much they made or how much of the drugs that they're holding for him."

"Which means that what's in Jimmy Nguyen's cargo ship might not be all there is?" Johnson speculated.

"I doubt it, Collins is a thinker, it's all about mind games with him. Who's smarter. He wouldn't put all his eggs in one basket." Jackson said.

"What about the money, that's above par for lab work?" Casteel asked.

"Let's see, add it up." Rothstein clicked a few keys. "It comes out to over two million."

"They must be holding it for him. He does that so that he can't be linked to it." Jackson informed.

"You guys didn't ask me if I wanted lunch." McCall observed.

"I got some cheese if you want it?" Holloman told him.

"Casteel, get this to Knox, we're going to have to move on these places too." Jackson ordered.

"Alright but the DEA has a hold on all evidence collected, she'll have to give it to them."

"Then make a copy first." Jackson told him.

"Already done boss." Rothstein informed. Holloman handed McCall the cheese to shove in his mouth.

When his phone started chirping the familiar sounds of

Sonny and Cher's *I Got You Babe*, Casteel reached into his pocket and retrieved it. He listened with the phone to his ear for a few seconds then thanked the caller and closed the phone.

"Get this, that was our guy watching the DEA offices." Casteel told them.

"Why is he watching them?" Holloman asked.

"Because we don't have any idea where Collins is and I was hoping the DEA might lead us to him." Jackson explained. "What is it?"

"He says that a fully loaded DEA Tactical team just rolled."

"Where the hell are they going?" Rothstein asked.

"I don't know but we'd better find out." Jackson returned.

"First time out?" Special Agent Pierce asked the agent steadfastly checking his M-4 assault rifle. He didn't have much room to work with the weapon safely inside the SUV but attempted to check it anyway, nervousness taking hold of him.

"That easy to tell huh?" The agent, Mark Baker, an inexperienced twenty-two year old with two children and a wife asked.

"It's alright, we've got a lot of firepower, these things always go well." Pierce confidently told him. Baker smiled and adjusted his utility vest to try to get more comfortable.

"We're approaching the target." The tactical team leader in the first SUV said over the radio. "Prepare to move."

"Everybody ready?" Pierce asked, he watched Baker and the two agents in the front seats give thumbs up before pressing the button on his radio. "Car 2 is ready."

"Car 3 is ready." They heard over the radio. When the SUV's turned onto the road that contained the church, they sped up, then broke fast, careful not to squeal their tires and came to a stop right next to a fire hydrant that was in front of the church. Three of the four doors opened on the SUV's concurrently and the Tac team got out and ran to the front doors of the church, their weapons pointing right in front of them.

One of the members of the Tac team took out a large hammer and slammed it into the door. Instantly the nine members of the team, including Pierce entered the church and scanned for threats. Once they were all in and finding no threats, they moved through the rows of pews slowly and carefully.

The point man approached the altar, Pierce, not far behind, stopped and looked down at the picture that Damon left for him. He got down on one knee and looked away from the sights of his rifle at the picture. Baker, who was next to him, lowered his body and continued to a better defensive position next to a pew where there was more cover.

The point man scanned the altar for threats but didn't find anything out of place while the second man watched the side door that was slightly cracked. The rear guard had his sights trained on the small balcony that overlooked the pews. Pierce reached down and touched the broken picture frame with his gloved hands.

Damon's five mercenaries were positioned perfectly for the attack. Scar, the oldest was with Carlyle behind one of the side doors that led to the alter, Damon was behind the other side door. Blood, a gangbanger, was positioned outside, camouflaged by some bushes under a stained glass window. Brute, the extremely large one, was with Musk, given his name because of his short, bulky frame, in the balcony.

A flashbang grenade rolled out of the cracked side door. Before anyone could react, the flashbang went off in a blinding and deafening array of sound and light. The rear guard was the only member of the team not blinded but his ears were ringing loudly. Panic struck him when he saw a grenade arch over the wall of the balcony.

"Grenade!" He yelled but no one heard him. He dashed for cover. The cracked side door opened wide, giving Damon a clear field of fire with his AK-47. The opposite side door also burst open allowing Scar and Carlyle to begin firing with their automatic weapons. Blood used the butt of an M-16 to knock out a pane on the stained glass window on the side of the church through which he could fire at his targets. Brute emerged from the balcony the moment his grenade exploded and aided by Musk, laid down devastating fire with the M-60 machine gun. Because of the close range, the 7.62 millimeter and 5.56 millimeter rounds ripped through the DEA agents, along with their body armor.

The attack occurred so fast and with such ferocity that the DEA agents barely had any time at all to return fire and what shots were fired went wild. Within ten seconds the entire DEA tactical team lay on the floor of the church, either dead or dying.

Upon hearing the flashbang explode, Olsen, who was sitting in the unmarked DEA car next to the body of the DEA agent who had been watching the church, hit a small red button on a detonator. The explosives placed in the fire hydrant rolled the DEA SUV's across the street, their own gas tanks exploding, killing all three drivers.

The group soon emerged from their respective covers, satisfied with what they'd accomplished. Wishing to inspect the work, Damon handed his weapon to Carlyle. He approached Pierce, who was attempting to crawl over Baker's bullet ridden body. He was attempting to take out his sidearm but several wounds up and down his body including shrapnel from the grenade was preventing him from doing so. Damon grabbed his bloodied utility vest and flipped him onto his back. He picked up the strategically placed photograph of his brother before placing a knee on Pierce's chest, causing blood to spurt out of his wounds.

"Special Agent Pierce?" Damon read the nametag on the vest and opened a pouch, removing Pierce's Leatherman Multitool. "It's nice to finally meet you in person." He told the man who was now choking on his own blood. "But I'm sure the pleasure is all mine." Slowly, he opened the serrated blade. "Give my regards to my brother." He spat in Pierce's face before slamming the blade into Pierce's throat and sawing it open. He placed the picture of his brother on Pierce's chest and wiped his hands on a piece of cloth he had taken from his pocket. "Bring the car." He said into a cheap two-way radio. The car, an old stationwagon pulled into the yard behind the church and the mercenaries quickly loaded their weapons into the back of it.

"We're ready, I've already called the trucks." Olsen told Damon from the driver's seat.

"Good," he said and turned to Scar, "you know what to do." Scar nodded, he, Brute, and Musk got into the stationwagon next to Eddie's former lawyer. Damon turned to Blood and Carlyle, who had just pulled up in the second car. He got into the backseat and the car sped away to the ominous resonance of sirens looming in the distance.

Owens took his cell phone out of his pocket, looked at the text message from Kimberly Mason that said she'd be slightly late relieving him and put it on the table so that he could more easily pour some coffee into the mug that he'd taken to using when staying at the Taylor house. He added three teaspoons of sugar and some milk before picking it up and taking it into the living room where Courtney was brushing her daughter's hair. Owens quietly sat down with his coffee and watched the primetime logo of the national network flash across the television. When Courtney saw it, she looked at the clock above the tv.

"It's time to hit the sack babygirl." She told Kaylee.

"It's still early." Kaylee argued.

"That's right and we have a doctor's appointment tomorrow morning and have to get up. So lets go."

Kaylee admitted defeat and left her mother's lap. Courtney expected her daughter to go straight upstairs, change and get ready for their nightly checks. Instead, Kaylee made a pit stop at Owens, whom she hugged and said goodnight to before going back to her routine. Courtney felt the sudden urge to smile, even though it was upsetting that Kaylee was taking to someone other than her. She was glad that Owens made her forget about the loss of her grandfather. Suddenly the thought hit her that Kaylee should be angry with him. Why wasn't she?

"Did you tell her that you wouldn't be coming around when this is over?" Courtney asked him while he sipped on his coffee. Owens didn't reply, though Courtney could tell that he was trying to formulate the right words.

"I wanted to talk to you about that." He told her.

"There isn't anything to talk about." She returned, mildly angry. "Do you understand what she's going to be like after you leave with no explanation whatsoever?" Courtney turned her eyes from him in disgust. "You're a coward." She added before going upstairs.

Owens put his coffee down on a table. Maybe she was right? Maybe he was a coward. Maybe he only decided to come back because he couldn't bear to know that Kaylee would be sad without him. Maybe that was cowardice. Then again he knew that either way was going to be hard. *Dave is right.* He thought. *It's not how long she's with us, it's what we do with the time she has.* Owens took comfort, however little, in that.

"Dave?" Casteel asked.

"Yeah." Jackson answered his cell phone.

"I found the DEA Tac team. They're out at a church in Shoreline." Casteel informed. Several more forensic detectives pushed by him, on their way into the crime scene.

"They get Collins?" Jackson asked.

"More like Collins got them." He replied with a sour voice. "It's a Goddamn massacre, and it's got Collins' picture on it...literally."

"Hold on." Jackson looked at his cell after he heard his call waiting chime. It was an unknown number. Jackson clicked over and recognized the voice.

"Hello David." Damon said jovially. "You should really look into who has your private information. Phone numbers, financial records, even home addresses are all up for grabs if you know where to look."

"It's done Damon, you're caught, the only way out of this is to give yourself up." Jackson told him, his voice angry at the mention of his home address.

"On the contrary, the DEA was just the beginning." Damon replied. "There are scores to settle and wrongs to avenge. I'm going to have my recompense from you, whether you like it or not." Jackson didn't reply, he knew that if Damon had killed the DEA Tactical team, he was indeed just beginning a much larger plan. "I'm glad you understand. The first part of making amends is to suffer the same grief you've given."

"You touch anybody, you'll seal your fate with me!" Jackson exploded.

"This my old friend is what you might call deja vu. It's ironic that you receive the exact same phone call as Rent, just hours before you die, like he did." Damon told him. Jackson listened, becoming angrier with every word. "Now listen up, we're going to play the same game Rent played. You took my family, now I'm going to take yours but just like Rent, you can get them back. All you have to do is sacrifice yourself for them, the same as Rent."

"I wouldn't have made you for a copycat." Jackson observed, anger in his voice.

"I'm broadening my horizons."

"When and where?" Jackson asked, his whole body shaking with a mixture of fear and anger.

"Not so fast, that's not the game. I don't wanna walk into a place where I'll be surrounded by one of your famous SWAT teams." Damon smiled in the joy of his manipulation. "Just like Rent, you have to find me. If you don't find me by two o'clock, game over." The line went dead.

The instant he saw that Damon was no longer on the line, Jackson bolted from the waiting room like a bullet. He knocked three lab technicians over and grabbed a uniformed officer's radio right out of it's holster in his flight through the lobby.

Screaming his home address into the radio, he darted through the parking garage to his Mustang. A turn of the key and yank of the shifter brought the muscle car squealing from it's parking spot, leaving tire treads halfway to the exit of the parking garage.

Frantically negotiating the busy evening traffic of Seattle, he heard the dispatcher sending units to his home. He sped through a red light, narrowly avoiding a pickup and causing a three car pileup. Seeing four full lanes of traffic stopped at another red light, Jackson spun the Mustang left and down a narrow alley full of boxes and dumpsters.

With its horn honking repeatedly, the Mustang skidded from the alley and onto another busy street. Jackson crossed into oncoming traffic to avoid another traffic jam and ended up causing two more accidents before he could get back in his own lane. Two more lights and one left turn put him on the street that his house was on. The patrol units hadn't arrived yet, Jackson was the first and stopped the Mustang in the front yard on top of one of his wife's prized flower beds.

Jackson quickly yanked open his glove compartment and removed a 9mm Beretta then rushed the front door of his house, his weapon in front of him, ready to acquire a target.

Slamming the unlocked front door of the house open, he moved in tactically, methodically going through the downstairs, keeping his gun trained on both his line of sight and possible threat points. He entered the kitchen and saw Marcy, in her pajamas, preparing some crackers and cheese to snack on. She turned to see him, let out a yelp and flinched hard.

"Where are the kids?" Jackson yelled at her. Marcy couldn't reply for a few seconds, the surprise of her husband entering the kitchen with a gun having scared her senseless. "Where are the kids?" He repeated.

"Up..upstairs." She finally blurted. Jackson moved instantly to the staircase, training his weapon forward during his ascent up them. Marcy followed, a few steps behind her husband. He checked the boys' room first. Both were awakened when their father burst through their door. Seeing no threat, Jackson heard the sound of a door slam from his daughter's room, he turned and rushed it.

Two patrol cars arrived simultaneously. Seeing the front

door wide open and the Mustang in the grass, both officers drew their sidearms and entered the house tactically.

A swift kick flung the door to Tonya's room open. Tonya dropped the telephone and screamed hysterically when she saw her father enter her room. He instantly pointed his gun upward and allowed his mind to work again.

"Lieutenant!" The patrolmen were yelling from the stairs. "Lieutenant, where are you?"

"Clear!" Jackson yelled. "We're clear here!"

"What's going on?" Marcy screamed at him. She wrapped herself around her crying daughter and comforted her in her arms.

"Wait a minute." Jackson said aloud, his mind churning a mile a second. "I didn't take his family." He thought a moment longer. "I took his brother!" Jackson grabbed the phone off the bed, cut off the call that was on the line, got a new dial tone and punched seven numbers. "C'mon, pickup, pickup!" He said to himself. "Get units to the Taylor residence, now!" He yelled to the patrolmen, then gave them the address.

Owens was looking out the front windows pondering what Courtney had said to him. Was she right? Was he supposed to give Kaylee up? He'd decided last night that he wasn't but Courtney clearly wasn't going to give him a chance to prove it.

The sound of his cell phone broke his concentration. He instinctively reached into his pants pocket to retrieve it, then remembered that he'd left it on the kitchen table. He crossed the living and dining rooms to the kitchen and picked up the ringing phone. Opening it he put it to his ear.

"Owens." He said but all he heard was a dial tone, the call had gone to his voicemail. He closed the phone, put it back on the table, then glanced up at the back door that led from the kitchen to the yard, it was cracked open, which was unusual. He slowly approached the door, listening intently. The ring of the phone once again broke the silence.

Damon stood in the laundry room, whose empty door frame was next to the rear kitchen door. He listened to the phone continue to ring, readied his Desert Eagle and prepared to attack. He started to move but was stopped by the barrel of Owens' police issue .45.

"Lookie what I caught!" Owens said, aiming his weapon at Damon. Carlyle came around Owens from behind. Before Owens knew he was there, Carlyle had slammed his elbow down onto Owens' gun arm and Owens' gun dropped from his hand. Blood seized Owens from behind and dragged him outside into the backyard. Blood and Carlyle proceeded to punch and kick Owens, causing him to slosh around on the ground.

Damon soon emerged from the house, Owens' gun in one

hand. When Blood and Carlyle saw him, they stopped beating Owens and turned him on his back. Damon tossed Owens' gun deep into the yard then put a knee in Owens chest to hold him in place.

"Rent would have never let himself get nailed like this. That's panache." Damon told him, then stood straight up and turned to Blood. "Do whatever you want with him, just as long as he dies." Blood smirked.

"You hear that?" Blood whispered into Owens' ear after Damon and Carlyle reentered the house. "You're all mine." Owens tried to reach up but Blood punched him in the face and he went back down. "You don't remember me do you? A year ago you busted me for intent to resell. What comes around, goes around, don't it?" Blood decided that to stay outside was too exposed so he grabbed Owens in a headlock and began dragging him into the house. When they passed through the kitchen, Blood pulled a large knife from it's stand.

"I'm going to cut me some country fried steak." Blood laughed. When they got into the living room, Owens got some traction with his feet and broke away from Blood's grip. Owens pushed Blood away, who swiped at him with the knife, barely missing him. Blood came back in with a downward stroke. Owens caught Blood's knife hand but Blood used his free hand to smash Owens in the face. His head already throbbing, Owens fell backward into the staircase, breaking the banister from it's base.

Before Owens could recover and get up, Blood slammed his

foot into Owens' chest, pinning him down.

Damon met Courtney coming out of her bedroom to check on Kaylee one last time. She started to scream but he leveled his gun at her and she stopped. He grabbed her by her nightgown and threw her in her room. "Get dressed." He ordered.

Kaylee screamed in horror when Carlyle came into her room. Owens heard the scream, couldn't bear it and got his second wind. Blood came in with the knife. Owens grabbed the broken banister and slammed it against Blood's knife wielding hand. Blood dropped the knife, was smacked in the head with the bannister and fell. Owen jumped up and stood atop Blood, beating him mercilessly with the large piece of wood.

"I guess you're going to get a country fried ass-whoopin instead!" He continued beating Blood, who was covering himself to minimize the blows.

"No! Get out!" Kaylee screamed. She held onto the bed frame as Carlyle tried to pull her from the room. Owens heard the scream and dashed up the stairs. He entered the room, swinging the broken banister like a baseball bat. Owens' first swing evaporated on Carlyle's forearm, which he got up to protect his head just in time. Carlyle grabbed the banister and the two wrestled for control of it.

"Jesse!" Kaylee began screaming out of worry.

Damon heard Kaylee's screams and left Courtney in her bedroom to investigate. He found Carlyle slamming Owens into Kaylee's dresser mirror during their struggle for the banister. Damon raised his gun to shoot Owens but before he could fire, Carlyle thrust him out the bedroom window.

Owens' entire body fell out the window and landed on the pitched roof over the back yard below it. He hung onto the bannister, Carlyle–who didn't want to let go while Owens was still alive–supported both their weight. Kaylee tried to run out the door but was caught by Damon's hand around the back of her neck. Furious, he pulled Kaylee to the window with him.

Owens saw Damon's Desert Eagle emerge from the window and knew that he'd lost this fight. Just before Damon fired, Owens let go of the banister and slid off the tiled roof, falling into some shrubs surrounding the house. The bullet missed Owens by inches, hitting the storm gutter instead.

Disappointed, Damon yanked Kaylee into the hallway, where he found Courtney, dressed. She could have escaped but wouldn't leave without her daughter. He motioned her with his gun to come along and dragged the little girl down the stairs.

Bloodied, his head ringing, his eyesight blurry and his chest in pain, Owens forced himself off his back. He rolled over and spotted the chrome of his gun reflecting the houselights. He quickly made his way to it, falling twice. Struggling to keep it out in front of him, he staggered around the house to see Damon, Carlyle, and Blood along with their hostages driving off in a sedan that his blurry vision couldn't make out. He fell against the front porch and prayed that someone had heard the shot and called 911.

14

"Warrants"

When conducting a raid, anything can go wrong. This was a lesson that the DEA learned, a little over an hour ago, painfully. Twelve DEA Agents, good men, patriotic, courageous, had perished. They'd been ambushed by a vengeful criminal who was determined to make right the wrongs he believed the world had committed against him. Damon Collins didn't care about the lives or the families of the DEA agents he took from the world. He didn't care about the lives of the hostages he was holding, to him they were simply bargaining chips. He had hoped to have killed Seattle narcotics detective Jesse Owens also but Owens had narrowly escaped the fate of his DEA counterparts.

Now, Damon Collins and his crew were on the run, they were

hiding, probably somewhere in the Seattle area. Why they weren't on a boat to Mexico wasn't certain, perhaps Damon really did want his recompense like he'd told Jackson? Jackson didn't believe that was what Damon was really after. Damon was too smart to bring down the heat he had over revenge, it was something he just wouldn't do.

If an escaped convict kills a patrolman who makes a traffic stop, a multi-state manhunt is automatically engaged. Law enforcement protects their own and will go to any lengths to find the killer of a cop. Damon Collins just killed twelve and not just street cops, federal Drug Enforcement Administration agents. He must know, he was smart enough to know, that American law enforcement, all of them, would hunt him unmercifully until he was dead. It didn't matter if he went to Guatemala or Istanbul or sat in the burnt out nuclear reactors of Chernobyl, law enforcement would pursue him to the ends of the earth now. Damon Collins had just signed his own death warrant and what was worse was that Jackson knew that Damon was intelligent enough to understand that. He knew Damon had to have planned it out, which scared him because one doesn't plan to mass murder federal agents and expect to be home in time to watch the evening football game. Right now, Damon Collins was capable of anything. So was Jackson.

Jackson was sitting at the long conference table catty-corner from Knox's office. Sitting on the other side of the table was Owens, who was holding an icepack to his head and had just downed half a bottle of pain killers. Sitting at the other chairs surrounding the table where the members of Narcotics Squads one, two, and three, which constituted the bulk of Seattle Police Department's Narcotics Division. All remained grim and silent, nobody spoke, most held their heads low. They sat at the table, some standing at the back due to the lack of table space, thinking about the events that had transpired in the last hour, some angry, others saddened by the loss of good men, peers, people in whose position they easily could have been.

Inside Knox's office was Knox herself, Assistant District Attorney Burke and Chief Tibbs. Every officer in the conference room struggled to make out what was being said through the closed door. They could see through the windows of the office that the conversation was quite lively, at least from Chief Tibbs' perspective. He was pacing the office, waving his arms, pointing angrily, and yelling. Not all of Tibbs' harangue could be made out, what could be heard didn't seem to be good. Knox and Burke each stood in front of the Chief, their heads lowered like children being scolded by a parent.

"One of the biggest dealers this city has ever seen..." Could be understood when Tibbs practically screamed it at the two subordinates, as was "An entire DEA Tactical team..." He continued yelling but nobody in the conference room could make out what it was, they did understand his last phrase of the rant. "And in my goddamn city!" They saw through the windows that Knox spoke to the Chief, followed by Burke, who handed the Chief something he eagerly took. Tibbs replied with something loud but not quite a yell. Knox opened the drawer to her desk and took some items out.

The grim trio finally opened the door to the office and entered the conference room. Chief Tibbs stood for a few moments, surveying his men. His face was expressionless, he didn't want his men to see his emotion at this moment but his eyes were covered in a vest of purposeful confidence which gave him away.

"Are you alright?" He quietly asked Owens.

Owens removed the icepack from his face. "Yes sir." He replied, equally quietly.

Tibbs pointed at Jackson. "You're back on the job effective right now." Knox carefully placed his badge and gun on the table next to him. Tibbs turned to the rest of his men and his voice turned from calm and quiet to loud and commanding.

"This is a fucking mess." He addressed everyone then looked at Jackson. "Fix it!" He slapped the folded papers he was holding onto the table and walked out with Burke in tow. Jackson looked up at Knox.

"I'm alerting the on-call patrols, they'll be at your disposal. I'm also giving you Air One. Captain Carrasco's SWAT team will be suited up and ready to move at any time should you need them." She told him. Jackson nodded. "Dave, if you cross the line, you're on your own." Jackson nodded again. "Good hunting, be safe." She said to the group before leaving the room.

Seattle Police Department's Narcotics Unit all looked at Lieutenant Jackson. He sat for a moment, staring at the large triple folded pieces of paper the Chief left. He slowly reached over and picked them up. Opening them, he knew what they were; Search and Seizure warrants for all five drug labs found on the memory stick, plus one for Jimmy Nguyen's cargo ship.

"Casteel?" Jackson said, reading over the warrants.

"Here boss." Casteel returned.

"Get'em ready. We're going to do this old school." Jackson ordered. Casteel nodded.

"Alright, you heard the man," Casteel yelled, "I want everybody downstairs and ready to move in ten minutes! Full Battle Rattle! Let's go people!" The unit picked themselves up from their chairs with purpose except Jackson who continued to read the warrants.

Walking out the door Owens dropped his icepack into a trash can. "Let the bodies hit the floor."

207 E. Harrison Street was a rundown apartment building in Capitol Hill. It was three stories tall, contained eighteen apartments per floor and a rusty fire escape on it's east side. It was the type of place where the tenants were forced to pay each month in advance and the police got 911 calls nightly.

Jackson led N.S.1 out of the staircase on the third floor.

Flushing down the hallway, each member chambered their weapons. They wore jackets which said "POLICE" on the back and bulletproof vests underneath. They had their badges clearly displayed on necklaces and had traded in their belt holsters for quick draw combat drop holsters that were fastened to their belts with a strap that hooked around their leg for added stability. Casteel's was the only pistol still holstered.

When Jackson arrived at the door, he said nothing, he simply pointed to it with two fingers. Casteel came around him with the shotgun. He aimed just below the top corner of the door and blew off the top hinge, leaving a giant hole where it had been. Pump. Bottom hinge. A powerful kick sent the door crashing to the carpeted apartment floor.

Within seconds, the entire squad was in the apartment securing three of the four men inside along with two underage girls. A deafening barrage of yells promptly erupted; "Police, let me see your hands!" "Show me your hands!" "Executing a search warrant!" "Drop that weapon!" "Get on the floor! Get on the floor!" "Move and you're dead!" The squad threw suspects on the floor, slammed them against walls, tables, counters, televisions, even the bathroom sink.

The fourth suspect ran to the bedroom window when he heard the first shotgun blast and thought he was making his getaway on the fire escape when he found himself staring into the barrel of a Smith and Wesson. "Where do you think you're going?" He was asked before being slammed violently on the metal grating and cuffed.

"We're clear, bring them in." Jackson radioed. Within seconds, N.S.3 arrived carrying boxes marked: *Paraphernalia*, *Money*, *Drugs*, *Weapons*, and *Personal Effects*. "I wanna be packed and ready to move in five minutes!" Virtually everything that wasn't nailed down in the apartment was thrown into the boxes. After only a few minutes, N.S.3 members were taping the lids of the full boxes with evidence tape, initialing them and hauling them downstairs. "I want forensics to print and analyze everything in here, no matter how small, make sure it gets done." Jackson ordered one of the patrolmen he'd been given.

"Dave." Owens got his attention. "This is Mr. Adams, the owner of this grand plaza." He stood in front of a blonde haired man in his twenties who was sitting in a chair, his hands cuffed behind his back. Jackson stepped quickly over to him, put his face inches from his suspect's and grabbed his shirt.

"I have a deal for you." Jackson stared menacingly into his eyes. "If I get what I want, I'll let you walk, no questions asked." Adams returned a scared look and swallowed. "Where is Damon Collins?"

"I don't know." Adams very much wished that he did know.

Jackson let go of him and stood straight up. "Get this piece of shit out of my sight."

6129 Beacon Street was a chop shop at the corner of Beacon and 15th Avenue. To increase their cash flow, they had turned part of their garage into a meth lab. The building was large, with many entrances and exits. Jackson chose to ram the Police Intelligence van straight through their garage doors. Within seconds, all three narcotics squads were sweeping the building, taking down any person on the premises, cuffing them and throwing them into the back of the van, which they had cleaned out.

The takedown went similar to the first, with a lot of yelling, threats, overwhelming force and intimidation. Jackson again found that no one at the location knew the whereabouts of Collins and again boxes were brought in to take the evidence away.

1301 Plum Street was a residence in a fairly nice neighborhood close to downtown Seattle. The neighbors were astonished when they looked out their windows to see the members of the Police Department's narcotics unit use a hand held battering ram to knock in the front door and enter the house.

Two suspects, the matriarch and patriarch of the family of six, were apprehended. The patriarch almost having to be shot because when the raid commenced, he'd grabbed for his sawed off shotgun. "Drop that weapon or you're dead!" Owens yelled at him. He quickly put the weapon down, was slammed on his wooden floor and handcuffed. The four children found in the makeshift crack cocaine factory which ranged in age from six months to eight years were handed over to the patrols to await the Department of Human Services personnel. The evidence in the house was bagged and tagged and after intense questioning by Jackson, it was determined that neither the mother nor the father knew where their business associate was.

The fourth warrant was for a shack on the outskirts of Jefferson Park Golf Course. It had been unused by the golf course groundskeepers for several years and two wily college students had commandeered it, turning it into a processing plant for the drug ecstacy. The narcotics units came out of the surrounding woods silently and before both students knew what had occurred, they were on the dusty floor of the shack, their hands cuffed behind their backs.

The evidence was packed into the boxes. Jackson interrogated the students but neither knew where Damon was hiding. Both students were scared out of their minds at having been caught with enough money, ecstacy and paraphernalia to send them to prison for twenty-five years and Jackson knew that if they had any clue whatsoever as to where Damon was, they'd have talked.

The fifth warrant was for an unused weight gym that had been abandoned when the company that owned it moved to a new location. One of the managers at the gym had moved in and was using it to manufacture illegal steroids, which he would sell to the gym members at the new location. He and two chemists that were splitting the profits with him were quickly taken down when the narcotics unit converged on them.

Once again the detectives packaged the evidence. Jackson took the gym manager into the locker room to ask him a few questions. Frustrated, Owens grabbed one of the chemists, hit him a few times, then slammed him on a table and put a gun to his head.

"Where's Collins?" Owens screamed at him. "Tell me or so help me God, we'll be picking your brains off the ceiling!"

"Jesse, that's not how it's done." Casteel told him, standing in front of the open locker room door. "You put a gun to somebody's head, they'll tell you anything, even if they don't know anything, you can never trust information gained that way. Besides which, the policy of this police department is to treat every suspect regardless of how much we know he's guilty with the dignity and respect that every human being deserves." Owens looked up at Casteel. "Take a lesson. Nobody and I do mean nobody knows how to treat a suspect with more dignity and respect than your boss and mine, Lieutenant David Jackson." In the doorway behind Casteel, Jackson violently slammed the manager into a locker, which buckled and caved.

"Where is he?" Jackson screamed into the manager's face.

"See." Casteel smiled to Owens without having to look

behind him.

Kaylee shuddered in fear every time she heard Olsen's voice. He was speaking a lot, which was causing her anxiety level to rise drastically. Both Kaylee and her mother were sitting on a bench at the amusement park, behind them was the Wildcatter ride, a weight drop roller coaster in which a four person car is hoisted up ten stories into the air and dropped along a ninety degree track in a freefall.

Kaylee struggled in her bonds, both her and her mother had been tied with electrical cord. Courtney tried to think but her mind was a blank, she didn't know what she could do, if there was anything, to try to escape. Kaylee wasn't thinking about escape, Kaylee's fear was causing her to watch with meticulous detail everything her captors did.

She watched Damon give orders to the two amusement park security guards on his payroll, then paid them off. She watched Damon have a second car loaded onto the Wildcatter ride. She also watched when Damon worked the controls and the very large thick chain pulled the first car to the top of the ten story drop.

Damon ordered Carlyle to place the two captives inside the second car. Once they were securely fastened in, Carlyle tied some additional electrical cord around their chests for added restraint. When Carlyle gave Damon a thumbs up, he pulled the lever next to the large red emergency stop button and the car, pulled by a second chain, began to rise. About two stories up, Damon pressed the lever back to it's original position and the car stopped.

Courtney felt a swell of relief when she realized that the height they were at wasn't very high off the ground. Even considering the situation and the men at whose mercy they were, Courtney felt a little hope in the situation. Below them was the runoff track for their car, since they were only 1/5th up the rollercoaster, if their car fell, it most likely wouldn't need a break to stop, the runoff would slow it down enough to save them. It was disparaging that they couldn't jump to safety, the runoff track would probably split them in half, but Courtney felt hope about that too. For safety reasons, when the ride was built, a steel ladder staircase was constructed along the side of the ride, so that in the event of an emergency, riders would be able to exit the ride fairly easily. Typically those riders weren't tied to the coaster car but Courtney felt that if she and Kaylee could free themselves, they could get off the coaster without many problems. These observations gave Courtney just a hint of security where before their had been none. That was until she looked up.

Directly above mother and daughter was the first car. It was at the absolute peak of the rollercoaster and it needed only a release of it's locking breaks to do exactly what it had been designed to do. Allow gravity, weight and a minimal amount of friction to drop it at incredible speeds straight downward. The only thing left out of it's design was the mother and child it would devour on it's way down.

Kaylee was still watching Damon down at the control platform for the ride. He was speaking to two men she hadn't seen before, Olsen was standing next to him but she could no longer hear his voice, which soothed her mind. Every word he spoke reminded her of that terrible day after school, where he told her that he would kill her mother. Kaylee wasn't scared for herself, she was scared of dying but knew that it wouldn't hurt, so it was easily put out of her mind. Her true fear, what scared her senseless at that very moment was the thought of losing her mother. She loved her mother dearly, even for all the faults she could already see in her and the thought of her mother being hurt scared her more than anything had ever scared her in her life.

"Is it ready?" Damon asked Musk on the platform of the Wildcatter, out of earshot of Courtney and Kaylee.

"Yeah, it's ready." Musk replied, looking at the buildings along the stretch of path behind Damon. He waved his hand in the direction of the buildings so that Damon could see. "Not even a tank could get through there."

"Good." Damon replied.

"Here's the detonator." Musk held out a large metal box with three rows of two buttons, each side by side down the rectangular box. "Press this." Musk flipped a switch on the top left hand corner of the box and a red light came on, then he shut it back off. "Then just hit the button of the bomb you want to detonate, I've wired them so that they go right down the list, right side of the box is right side of the street."

"Give it to Olsen, he'll be operating it." Damon ordered, Musk handed the box to Olsen. "Get with the others, you have to hold off Jackson's guys until we make the trade, got it?"

"Got it." Musk replied.

"Good, we'll see you at the plane, don't be late, we'll be in Mexico by tomorrow night." Damon said, Musk turned and stepped off the platform, on his way to meet up with the others. "You know what to do, anybody comes down that street before I get back, blow them to hell." He ordered Olsen.

"Yeah, what about them?" Olsen pointed to Courtney and Kaylee.

"I don't care about them, you could say they're in God's hands now." Damon said.

"They can identify us." Olsen told him.

"Who cares, they'll never find us in Mexico and besides which, even if they do, I make some payoffs and the Mexicans will never let them near us."

"I want them dead. There's got to be an easier way to kill them." Olsen demanded. Damon responded by slapping him on the side of the head.

"That's the point you moron." He chided, pointing to the

lower car. "The cops will break their own necks trying to save them while we escape. I want Jackson and his shitbird hick partner to die, it doesn't matter what happens to these two." Damon started to walk away, then turned around briskly. "So help me God, if you screw this up!" He turned back around and continued walking.

"Status?" Jackson crawled on his belly to the plain clothes officer watching the cargo ship.

"Nothing, no activity all night." The officer told him on the roof of the building overlooking the pier. Jackson had placed surveillance on all six targets the moment he began the raids and unlike the DEA, he checked in with them personally before he made each raid.

"There should be a sentry at that boarding plank." Rothstein crawled up next to Jackson.

"Alright, stay sharp." Jackson told the officer before he and Rothstein crawled off the roof and stepped down the fire escape to the alley where his teams waited. "It's all quiet here. Let's keep it that way, we'll go in stealth, then go loud when we encounter the suspects, intel only puts two of Jimmy Nguyen's guys here but stay alert for others, he could've reinforced."

"M-4's." Casteel ordered. "We don't have to worry about rounds going through walls but be careful of ricochets." Each member picked an M-4 out of the weapons SUV, locked and loaded, then checked their earpiece radios. "We're ready boss." Casteel told Jackson when all the members had checked in through their earpieces.

"Ari, you and Kim know the layout, you're point. One, you're first, with me and Owens, two you're right behind us, three you're on perimeter. Stack up." Jackson ordered. Everyone lined up on the side of the building and took their rifles off safe. After each team leader gave Jackson a thumbs up, he tapped Rothstein on the shoulder.

Rothstein and Mason moved out of the cover of the building first, training their weapons at the top of the boarding plank during their approach. Jackson and Owens moved briskly behind them, each training their weapons on various threat points. Casteel, Holloman and Johnson brought up the rear, followed by N.S.2, several steps behind, and N.S.3 even further back, spread out very thinly.

N.S.1, along with Jackson and Owens ran quietly up the plank while N.S.2 covered the threat points, then N.S.3 covered N.S.2 as they boarded. Within a minute, N.S.3 was aboard ship, securing the deck as N.S.1 approached the hatch. Mason slowly and quietly opened the hatch allowing Rothstein to move in first, followed by Mason, Jackson and Owens, then the rest of N.S.1. They cautiously made their way down the stairs and entered the closed hatch to the cargo hold.

The massive cargo hold that seemed so full when it was filled with drugs now seemed like a void without them. All the pallets were gone and when N.S.1 entered it, they observed that the only thing left in the hold were two corpses, which were surrounded by blood pools.

"Either one Jimmy Nguyen?" Jackson whispered to his team. Owens bent down to look at one's face. He shook his head and they continued to the second corpse. He wasn't Jimmy Nguyen either. "Collins must have been here right after the DEA attack." Jackson lowered his weapon.

"But how'd he get the drugs out so fast?" Owens asked.

"I don't know but it must have been before we got eyes on, we've got to alert..." Everyone suddenly turned their weapons to the cracked hatch at the far end of the cargo hold when they heard a sound emanate from it. Jackson used hand signals to instruct the various members of N.S.1 to cover some possible ambush points before speaking into his radio. "2, sweep the hallways around the cargo hold."

"Roger that, moving." N.S.2 replied. Jackson and Owens kept their weapons trained on the hatch and approached it. They each hugged the wall on either side of the hatch, their weapons at the ready.

"Remember this?" Owens whispered to his partner. "Last time we were in this situation, I got shot. Would you mind going first this time?"

"Yeah, I'll do that." Jackson smiled cynically. He propped his M-4 rifle on the wall next to him–it was too long and bulky for what was going to be a relatively small room–and drew his pistol. Owens did the same. Jackson counted to three with his fingers and burst into the room with Owens right behind him. They scanned quickly for threats and found only one. Behind the desk of the cargo office was someone sitting in a large backed chair, facing away from them.

"Let me see your hands, show me your hands!" Owens yelled.

"I assure you detective, that is quite impossible." It took a moment for the person in the chair to reply. Owens shot a glance at Jackson, who nodded.

"Turn around, very slowly!" Owens ordered. The person in the chair used his feet to slowly swivel the chair around. "Eddie's lawyer?" Owens exclaimed upon recognizing the man with his hands tied to the chair's arms with electrical cord.

"I was kidnaped." Lynch told them.

"Sure you were." Jackson grumbled.

"In fact, I believe that the only reason that Mr. Collins left me alive was so that I could deliver a message to you, Lieutenant Jackson." Lynch informed.

"I'm listening." Jackson replied.

"Mr. Collins wishes to thank you for recovering his money for him, it was a problem which he had much difficulty solving. He says that if you bring yourself and the money to the Enchanted Village amusement park and if you come alone, he will release his guests. If you refuse, he will kill them." Listening to Eddie's lawyer, Jackson felt a tornado of anger fill up his stomach.

"What about the drugs?" Owens asked.

"Yes, Mr. Collins has decided to bestow upon you an additional dilemma. The drugs have been loaded onto freight trucks and shipped to their destinations across the United States, the locations of which are known only to Mr. Collins himself and the truck drivers. I can personally tell you that they left some four hours ago and were given instructions not to use the main highways. If you're lucky, they may still be in the state." Jackson and Owens' minds raced, trying to figure the situation out. "Mr. Collins also made something else perfectly clear." Lynch added. "That if Lieutenant Jackson and the money were not delivered to him at the base of the Timberhawk rollercoaster by exactly two a.m., the girl and her mother will die." Lynch read the hands of the clock that had been conspicuously placed on the desk in front of him. "You have twenty-two minutes."

15

"Through the Fire"

The three teams scurried down the boarding plank of the cargo ship. Jackson was in the lead. When he reached the bottom, he was met by a uniformed patrol officer.

"There's a suspect tied up in the office of the cargo hold, take him down to interrogation." Jackson ordered.

"Will do." The patrolman replied.

"Enchanted village is fifteen minutes from here." Johnson informed. Moving quickly they made their way around the buildings to their vehicles.

"Four hours on back roads, we've got a good chance of catching up to those trucks before they hit the state line." Casteel thought aloud.

"Get Knox on it." Jackson ordered him.

"Way ahead of you boss." Casteel replied with his cellphone already to his ear.

"I want N.S.2 on docks, airports, bus stations, train stations, ferries, if there's a way to get out of this city, I want you to cover it, Collins has an exit, find out what it is and block it!" Jackson ordered the N.S.2 team leader. "3, I want you to check the local trucking businesses, everything from Tacoma to Vancouver. Collins didn't have time to bring in trucks from out of state. I'll bet he's using somebody here, if he is, they know where their trucks are headed."

"On it." N.S.3's team leader announced. The large group arrived at the SUV's.

"Marcus?" Jackson asked, Holloman nodded that he was listening. "You still have Vera?"

"My little manhunter, sure thing." Holloman replied.

"You're in Air One." Jackson ordered. Holloman opened the back of the middle SUV and pulled a long rifle case from under the back seat. Vera, everyone's affectionate nickname for her, was a Heckler and Koch PSG-1 police special sniper rifle that fired a 7.62 mm round. The weapon had been specially designed for increased accuracy (even moreso than similar rifles used by the military) at shorter ranges and possessed a Hendsoldt 6 x 42 mm telescopic sight. Her user Marcus Holloman was twice Seattle Police Department's rifle target shooting champion. After picking up the rifle case, Holloman opened a box of handheld flares, took one and ran to a suitable location where he could direct Air One to land and pick him up.

"Ari, you and Kim take that money out of the boxes and put it in a bag." Jackson ordered. Rothstein grabbed a gym bag from the back of the SUV and emptied it while Mason started bringing the boxes marked "money" to him.

"I got Carrasco on the phone, from their staging point, they're thirty minutes from Enchanted Village." Johnson told Jackson. Owens walked up beside him.

"Get him moving." Jackson ordered. Holloman was directing the helicopter down. The sounds of the whipping blades were deafening so Johnson put a finger in his non-listening ear and stepped away to speak on his cell .

"He played us like a fiddle." Owens commented to Jackson.

"Now we're going right where he wants us and there's nothing we can do about it." Jackson conceded. "He knows we don't have time to get any kind of backup to the park, plus he knows that we have to put everything we've got on finding those trucks. He thinks he's outsmarted us again."

"It's always about who's smarter with him." Owens observed.

"Yeah." Jackson muttered, he watched Holloman direct the helicopter to the darkened dock with his flare, the immense wind whipping up dirt from every crack in the concrete. Holloman was being especially careful to direct the helicopter away from the various power lines in the area. Suddenly an idea hit Jackson. Collins thought he was so smart, why not make him think he's won? "Hey! You two!" Jackson yelled to Rothstein and Mason. "Take the clips off that money, I want it loose in the bag." The two detectives complied by taking out their pocket knives and cutting the paper clips off the thick blocks of cash. Jackson whirled around and addressed the team. "Jesse, you and I are in the first car with the money, everybody else is in the others! I wanna be on the road in two minutes, let's move people!" Jackson yelled.

"Yes I know what that means!" Knox spoke loudly into her telephone. The reply that she got was one that she didn't like. "Look, there are five trucks headed out of state, they have in them tainted drugs that will be sold through pharmacies, we can't, under any circumstances allow them to get out!" She told a Captain of the state highway patrol. "Look Bill, I'm hitting the 'oh shit' button here. We need every cop in the state, highway patrol, Sheriff's departments, WBI, local, federal, Christ even get parole officers and the corrections guys out on the roads! We have to stop and inspect every semi! Do you understand me? Every truck!"

Within minutes of Knox's calls, law enforcement agencies across the state of Washington commenced to stopping all of the tractor trailers they could find. Roadblocks were set up on all of the back roads that led out of the state, as well as state and federal highways. Idaho, Oregon, Montana, and Canada were also informed of the dangerous trucks that had departed the Seattle area only four hours before and they too set up roadblocks to try and find the poisonous drugs. The border patrol and Coast Guard were also informed and assisted the local agencies.

Cops all over the state were being awakened from a normal night's slumber and ordered to report for duty. City patrols were directed to stop any and all trucks they encountered. Because of an ingenious computer technician at the Washington Bureau of Investigation, a statewide command center was established at the WBI headquarters. There, all information about which trucks were stopped and when would be routed via either radio, computer instant message, or by phone. Technicians would then log the information into a computer and would be able to pull it up at a moment's notice, thereby reducing the chances of wasting time by checking the same truck twice.

Jackson's plan was simple, Damon belonged to him. Everything else was about finding Courtney and Kaylee. Jackson would distract Damon by meeting him at the Timberhawk ride per Damon's demands, meanwhile, N.S.1 would clear the park of

hostiles from the west, and Owens–who could more easily avoid
detection on his own–would attempt to locate Courtney and Kaylee,
which Jackson assumed would be close to the meeting point.

Two streets before they got to the parking lot of Enchanted
Village, the two SUV's carrying N.S.1 split from Jackson and
Owens, they maneuvered the roads surrounding the park to get to the
west side, there, outside the park, they dismounted their vehicles and
entered the park, each carrying their M-4 rifles.

Jackson and Owens dismounted in the parking lot on the
north side and silently moved up to the gate. "I'll catch you on the
flip side." Owens nodded to his partner. Jackson nodded in return.
They mashed their fists together and went their separate ways,
Jackson towards the entrance, bag in hand, and Owens to a darkened
portion of the fence to clandestinely infiltrate the park.

Time was up, Jackson only had one last play that he could
make. He approached the Timberhawk ride in silence, only the
quietness of carefully placed footsteps emanating from him. His
breathing was calm and controlled. If anything, Jackson was always
collected under pressure.

The Timberhawk rollercoaster was one of the largest wooden
rollercoasters on the west coast. It's massive wooden frame was
supported by an infrastructure of scaffolding that was so thick that in
places the individual boards became indistinguishable from each
other. It was over 75 feet tall and at it's highest point the track
circled almost 360 degrees, making the towering behemoth look

similar to the Roman Colosseum. It's sturdy wooden frame was reinforced with long steel rods that attached to the top of the round circle. The rods were meant to keep the rollercoaster from shimmying during high winds and thus only connected to the ground and the very top of the ride.

Jackson approached the base of the large wooden ride slowly. His gun remained in his drop holster, though it's security strap was left unbuttoned in case he needed to draw it quickly. Jackson knew that if he approached the meeting point with his weapon drawn, Damon would not hesitate to kill him and he needed Damon to talk. The area was dark, almost none of the park lights were on. Jackson figured that Damon must have turned them off. He stepped carefully into a patch of light created by the moon and heard Damon's all too familiar voice.

"That's far enough." A voice said to his left, at a distance, in the shadows. Jackson stopped, careful not to make any sudden movements. "Is that my money?"

"Maybe." Jackson remained noncommittal. "Where are the hostages?"

"All in good time." The shadowy voice replied. "Your gun." Jackson looked at the darkened shadows where the voice was coming from, he couldn't even make out Damon's outline, a shot was impossible. He reached slowly and deliberately for his gun. "Ah, ah, two fingers." Damon ordered. Jackson complied, taking the gun out of the drop holster with only his thumb and middle finger. He tossed it to his left, across his body. The sound of the weapon smacking against the pavement and sliding a few inches echoed through the wooden scaffolding of the Timberhawk. "Good." Damon said, crossing the meridian of the shadows and moonlight. "Now we can talk."

"I want the girl and her mother, now." Jackson demanded.

"After I get my money I'll tell you where to find them." Damon said, aiming his .50 caliber Desert Eagle at Jackson's head. "No tricks."

"Just give me the hostages and be on your way." Jackson replied.

"You forget, the deal was for the money and you. I have you, now I have to make sure that's my money you're holding."

"Alright, I'll give you you're money." Jackson lifted the bag to his chest with his left hand, unzipped it with his right, placed his right hand into the bag, grabbing ahold of something. He switched his left hand to the bottom of the bag and tipped it end over end, allowing two million dollars to be carried to the ground by gravity.

"What are you doing? Stop!" Damon ordered but Jackson didn't comply. Damon's first instinct was to shoot but Jackson had surprised him. He readied to fire but Jackson suddenly slammed the bag against his knee causing a bright red glow to fill the bag. Jackson ripped the bag from his right hand and threw it aside. There, his arm fully extended over Damon's large pile of cash was Jackson, holding a flare. Damon hesitated shooting, he tried to think quick.

"I wouldn't do that if I were you." Jackson warned. "You shoot me, I drop this, you're broke!" The two stood, staring at each other, stalemated. "What's that smell?" Jackson asked, taking a whiff. "Oh, that's lighter fluid." Jackson smiled. "I've been looking for that, my zippo's been out for weeks."

"Maybe it's worth it." Damon's anger reaching an apex but he was trapped; he couldn't kill Jackson without losing the money.

"We both know it's not." Jackson replied, calling his bluff. "Besides, this is really what you want, I'm still offering you an opportunity to get everything you asked for, me, the money, to escape. It's just going to be slightly more difficult than you anticipated, now isn't it?" Damon's gun began shaking, his anger showing itself. "Be honest Damon, you didn't want to do this with a gun anyway. You wanted to do it up close and personal. To look into my eyes as I die slowly, to truly avenge that little cumstain you called a brother." Damon's eyes filled with rage. "It's your money Damon and you can have it, if you can get through me."

"I'm gonna fucking kill you!" Damon screamed.

"Then lets do it." Jackson replied. Damon released the magazine from his gun and ejected the round in the chamber before throwing the weapon aside. Jackson smiled and dropped the flare into the pile of money. "Butterfingers." Jackson bemused. Damon's eyes went wide. Damon's attention shot to Jackson's gun, which was still loaded. He dashed for it. Jackson answered with his own rush but not for his gun, for Damon. Jackson collided with Damon with the thunderous force of speeding locomotive, performing a near perfect tackle.

"Hostiles at your nine!" Holloman yelled into the radio from the helicopter. N.S.1 was on the ground, sweeping around several of the park's buildings. Casteel faced his M-4 to the nine o'clock position and was struck in the side of his stomach by a round from Brute's M-60 machine gun. All five mercenaries began firing at the team from various positions on and around the Zooma Falls ride, a massive water slide that twists and turns its way down into a large wave pool.

The round went straight through Casteel's kevlar vest, sending him to the ground. Two additional rounds were caught by his M-4, sending fragments of the weapon into his face. Johnson, who was behind him, caught his fall and lunged backwards, hoping to fall into cover. Once on the ground, Johnson pulled Casteel back, out of the kill zone. Casteel instinctively dropped his rifle, which was useless now, drew his pistol and returned fire.

Blood and Musk opened up on Mason and Rothstein, who were on the other side of the building but fortunately they'd heard Holloman's radio transmission in time to take cover from the ambush. Both found separate firing points and returned fire.

Holloman's only target was Brute, who was the only

mercenary that Holloman could see was without adequate cover. He lifted Vera to his eye, took aim and fired. The instant he pulled the trigger, the helicopter shifted position. Carlyle was firing at it from atop the ride and the pilot had jerked the stick. Holloman's round struck far right, missing Brute entirely.

"We're taking fire, we're taking fire." The pilot screamed, slamming the throttle.

"Bring us around!" Holloman ordered. The chopper swung hard to the right to avoid being hit.

"We'll have to circle high!" The pilot told him and flew out of range.

Owens made his way through the maze of pathways and streets within the park. Courtney and Kaylee weren't difficult to find. Owens saw the car at the top of the ten story Wildcatter ride easily and knew that it wasn't supposed to be there. Using the buildings, shrubbery and signs for cover and concealment, he made his way to the wide path that the Wildcatter was on and positioned himself next to a tiny food stand housed in a concrete building. From his vantage point he could see Courtney and Kaylee in the car about a third of the way up. What really got his attention was the red light that suddenly appeared inside the open doorway of the food stand.

"Not again." He took off running. The stand exploded into a

huge plumb of smoke, throwing debris behind him. Then the food stand on the opposite side of the path exploded and Owens found himself in a gauntlet. Knowing that he had no cover to run to, his only chance was to outrun the explosions. He sprinted with all of his speed and strength up the path while three more buildings–on both sides of the street–exploded behind him.

Shrapnel of all kinds struck both him and the area around him. He fought through the pain to keep moving. The last explosion was the only one he wasn't able to outrun. A small wooden maintenance building next to the Wildcatter blew into a large fireball, sending giant flaming splinters in every direction. Several pieces of fire engulfed boards rocketed into a group of barrels which contained the special oil used to lubricate the Wildcatter ride. The concussion of the blast knocked Owens across the path into some bushes; a large flaming plank cutting into the grass just inches from his head.

Olsen slammed the detonator on the pavement, grabbed his shotgun, which he'd propped up on a light pole and proceeded to finish the task he started. Courtney and Kaylee watched the explosions in fear, Kaylee feeling a slight sense of relief that Owens was there, even though she wasn't sure if he was alright.

Blood, Carlyle and Musk were now firing almost exclusively on Casteel and Johnson's position. They tried to maintain the lowest possible profile while the armor piercing rounds tore through the brick building they were using for cover. Casteel continued to fire his pistol with one hand while he held his wound with his other. Johnson had just run out of amunition for his M-4 when Casteel ordered him to find out how long it would take for backup to arrive. Laying flat on his back, while continuing to fire with his Smith and Wesson .45, Johnson radioed in their position and their pressing need for assistance.

"Lock and load!" Carrasco yelled after acknowledging the radio transmission. The three SWAT vans were racing to the amusement park, sirens blaring. "We're going in hot!"

"We can't stay here!" Rothstein yelled when he fired his last round of M-4 ammunition. Mason looked bewildered for a moment, then he pointed to Scar and Brute, who were switching positions, probably to try and flank them.

Mason nodded, then finished off her own rifle ammunition and they ran to new cover. Rothstein saw an open door in the auditorium they were next to and tapped Mason on the shoulder. She followed him in.

Damon struggled violently to free himself from Jackson's grasp. The two wrestled on the ground for a few seconds, neither able to gain the upper hand, until Damon caught Jackson in the face with a hard elbow. The strike stunned his attacker enough for Damon to break free his grip and get to his feet. When he approached Jackson's gun, Jackson pushed him against a light pole and kicked the weapon. The kick flung the weapon across the street and into a storm drain.

Damon turned around and nailed Jackson in the face. When Damon attempted to land a second punch, Jackson parried, reached behind his back, removed his handcuffs and slammed one of them onto Damon's left wrist.

Twisting the handle of the cuffs unnaturally, he wrenched Damon's arm backwards, contorting the elbow, then switched directions and rotated the arm in the opposite direction, flipping Damon onto his back. Jackson backstepped, dragging Damon along the ground.

Again using the handcuff for leverage, Jackson slammed Damon into a park bench, then a tree, then some bushes, part of which Damon broke off and smacked Jackson in the face with, causing him to let go of the cuff.

Damon jumped to his feet and darted for the Timberhawk. Jackson shook off the hit and followed. There weren't many places for Damon to hide, he knew that Jackson had the benefit of extra strength to enhance his skill. He needed something to even up his odds. He jumped onto the track of the ride and headed up. Jackson followed.

Olsen moved forward with his shotgun, shooting wildly at Owens from a distance. Owens hurled himself into a front roll and back to his feet again, running for the coaster even though he'd caught several pellets with his arm and side from Olsen's shots. Olsen saw that Owens was closing on the bottom of the coaster and headed for the control platform.

Olsen reached the controls and slammed his palm onto the button controlling the top car. The brake holding its chain released and the car started to drop.

Owens saw the chain whirling by him and thinking quickly, picked up a two foot wrench stored on the side of the ride and jammed it into the chain. The wrench quickly spun away from him, crashing into the sides of the large shaft that housed the chain mechanism. The wrench held at the entrance to the shaft, stopping the chain and the top car crashed down two stories but stopped.

Kaylee looked up at the car that had almost fallen on them and panicked. She hadn't realized the danger that car wrought until it had started to fall, now fear seized her. She began jerking violently in the electrical cord tied around her. "It's ok baby, it's ok baby!" Courtney tried to comfort her but the words had no effect.

Owens turned and took aim at Olsen, who was hitting the

controls, wondering what had gone wrong. Owens carefully sighted-in the far off target, closed one eye and squeezed the trigger. He watched Olsen spin around and fall.

Twenty yards from the platform, a wooden board stuck in a barrel of lubrication was still aflame. It's fire burning downward to the extremely flammable liquid.

Scar and Brute covered each others run to the side of the auditorium building. Once there, they hastily moved around the building in an attempt to entrap Rothstein and Mason, who were coming out of a side door behind them. When they exited, Scar and Brute heard them, turned and fired. The cops had the drop on them though and fired a split second before their adversaries. Mason put two rounds in Scar's heart and Brute took one of Rothstein's rounds in the lower stomach. Both men fell and Mason rushed up on them, kicking away the M-14, while Rothstein tossed the M-60 away from the wounded Brute.

Carlyle turned to see his comrades fall and took aim with his AK-47 assault rifle. From his position perched at the top of the Zooma Falls ride, he had a clear line of fire to his targets. Mason was hit in the shoulder and dropped her weapon when she fell. Rothstein bolted for cover and Carlyle turned to him.

Rounds slapped the ground around Rothstein's feet as he leaped behind a dumpster. He picked himself up and aimed for the sniper but knew that his pistol wouldn't reach the distance needed. He had to get to Mason.

With Rothstein out of sight, Carlyle turned back to Mason, who was attempting to get back inside the door she and Rothstein had exited from. Carlyle anticipated her move and threw a flurry of rounds into the open door causing Mason to skid to a stop. She tried to turn around and head for the opposite corner but with her wound making her light headed, she tripped.

"I got you now bitch." Carlyle said, putting his eye to the weapon's sights. Suddenly, a 7.62 mm round smashed through his head, showering the area around him with blood and brain fragments. Holloman took Vera's telescopic sight from his eye and worked the bolt back then forward again, loading a fresh cartridge to be fired.

Using the maintenance path which ran parallel to the rails of the Timberhawk, Damon, with Jackson hot on his heels, made his way up and down the windy curves and hills created by the massive wooden construct. In order to reach the top circle of the coaster, the two had to climb a very steep grade. Damon's hope was to tire Jackson out so that he could be easily taken once they reached the top. He believed that Jackson's bulk would become a hindrance to him during the climb. By the time Damon reached the top circle, he realized that Jackson hadn't tired nearly enough.

"C'mon!" Damon turned and taunted when he reached the top of the huge circle. Breathing heavily from the climb, Jackson rushed him and the two opponents engaged in a bitter punching match, each man's anger absorbing the other's blows.

Though Damon had taken several devastating punches, he gained the upper hand when he lashed out with his foot to Jackson's knee. He slammed his opponent in the face with a rabbit punch and pushed him back against the railing. Damon flicked his cuffed wrist and brought the free handcuff into his palm, grasping the edged portion of the cuff between his fingers, he brought it down toward Jackson's eye. Jackson's strength just barely stopped the cuff from plunging into his eye and because he was tired from the climb, he couldn't push Damon's substitute weapon away, just scarcely hold it in place.

Owens was one story up when the barrels exploded in a deafening roar that everyone felt more than heard. The gargantuan fireball that erupted crossed over the top four stories of the Wildcatter, further weakening the chain holding the top car. It also sent hundreds of flaming chunks of oil and shrapnel into the area around the control platform for the ride.

Owens was knocked on his side but quickly recovered and made his way to the second story where he found the two hostages.

Kaylee was still trying to dislodge herself from the electrical cord.

"I'm here!" He yelled to her. The ten year old was in a panic, all she could think of was getting her mother to safety. A second after she heard Owens' words, the ligaments in her shoulder gave way and it dislocated. With the new shift of her body, she slid her hips downward to slide out of the electrical cord but her traction was poor and she slipped right out of the car.

Owens lunged over the emergency rail and holding himself in place with one hand, used the other to catch the electrical cord binding Kaylee's wrists. "I've got ya!" He noticed the electrical cord sliding up her tiny hands. "Grab my hands, grab my hands!" He yelled but it was too late, the cord released it's clutch on the little girl and she fell.

"Kaylee!" Courtney screamed hysterically. Kaylee fell between the two lethal rails of the coaster to the dirt below. She landed on her feet, breaking her left ankle and sending her face hard into the dirt, fracturing her nose.

Owens righted himself, he knew he had to get Courtney out before he could see about Kaylee. He had just reached over from the emergency stairs to Courtney's electrical cord when he was struck from behind.

Olsen, a gash on his forehead where Owens' bullet had nicked him, jumped on his back, sending them over the rail. Owens grabbed the car's safety rail in front of Courtney and hung on with both hands. Olsen twisted an arm around his neck. The two hung from the car, neither sure what to do next.

Musk's round hit a light pole, ricocheted to the ground, skipped twice and slammed into Johnson's pelvic bone, shattering it. Johnson shrieked in pain before his legs completely gave out and he thumped on the asphalt, firing his last shot into the air. Casteel grabbed him with the bloody hand he was using to put pressure on his own wound and pulled him to better cover. Both were now completely out of ammunition.

Blood heard the whiz of the helicopter over Musk's constant firing and switched from Casteel and Johnson to Holloman. His AK-47 struck the chopper three times, twice in the fuselage and once in Holloman's leg.

"We're hit, I say again, we're hit!" The pilot radioed when smoke started filling the cabin.

"Roger that, there's an emergency landing site in the parking lot." Carrasco came over his radio. "We'll take it from here." Carrasco took his hand off his LASH radio and waved the SWAT team forward in a two man covering maneuver. The team advanced, firing their M-16's, their laser sights not able to get a bead on the two suspects who had good cover on top of a building which housed a pair of restrooms.

Blood and Musk both returned fire with their rifles by pitching them over the concrete wall of the roof and firing blindly.

Several of their rounds went through the various covers that the team was behind, hitting two team members but not seriously.

"Alpha One, we're taking fire from armor piercing rounds." Bravo team leader reported over the LASH.

"Roger, sending alpha to alternate cover, suppressive fire on my mark." Carrasco ordered over the radio and gave hand signals to two of his team members. "Now, covering fire!" He yelled, both to his men and over the radio. Simultaneously, every member of the SWAT team fired on Musk and Blood's location, the intense fire meant to make the suspects keep their heads down and not fire on them when they moved. Two members of Alpha team split left and took cover by a pillar on the side of the auditorium building. Carrasco now had everyone in place. "Gas, gas, gas!" He ordered.

The man behind Carrasco took the 40 millimeter grenade launcher from the back of Carrasco's utility vest, loaded it with a single gas grenade, aimed and fired. The two members of Alpha team that Carrasco had just moved also fired a grenade. Bravo team did the same. The three grenades exploded in a cloud of white smoke that burned the eyes, nose, ears, mouth, and throat of anyone it came into contact with.

"I'm gonna mount your head on my wall!" Damon continued to push the tip of the handcuff toward Jackson's eye.

"I wouldn't hold my breath." Jackson replied and slammed

his knee into Damon's ribcage, pushing him back. Jackson stood straight and when Damon came in with a punch, Jackson proved faster with a punch of his own. Damon tried again but again Jackson was faster. He tried a third and fourth time but each time he found himself smacked with another painful blow to the face.

Damon turned and ran. Jackson followed but stopped when Damon climbed onto the guardrail and jumped. Jackson ran to the side and looked over. Considering for a moment–he wasn't going to let Damon get away this time–he decided to follow. Jackson jumped from the guardrail into the immensely thick scaffolding below, whacking Damon in the back with his knee while the criminal tried to climb through the bowels of the coaster.

Olsen pulled a knife from a scabbard attached to his belt and stabbed it deep into Owens left shoulder, causing him to let go with that hand and painfully yelp. "I'll take you with me!" Olsen screamed up at Owens.

Owens knew that he couldn't hold both of them with just one hand and felt his grip slipping. He looked up at Courtney, who had gone into a frenzy of screams. He knew that Kaylee was below him and if she survived the fall, she'd need immediate help.

Olsen removed the knife from Owens' shoulder releasing a river of blood that flowed down his arm. His grip was quickly coming loose, he had to act. Working through the pain, Owens put his bloody left hand into his jeans pocket, removed his own knife, used two fingers to open the folding blade and smashed it into Olsen's stomach. Olsen squealed but Owens still pulled the knife across his stomach and being weakened; he let go of Owens. The blood from his wounds saturating Owens' hand and making the handle of his pocket knife slick, it slipped out of his grip.

Olsen, the pocket knife still in his stomach, fell directly onto the tracks, the force of the impact snapping his spine like a twig, leaving him unable to move and just conscious enough to realize that he would bleed out within a matter of minutes.

The wind was now moving the gas through the cover that Casteel and Johnson were taking shelter behind. Blood and Musk were happy to see that the gas was finally subsiding, however when Musk lifted his head to continue firing at the SWAT team, he found that they'd used their time wisely and taken up perfect firing positions on the two. The first round went straight through Musk's cranium. Blood didn't stand but stayed kneeling and continued to fire, unaware that half a dozen laser sights were eating away at his chest cavity. The harmless laser beams were followed by a barrage of 5.56 mm ball ammunition that virtually ripped him in two.

Rothstein rounded the corner, helping Mason along by her

good arm and found Casteel and Johnson lying on the ground, coughing, trying to cover their wounds.

"I'm out!" Casteel yelled to Rothstein and Mason, unaware that the firefight had ended just moments before.

"I'm out too." Johnson said. Rothstein placed Mason on the ground next to the building. Checking his gun, he took out his magazine. One round was in it. "I've got two left." He informed and was hit hard from behind by Brute. Both the .45 and it's magazine were flung into the air in separate directions.

The .45 landed a few feet from Johnson but with his legs useless, he had to crawl, using only his arms to reach it. Brute picked Rothstein off the ground and Rothstein tried to return by sending a backfist into Brute's face, which had no effect. Brute allowed Rothstein to land a full force punch to his face, also no effect. Casteel and Mason tried to get to their feet to help but were too weak. Laughing at him, Brute hit Rothstein with a punch that spun him around several times before he hit the ground.

"I'm going to teach you a lesson you fat little bastard." He told his prey. Johnson reached out for the gun but Brute inadvertently kicked the .45 away from him and into some dirt when he picked Rothstein back up. Brute spun him around, hit him several times in the stomach and threw him into the wall of the building.

Rothstein looked in front of him, dizzily, to see his .45. He quickly got to his knees and lunged for it but was grabbed by Brute.

His fingertips dug into the dirt behind the weapon as Brute pulled him away. Brute placed both his gigantic hands on either side of Rothstein's head, lifted him up and slammed him into the building several times.

"I'm gonna pop your head like a balloon." The ogre informed. Rothstein tried hard to stay conscious and in so, noticing that his feet were freely kicking back and forth about a foot from the ground. He pulled his right ankle up to his hand.

"I'll teach you something." Rothstein muttered through the pain in his head. Brute suddenly felt the muzzle of a .38 Police Special snub nose under his chin and immediately thereafter heard the hammer click into firing position. "Fat guys carry backups!" With the pulling of the trigger, Brute's head erupted in a fountain of blood. Rothstein was pulled by gravity to the ground and arrived just slightly before Brute's corpse. "There endeth the lesson." He commented with a headache. "And I'm not fat, I'm pudgy."

Damon knew he'd won. The in-close fighting produced by the Timberhawk's scaffolding had nullified Jackson's powerful blows. Damon was easily more agile than Jackson and used the scaffolding to his advantage, pummeling the cop with vicious punches and kicks while gliding around acrobatically.

Jackson tried to grab hold of Damon but he used the scaffolding to his advantage, avoiding Jackson's grasp. Damon grabbed hold of the beam above him, pulled himself to it, then whirled himself over it, coming down with both feet onto Jackson's chest, knocking him against the beam below him.

The metal housing of the shaft that held the chain gave way. The large wrench clinked and clanked up several feet until it was caught in a narrow wheel designed to hold the chain in place. The top car shuddered and fell several feet before stopping.

Kaylee lifted her head from the pool of blood collecting on the ground around her nose when she heard the noise. She could see that the top car was about to fall. Owens had just climbed in the bottom car, perhaps he could get her mother out in time. But something was wrong, neither were leaving the car.

Owens worked ferociously on the knot of electrical cord around Courtney's body. A combination of blood on his hands, his very limited use of his left arm, and the slick nature of the cord kept Owens from getting any type of grip whatsoever on the knot. He looked up at the top car that inched downward as the metal wheel chewed into the wrench.

Kaylee watched the scene with horror. Her tears fell into the pool of blood under her face. The last two people in the world that she cared about could be killed at any second and she was down on the ground, helpless. Helpless, like she had always been.

"Goddamnit!" Owens said, continuing to try to get a grip on the knot. Courtney cried sorrowful tears, she was beginning to believe that his attempts would be fruitless, she could tell that he wasn't having any luck and consigned herself that in a few short seconds, she would be dead.

The top car inched down again after the wheel further gnawed into the weakening metal of the wrench. Kaylee couldn't watch it any longer, she refused to become a spectator to their deaths. She refused to be helpless. She turned her head away and saw the control platform engulfed in flames. Suddenly she remembered watching Damon use the controls earlier.

"Jesse?" Courtney said calmly, alarming him. "Jesse, I want you to do something." She swallowed. "I want you to promise me that you'll take care of Kaylee and then I want you to go."

"Don't talk like that." Owens ordered. "I'm going to get you out, just give me a minute."

"We don't have a minute, that thing is going to fall anytime, Kaylee's down there and she needs at least one of us. You have to go." Courtney ordered. "Promise me and go!" Owens ignored her and continued to work on the knot.

Kaylee looked up at the two people she loved, then at the platform, then back at Owens and Courtney again. Her eyes left them for the platform and changed from fear to determination. She put her hands next to her chest and lifted herself onto her knees. The instant she got to her feet, her broken ankle gave way and she stood on the bottom of her calf bone. She took a step, a pronounced limp because of the new difference in the length of her legs, her foot unnaturally flopping around next to her leg.

"Go!" Courtney ordered forcefully. Owens worked on the knot, still not having any luck. "Just go!" She cried.

Frustrated, Owens stopped his work, put his face in front of hers and connected their eyes. "I am not leaving you!" He yelled at her then went back to work. "If that thing falls, I want you to get as low in the car as possible, its got a thick metal back, that might help some." He said, still trying to get a grip on the knot.

The wheel munched down a little more, bending the metal wrench. The top car shuddered because of the slight move in the chain. Kaylee heard it but didn't look up. She continued, limping, crying, toward the smokey fire surrounding the platform. She was no longer scared, she was purposeful, she knew what her destiny was, what had to be done.

She crossed into the fire and the smoke began to make her eyes water. She pulled her bloodsoaked nightgown over her nose. The fire singed her skin with every step.

The wheel bent the wrench into a horseshoe shape, it's metal further weakening.

The three hot metal steps kept the skin from Kaylee's left foot and right ankle when she staggered up them. She crossed through another oil soaked lob of flame, which charred her legs even more, creating huge bubbles that filled with pus. In her path was only one more oil fire created from the exploding barrels. It was directly in front of the console. She could barely see the controls through the smoke it created and though she'd watched Damon work them, she knew not which one to use. She reached her hand through the flames, standing on her good foot's tiptoes to reach the buttons.

The wheel finally bit through the wrench, splitting it in two and sending both pieces rocketing out in opposite directions. With nothing obstructing it, the chain now free flowed through it's path.

Owens grabbed Courtney and pushed her head into her lap while covering her body with his own.

Kaylee reached through the fire which cooked her skin.

"Close your eyes!" Owens ordered as the top car fell toward them, picking up speed.

Red means stop.

Kaylee slammed her hand onto the large red emergency stop button. The brakes on the top car promptly engaged and the car slowed but had been going too fast and could not be stopped right away. It continued to skid down.

Owens held onto Courtney for dear life while he listened to the top car approach. He closed his eyes. Everything went black.

Several seconds later he opened his eyes. Everything was dark, Courtney was still there. He breathed in some air and realized he hadn't done that in fifteen seconds or so. Wondering what had happened, he lifted his head.

"Ow." He said, slapping his head on the bottom of the top car.

Damon reached outside the scaffolding, grabbed the long metal pole that stabilized the top of the coaster with the ground, lifted himself out, spun around the pole and nailed Jackson with both feet. Bruised and battered from Damon's constant flurry of attacks, Jackson lost his traction on the wooden frame and fell against a horizontal board.

Still holding onto the pole with his left hand, Damon kicked Jackson in the face once for good measure, then propped his knee on his opponent's chest to hold him in place. Jackson spit out air and gasped from the attack. Damon reached over with his right hand and delivered a series of punches to Jackson's face, then grabbed his throat, choking the life out of him.

"I've been waiting for this for a long time! I'm gonna watch your soul leave your body!" Damon yelled with malicious anger, holding Jackson in place with his knee and himself in place with his left hand on the metal pole. Jackson reached for the hand Damon was using to steady himself with on the long metal pole. He hoped to destabilize Damon and knock him over but he couldn't reach, coming just an inch short. It didn't matter.

Damon saw a smile develop on Jackson's face, confusing him. "What's so funny?" He loosened his grip so that Jackson could speak. Jackson let out several quick coughs before he could vocalize.

"I finally got the cuffs on you!" He told Damon in a gravelly voice. Damon's eyes shot at his left hand, the loose cuff freshly secured around the pole. "Now lets see if they stick!" Jackson added and flung his fist into Damon's face. The strike sent Damon reeling into the air, his head catching a low board on his way off the scaffolding. The cuff stopped his momentum horizontally and began his momentum vertically. It guided him all the way to the asphalt. He landed head first, his skull breaking open on impact and his brains scrambling around his body like an egg.

Owens and Courtney made their way down the steps hastily. They found Kaylee sitting on a park bench near the still burning platform, her right leg crossed squarely over her left and holding her ankle. Burns blistering and bursting with pus, then gradually hardening into a leathery form all over her legs arms and face, her nightgown charred in several places, Kaylee's face held a curious expression while she examined her ankle. Owens stopped at the bottom of the stairs and let the girl and her mother have their moment. Courtney ran frantically to her daughter.

"I think it's broke?" Kaylee commented. She dropped the foot and watched it hang freely and unnaturally by a thin layer of skin. "Yep, it's broke." She observed dryly. Courtney grabbed her and pulled her close, weeping.

Owens stood, grasping his wounded arm, watching the scene with a feeling of euphoria coming over him. He saw Carrasco's SWAT team tactically sweeping the area down the path. Taking his necklace off, he stepped to the center of the path and waved his badge in the air to get their attention.

"It's me! We're clear here!" He yelled.

"Secure the area." Carrasco ordered, signaling the men that had come with him. He approached Owens, took off his helmet and balaclava, then smiled. Glad to see he'd made it.

"How's everybody else?" Owens asked.

"Pissed." Carrasco returned jokingly. "But they'll live." Digging into one of the pouches on his vest, Carrasco removed a large bandage and held it firmly on Owens' knife wound. "I could make a career out of patching you up boy." He commented.

"I reckon you could cap'n." Owens laughed in an accentuated southern draw.

"Where's Jackson?"

Jackson sat on the scaffolding, his back against one of the vertical boards and his leg propped up in a relaxing pose. He was admiring the beauty of the smoke from the fires that was congregating and reflecting the twirling red and blue lights of the emergency vehicles against the cloudless, starry night's sky.

"Rest in peace Carey." He told his deceased partner. "We got him."

Epilogue:

All five trucks were found. Two had gotten out of the state before the roadblocks were set up, the other three were stopped, one by a patrol officer near Spokane, two by the roadblocks set up in the southern portion of the state. N.S.3 found the trucking company that Damon Collins had hired fairly easily and once their destinations were determined, the trucks were apprehended making their first deliveries.

The drugs found inside the trucks all tested positive for the leftover chemicals found on the ship. Since the trucking company had records of all the pharmacies that were to take the drugs, each was investigated thoroughly and Damon's accomplices arrested. It was found that the pharmacies were located across the country, in twenty-six states and had the drugs gotten to them, they may have been placed on the market the very next day.

In Scar's pocket a sheet of paper was found detailing in which airport and hanger Damon's escape route had been placed. A thorough examination of both the airport and hanger revealed no possible planes that could have been used. It was first assumed that Damon had never planned on escaping the Enchanted Village amusement park at all. But when one of aliases turned up on the roster for a freighter headed to the Philippines, it was instead determined that he intended to pull a fast one on his own guys and leave them to either die by the hands of the police or get caught. Either way, it didn't matter to Damon because they knew nothing of his real escape plan.

The routing numbers on the invoices led to an off-shore bank account in Switzerland. With the bank account information, Damon would have the opportunity to withdraw the funds at any time. What the investigators didn't find was that Damon had planned to purchase a cottage just outside Manilla. With the low cost of living in the area, Damon would have been able live out his days like a king.

Kaylee's wounds were extensive. She had first, second, and third degree burns over much of her body, the cartilage in her nose was fractured and the ligaments in her right ankle were almost completely destroyed due to her march to the control platform. Her right foot had to be amputated because of the lack of blood that had gotten to it. Three of her fingers also had to go because of an infection that set into the burns she'd received. Her face, legs and arms would be scarred for the rest of her life.

Kaylee took all of it like the spunky young lady she was. She watched the doctor amputate her foot and fingers, making jokes the entire time. She didn't care, it was a trade off she was happy to make; a foot, a few fingers, some cartilage and scar tissue for the lives of her mother and Owens. To Kaylee, it was a no-brainer.

Courtney's scars were internal and would last much longer. She constantly had nightmares about the traumatic incident and would even awake in the middle of the night with full screams. Kaylee was always there to comfort her and her daughter's presence seemed to sooth her tormented spirit.

Courtney accepted Owens as a part of Kaylee's life; she came to terms with her insecurities about him and Owens became a daily fixture around the house. He visited Kaylee on an almost daily basis, the little girl becoming his best friend and him hers. Kaylee was delighted at the arrangement, to her, she had everything she could have wanted. Her friend Jesse was around and no longer in conflict with her mother, whom she loved very much.

Much to Marcy Jackson's annoyance, the five members of N.S.1. congregated at her house everyday, turning the family home into a hospital-like clinic full of changed bandages and crutches. Though none of their wounds were fatal, several were serious, including Johnson's which would put him at a desk for the rest of his career. Johnson didn't seem to mind, the firefight in the park had jarred him and he was relieved at not having to go into the field again. Jackson and his team didn't disapprove of their respite. They sat around and watched ESPN all day long for the month they were out of work. They were all on administrative leave.

It was three months later, shortly after ten at night when Owens received the frantic call from Courtney. He rushed to the hospital and met Kaylee's mother outside the room in the white hallway. Courtney was pale, her eyes and nose red, her age showing in her frown. Her hair was natty and tangled.

"It's her appendix." She told him, her voice breaking.

"But they took it out, didn't they?" He asked, hoping the answer would be different than he thought.

"She didn't even know it was inflamed." Courtney stopped, gathered more air to speak the words that she dreaded. "Jesse...it burst. There's nothing they can do." Owens heart sank. He'd consigned himself to this moment but was not prepared for it. He stumbled backwards a step and struggled to right himself. Courtney watched his face turn as pale as hers. The two embraced, holding, comforting each other.

Kaylee was lying in the dark, all her movement concentrated in her eyes. The faint rays of a half-moon shined between the curtains of her modest room. Her eyes shot to the door when it opened revealing the two people she cared for most in the world. They entered quietly, taking position on the left side of her bed. Courtney sat on a small stool and Owens pulled up a chair next to her.

"Jesse." Kaylee said weakly while Courtney held her hand.

"I'm here little sister." He said. Kaylee smiled. Her face was becoming gray, her eyes glossing over, her pupils dilated. She felt weak and couldn't move very well.

"They said I get to go to heaven." She told them a few minutes later.

"That's right babygirl." Courtney could barely say the words.

"What do you think heaven will be for me?" She asked, slowly, faintly, several seconds later.

"It's whatever you want it to be." Owens replied, seeing that Courtney couldn't muster any words.

"I want," Kaylee thought a few more minutes, "I want to go home." She whispered. "And I want you to be there." She said to her mother first. "And you too," She told Owens, "and I want Grampa there. Will you all be there?"

"Yeah, baby, we'll all be there for you." Courtney broke down.

"I wouldn't miss it for all the tea in China." Owens agreed softly. Kaylee smiled again.

"Mommy?" Kaylee asked, closing her eyes.

"Yeah, baby?" Courtney said rubbing her daughter's hand.

"Mommy, it hurts." Kaylee told her.

Kaylee never opened her eyes again. She kept talking for several hours. She talked about the time they'd all spent together, she told stories about her grandfather, she talked about her favorite television shows and her experiences at school. As the night went on, her rambling became more and more incoherent. By the time she fell asleep, her words no longer made any sense whatsoever. Her mumbling slowed and eventually her whispers melted into silence. She slept for over an hour until her heart gradually slowed to a stop.

Courtney held her face to her daughter's hand, she kept it there all night, sobbing quietly. When the machine monitoring the little girl changed from a sporadic beeping sound to a single monotone hum, Courtney finally allowed herself to completely break down.

Owens got up from his chair, rubbed Kaylee's forehead with his hand and kissed her on the cheek. He put his hand on Courtney's shoulder and squeezed it slightly, her face laying on the bed touching her daughter's hand.

Owens opened the door to the room, stepped out, silently closing the door. He looked up to see Jackson standing in front of him. They said nothing. The look in their eyes told each other everything. Jackson nodded, subtly. Together they walked down the hallway. Side by side. Friends.

About the Author

Already the author of *America's Martyrs*, Richard Hodgkinson
resides in Murfreesboro Tennessee.

Coming Soon From Richard Hodgkinson
Wicked Lies
Wicked Games
Wicked Motives

For more information, pictures, blogs, news, ordering information
and much more, go to
www.myspace.com/richardhodgkinson